Benedict Kiely was born in 1919 near Dromore, Co. Tyrone. He grew up and went to school in Omagh and is a Freeman of that town. Apart from some years in the United States, most of his life has been spent in Dublin. He graduated from University College, Dublin and worked as a journalist, broadcaster and lecturer. He is past-president of the Irish Academy of Letters. His first book of memoirs *Drink To The Bird* was published by Methuen in 1991.

GW00482005

HONEY SEEMS BITTER

To

Marnis

Good to see you

New Year 1999.

Marianne

By the same author

Benedict Kiely

HONEY SEEMS BITTER

MOYTURA PRESS • DUBLIN

First published in 1949 by
Jonathan Cape, London

This edition published in 1992 by
Moytura Press, Ormond Court,
11 Lower Ormond Quay, Dublin 1.

© Benedict Kiely 1992

BRITISH LIBRARY CATALOGUING IN PUBLICATION DATA

A catalogue record for this book
is available from the British Library.

ISBN 1-871305-10-1

Printed in Ireland by
Colour Books Ltd, Dublin

Contents

In memory of
E.J. Crowley

Introduction

And Jonathan Cape, the great publisher said to me: 'You will write yet your breakthrough book'.

The great man said that to me in the year of 1952. Wasn't that Holy Year when Brendan Behan and Anthony Cronin set out on sandals with staves in hands and cockleshells in hats, on pilgrimage to Rome: and never got there? See through laughter and tears, the classic story in Cronin's *Dead As Doornails*.

As for Jonathan Cape and myself: At that time he was holding but not for the moment wishing to publish a manuscript novel, or something, of mine, called *The Cards of the Gambler*.

At the same time a learned friend of mine and, in the nature of things, more learned than ever, except in the unlikely event of his having forgotten more than he ever learned. That learned friend, I was about to say, was, at that time, bound for Peterhouse, Cambridge, to do his doctorate. So for old friendship, and for the joyride, I went with him and we had a merry time on the way. On the evening of the day on which I left Cambridge to find my quiet and respectable way back to Dublin, I had an appointment with Jonathan Cape: for six o'clock in his fine apartment at a corner of Bedford Square. He kept that apartment to meet authors and others, close to the office but a little away from the office atmosphere: and, in the evening, when the office had formally closed, he could sit in the apartment and talk to guests, or read typescripts, until the rush had died down in the Tube and he could go home in comfort.

How and ever: My learned friend and myself are in Cambridge in the morning walking from Peterhouse to the railway station just when the boozers are opening. We step in for a half of bitter. My friend says: 'We will have one for your road in the pub at the corner'.

He is, of course, staying on in Peterhouse. I must rise, as the old song says, and he need not. From behind the counter the proprietor of that boozer says: 'Wouldn't if I were you. The pub at the corner, I mean. Full of Irish farmworkers from a place called Mayo. Eat you alive'. We did not tell him. That would not have been playing the game. My friend had no noticeable Irish, nor any other accent, except when he was pretending. And because of the vowel sounds of my place of birth I have frequently in Southern England passed as Scottish. Although North of Carlisle the natives would immediately notice the difference. But we did look into the pub at the corner and find it, for us, the mere Irish, perfectly normal.

And in that pub I met a tall, young man the wreck of something that had been magnificent, a deserter from the Irish Guards, shabby, in ill-health, wearing an overcoat that was long, even for him. And the neck of a bottle of wine (non-vintage) stood up out of a pocket of the coat: as plain to be seen as the Eddystone lighthouse. A civil, sad, lost man. He gave me a message for his brother in Ireland and, later I am to pass on the message and get little thanks for doing so: and I am never again to see that sad young man. But if you search around you may find his shadow in this novel.

All the way on in the train to London I was reckoning that since Jonathan Cape had asked me to call on him at six in the evening he might be good for a free dinner. That was of the utmost importance. My money, such as it was, was running out and I had to catch the Irish Mail at Euston Station, at nine o'clock or there abouts. If, I think to myself, I go down to Fleet street, to the immortal company of Terry Ward and Con O'Leary, I can raise any God's amount of money. But then I would be happy in Fleet Street as Dr. Johnson was before me, for the next week. And I am expected back in Dublin. Out of the Cambridge and Peterhouse jollification I had hoarded enough money to get me to Euston Station, to pay on the ship from Holyhead to Dun Laoghaire, to pay my bus fare from Westland Row terminal to Dollymount, North Dublin City, where I then lived.

The door of Cape's apartment was opened to me by a charing middle-aged lady from Galway, of all places, who was a member of the staff. She made me feel almost happy by, obviously having read a previous novel of mine: *In a Harbour Green*.

As always: the great man was gracious! He produced three varieties of whiskey or whisky: Bourbon, Canadian Rye, Powers'

Gold Label. The Gold label was a gift from Paddy, the Cope, Gallagher, great son of Donegal, who was at that moment dignifying London by a visit. Cape had published his fine book, *My Story*.

So Jonathan and myself, sip as soupçon, of all three whiskies. The Canadian Rye was, as far as I can remember, a presentation from Morley Callaghan. And we nibble at a thing called Gentleman's Relish i.e. bits of toast with stuff on them. The stuff is the relish. That's the good news. The bad news is: no mention of dinner. It's a long long way to Holyhead. Whiskey is only a temporary relief. The worse news is that he thinks that I should sit on *The Cards of the Gambler* for a bit. People won't know what it's about. My next novel, he assures me, may be my breakthrough novel. And, after that, he will be able to sell anything with my name on it.

'But', I plaintively cry, 'I've written the bloody thing. And I need money'.

'Oh money, money, money', he said. 'Belloc was always annoying his publishers about money. For his boats. And his wines. Yachts and champagne. Ernest never bothers me about money'.

He was, sure as God, dead serious. And, at that realization, and even in such a presence, my patience broke. Three nationalities of whiskey on an empty stomach. Mercy of God, Neil Gunn and Yukio Mishima were not, in that year, among his authors.

So I rose with dignity, I hope, and said: 'Mr Cape, sir. If I had as much money as you and/or Mr. Hemingway I would not be here with my hat in my hand'.

No hat did I possess.

Ernest, God rest the mighty man, was then financially quite comfortable in Havana, Cuba. And had, I felt, provided the Bourbon. All honour, also, to the mighty Jonathan. For we parted smiling and, as I said, and in spite of my ill manners, we remained friends.

Long afterwards he said to me: '*Honey seems Bitter*, was your breakthrough novel. You should have been with me then'. So I told him about the deserter in the pub in Cambridge who had found his way into that novel. That interested him: and it interested me to think that he would bother to read the books of those who were no longer with him. A deserter like myself. But who deserted whom? Or did he read the novel just to prove to himself, and to be able to tell me, that he had been right.

Honey seems Bitter, was my fifth novel, I think. Michael S. Howard wrote: 'For Jonathan a fifth novel held an almost mystical significance. He believed that it established firmly an author's reputation, or made a breakthrough to success if the beginning had been slow'.

Well, what I ever did break through to I never did find out. Being young at the time and my head, such as it was, still echoing from the classics, I delicately picked my title from Marcus Aurelius. No better man. When Dell paperbacks did an edition in the U.S.A they, with my assent, changed the title to *The Evil Men do*. Still good, and quite respectable. But one Dublin newspaper, at that time a conservative organ (if that's the description I'm searching for) gave the novel a brief, hostile review at the bottom of a single column and under the headline: 'A Nasty Novel'. In that famous backroom in Fitzwilliam Square the wise heads of the Censorship of Publications agreed with that review. And for the second time I achieved the litarary laurel for being in general tendency indecent or obscene.

Well go ahead and read and pick your own title.

BENEDICT KIELY

One

From the wobbly stile on the grassless summit of the fair-green I saw the bus waiting outside the hardware store, and felt through still morning air the impatient vibration of the engine. Summit? And a grassless green? Well, yes, because up above one end of the village street this thing, green or muddy mountain, soared steeply. The piles of silvery buckets outside the hardware store seemed to vibrate in metallic or magnetic sympathy with the engine. So I started to run, watching my steps as carefully as I could to avoid skidding in mud or tripping over stones. The weather was dry. But the day-before-yesterday's dung and slush were still on the slope, in the marks of hooves and farmers' feet come together for a fair that tradition kept alive. A strong rural tradition too, even if the city's boundaries were only twelve miles distant.

I shouted and waved my arms. The driver didn't see me or pretended not to see me. The bus moved and the silvery buckets, I'll swear, laughed at me and were glad. There was nobody on the street to relay my wait-for-me message. No head looked, sleepily curious, out over a half-door. The villagers were in bed or at breakfast; and the bus turned the chemist's corner and vanished just as my feet, all clabber from the descent, hopped on to the old blue pavement. I ran to the corner and looked up the city road after the vanishing bus. Perspiration like paraffin oil on my forehead. Phlegm, thick and immovable, choking my throat. Heart going like the toes of ten tap-dancers. I shouldn't run like that. Health. That's what I'm here for—health. Turning from the corner, prepared dismally to wait two hours for the next bus, I saw the one other belated traveller, still running and with a fine, long, healthy, enviable stride. He carried a brown leather briefcase. His rainproof, draped cloakwise around his shoulders, was caught at the throat by one button, and the sleeves as he ran flapped like wings. He said, not too breathlessly: 'Has it gone?'

'There it goes.' Waving my hand at the empty road where high hedges had closed like curtains behind the departed bus.

'There's a train in fifty-five minutes.'

'But it's a two-mile walk to the station.' The perspiration was, in the cool early air, drying rapidly on my forehead and for reasons connected with my illness I didn't like the idea of walking two miles along a country road. 'It's a fine morning,' he said, and he breathed deeply, taking wine out of the air, filling his healthy lungs until his chest visibly expanded and he laughed a loud, sane, likeable laugh. 'Walk with me,' he said. 'I'll show you a short cut across the fields.'

'But I'm really in no hurry. I could wait for the next bus.'

'It won't be here for two hours. You can't walk up and down this street all that time. And it'd be less exhausting to walk to the station than to climb back over the fair-green to your cottage.'

'You know where I live?'

'Oh, well. It's a small place. The fact that it's so near the city makes it seem smaller. Nothing much ever happens here. A stranger is a big event.'

'I'm down here for health.'

Almost without my knowing it we had started walking away from the village towards the railway station. He carried his brief-case securely under his right oxter so that it was half concealed by the cloakwise rainproof, and his left hand was deep in a pocket of his expensive well-creased gabardine pants. 'Too bad. Was it lungs?' That was a bit over-familiar, a bit crude, and it was a wrong diagnosis; but I couldn't feel angry, for he clearly meant no harm and anybody seeing my hollow-cheeked pale face, unkempt dark hair, and the way my wobbly limbs had shrunk away from my suit would have thought sympathetically: Lungs, poor bugger. But only in villages do people voice such thoughts. 'No,' I said, 'it was nerves.' The beauty of being a nervous case is that you're not ashamed to say so.

'Nerves are bad,' he said. 'They give you a hell of a time. That's what I hear. Can't say I ever suffered from them myself.' Looking at him through a telescope and from the top of a distant mountain, it would have been clear that never in his life had he suffered from nerves. He was a little over six feet in height, broad-shouldered, and he walked with a long stride and an easy, confident swagger. Dark curling hair, with the rhythm of his swaggering walk, bobbed this way and that way above his forehead. The lines at the corners of his eyes and mouth hadn't been viciously chiselled by twitching nerves; they were happy mementoes of drink, laughter, dances, and triumphs with women. 'The worst of it is,' he said, 'that everybody says to you that the cure depends on yourself.' That showed insight. Although he was so much that I wasn't and wanted to be and could be, I still found it impossible to resent his superiority. He was warm with good nature. You felt that instinctively. And he did understand.

'You must know something about it.'

'I had a friend once who suffered hell that way.' 'One learns a lot from watching friends suffer.' 'One does.' We walked without speaking around the first corner and still without speaking past the gaunt ruins of an old mill. Morning sunlight spilled like yellow wine through the staring holes where high windows had once been. An ash sapling had burst out from a crevice in the wall above the motionless rusted wheel and a blackbird sang from some hidden place in the jungle of shrubbery bordering the stagnant mill-race. He said: 'It's a heavenly morning,' and breathed deeply again and said: 'It's a curse to have to go into town today.' I wanted to talk about my illness, about the recurrent inability to lie in bed at night and the necessity of going out walking or cycling on silent roads; about the choking sensation as if bundles of phlegm large as tennis balls and tough as gutta- percha were lodged in the throat; about those supremely awful moments when the earth rocked under the feet and sweating hands reached out to touch steady walls or the elbows of confident friends. I wanted to tell him that it was true that people had gone blind from nerves, just fears and nerves and neuroses until darkness, self-impelled, came down around them like a suffocating mist. But it wouldn't bc wise to impose such confidences on a complete stranger. His face might show boredom or impatience or disgust, as the faces of so many of my friends ultimately had. Instead I said: 'I have to go in to cash a cheque. Then I'm free.'

'Lucky you.' A blue car driven by a pretty girl went back towards the village. She waved a hand and easily, gallantly in return he blew her a kiss, then walked in silence for a few minutes as if he was meditating on the swallow's flight of the girl in the blue car. We passed a cross-roads and a quietly awakening farmhouse, blue smoke like Indian signals puffing up from a squat white chimney, a cow lowing, a belated cock crowing raucously from a bedraggled pile of straw in a spindle-legged shed. Far away down the side road to the right a farm cart truckled lazily. If peace could soothe my nerves my cure was here. 'I work all day and I work most nights,' he said—an overworked man suddenly, a man with a grievance. 'During the day I work in an advertising agency. Three or more nights of the week I'm reviewing films and plays for a fashion magazine.'

'Lucky you,' I said, not really meaning it, for the level of theatre criticism possible in a magazine about women's clothes was hardly capable of inspiring awe in a reader of Pascal and Papini. But I did envy him the physical ability that enabled him to work days and most nights, to walk with a swagger, to wear his coat like a cloak, to laugh loudly but melodiously and in complete harmony with a Monday morning in late mellow August. 'To make things more unpleasant my car's off the road. Being rebored. I'll be late in town tonight.' He looked at me speculatively, weighing me up, I felt, as a possible companion. 'Would you care to do a theatre with me? It's not much of a show, I'm afraid. A West End success, God help us, transported over here by a travelling company. One visiting star. Billed to blazes as the year's best, and nobody in London, outside the lesser agencies, ever heard of her.'

'I'd like to.' Theatres were places I didn't or couldn't go to on my own: the darkness, the loneliness, the emphatic unreality, worse even than the unreality of a busy street when the pavement rocked under the feet and one suffered the horrors of an earthquake that affected nobody else or nothing else, neither houses nor buses nor people staring complacently into shop windows. 'I genuinely would like to. But as things are I can't afford late nights.'

'Do you all the good in the world. Take you out of yourself. That's what you need.' He was right, as everybody should know who claims to know anything about the workings of my malady. The specialist, a charming brown-haired woman, had said that. My friends and relations had echoed the specialist until I hated the sight of them and the sound of their voices. The old priest I went to see in a solemn-chanting monastery in the south of the country had said so too. But I couldn't accept an invitation as readily as all that. Might give this healthy, friendly stranger the idea that my company could be had for the asking. So to break off the conversation, temporarily, for I meant to say yes as if reluctantly when we were waiting on the station's wooden platform, I stopped to lean over a stone bridge, to look down into a small stream that came sluggishly from an artificial lake in the grounds of a big Georgian house on the left of the road. 'Magnificent place that,' he said. 'The blonde in the blue car belongs there. A smart bit. Pots of money.' Resting, backs to the bridge, we looked across the road, over the lake fringed with pampas grass and canopied with willows, across a level green field to the distant spacious house. Two cars were parked before the door. Ivy clothed one-half of the walls. Behind us the ascending sun shone glitteringly through a wood of smooth-boled beeches. 'God, this is peace,' he said, touching my thoughts. 'It should never be broken.' And just then it was broken with as piercing a woman's scream as ever came out of the sort of Whitechapel fog made specially for Hollywood films about Jack the Ripper or the picture of Dorian Gray. We suspected the big beautiful,house because we happened to be looking that way and there is some theory about eyes following sound or sound following the eyes; and tensely erect, snatched from our easy buttocks-against-bridge repose, we stared at it, waiting probably for a window to burst open and a burning body to come hurtling to the ground. But when the second scream came we whirled around, our backs to the big house, and looked where a path went away from the road through the iridescent beechwood.

It was a small wood, not more than a hundred trees, all smooth as young girls and well spaced on a short-grassed slope unmarred by prickly undergrowth. The stream twisted along at the foot of the slope. The path ran away from the stream, winding up the slope and delicately between the trees like a humble skivvy careful to avoid brushing against well-dressed heiresses. Then it dropped out of sight towards the place from which the third and as yet the loudest scream came. The big man in a jump crossed the stile at one end of the bridge and went running along the path towards the sound. I followed as well as I could. Two sprints in one morning would be the end of me; and as I ran or tried to run, listening for more screams, I saw so vividly that they'll stay in my mind for ever, those beech trees on a green hill, graceful branches pushed westwards gently by the wind, and above them, black in a blue sky, one lone rook rising and falling, rising and falling, playing at exile from a ragged nest.

Then the old running, screaming woman met us on the path.

She was dressed in a long night-shift of cheap blue calico, scrupulously clean but ragged enough to show here and there small patches of yellowing skin. Sixty years or thereabouts. At her age, and screaming with panic or something and dressed or undressed as she was, she didn't look her best. Yet it was possible by using a little imagination to see her as she had once been—a pretty plump woman. Her hair escaping from underneath an unbalanced cotton night-cap had gone almost grey, but flashes of odd yellow showed how beautifully blonde it had once been. She had wrinkles and two chins and a mole and faded blue eyes that would have been contentedly goodnatured if they hadn't been gelid with horror. Something vaguely familiar about her appearance set me thinking I had seen her somewhere—on the village street or in the bus or buying something in a shop. When she saw us she opened her mouth for what might have been the loudest and shrillest of all her screams; but the big man caught her firmly and gently and said: 'What is it, Mrs. Morgan? What's the trouble? Calm yourself now. You're with friends.' He held her as carefully as if she were a beloved child or a precious tantalizing piece of nineteen. Leaning breathless against the trunk of the wood's hundredth tree, I envied him his power to hold her, to calm her, talk to her soothingly until the east-wind fit of screaming passed and tears came like rain. She leaned against him as once she might have leaned against a lover, and again I felt she was known to me already. She said: 'Mr. Butler, Mr. Butler, she's dead, she's dead, my precious Lily's dead.'

'Who's dead? Calm yourself, Mrs. Morgan. What is it?' I had flickering montage memories of George Washington saying farewell to his mother or the Irish soldier boy patiently at attention while his mother with loving arms tied round his waist his bandolier. He was big and sympathetic, but he did it all with a touch of ostentation that made one want to laugh and at the same time to slap his shoulders in friendliness and congratulation. 'She's dead. Lily. My poor girl. My poor child. Dead half in and half out of her bed and black marks on her poor throat. Oh. Oh. Oh. Oh. Oh.' It sounds a ludicrous and impossible exclamation, but squeezed from the lips of an agonized woman on an August morning in a sunny wood it was more terrifying than all the shrieks of hell. Then she fainted in Butler's arms. 'Run,'he said,' for God's sake run to the house and see what in hell is wrong. I'll try to carry her there.' His voice, and not without reason, had lost all its heartiness; it was shrill and strained as with an effort he lifted the old woman off the ground and started to walk, staggering a little, away from me. I didn't like the idea of being the first person after the old woman to find out what was wrong. But for shame's sake I couldn't loiter, so circling around the big man and his burden I took the lead and began my third sprint that morning.

Fifty yards away where the path ended in the heart of the fields I saw the house. Oh, the genuine article: white as snow except where roses climbed the walls; green grass all around and low neatly clipped hedges; green-and-white wooden railings guarding patches of all the things that should grow around such a cottage— nasturtiums, marigolds, sweet pea, and pansies, lupins, carnations, and snapdragons, poppies, geraniums, and hollyhocks. It was like a page from an E. V. Lucas essay on seed merchants' catalogues. It was just the sort of place for a widow and her virtuous simpering daughter who might know about sorrow but not about sin and certainly not about screams.

I trotted the fifty yards, leaving Butler farther and farther behind. I went up the inevitable sanded path limited and ornamented by egg-shaped seashore stones all carefully whitewashed, then through a red-tiled porch, stained glass in two narrow side-windows, through a clean kitchen where a kettle irrelevantly puffed from a gleaming range and breakfast things were laid on a white table, into a bedroom opening off the kitchen, to see a girl half-naked and, as the old woman had said, half in and half out of a rumpled bed. That was the first time I'd seen a dead girl. It was also the first time I'd seen the results of murder. It was a staggering shock.

II

To a fellow with nerves, I repeat, it was a staggering shock. To make it more awful I had once met and spoken to the girl. In this way.

Six weeks previously I had been coming to the end of a stay in a convalescent home on the south of the city. One wing of the building for men and the other for women, good nuns in charge and no contact between the sexes. At least that was the theory, and I found it easily acceptable, for women were of little use to lean on. The other young men, pimply with convalescent prurience, found various ways of evading the religious rule of segregation and they had the cooperation of most of the young women. They made assignations and kissed and cuddled in corners behind clumps of rain-sleek rhododendrons or, if they were permitted and had the strength and the money, they walked a half-mile to the cinema in the nearest suburb. I walked or wobbled alone between the rhododendrons. There wasn't much congenial company in the place and nobody who could talk about books except a poor man in some stage of creeping paralysis who wrote poetry in a handwriting so shaky as to be completely undecipherable, and who said over and over again that 'Lalla Rookh' was the world's greatest epic. I walked or wobbled to the suburb and sat and suffered alone in the cinema, meeting occasionally one female patient who like myself seemed to shun company. She was curiously foreign in appearance. Dark hair parted in the middle, combed tightly away from the parting and gripped securely in a round steel comb just on the nape of her neck. Her face, if it had been brown, might have been the smooth, perfectly moulded face of some Egyptian or Indian child-princess with unworldly brown-eyed beauty making her seem older than mortal sin or the days of Cleopatra. But her face wasn't brown. It was unhealthily white. She had been ill—well, obviously, or she wouldn't have been in that place—and I sympathized because her illness, like my own, had clearly more to do with the mind and the sensibilities than with the body.

We exchanged glances on a few occasions, shy glances that touched and then fled away like timid animals nosing and startling each other by the contact. Her clothes, like my own, were shabby. The other girls brazened out their illnesses by dressing with increased flamboyance and by daubing their pale cheeks. So we passed each other, glanced and glanced away again, but never had the courage to speak until the day she left the convalescent home. Coming back from the brief escape of the suburban cinema, I met her fifty yards from a bus-stop. She walked slowly and almost noiselessly. She carried a blue zipper bag stamped with an airline crest.

'Are you leaving us?'

'Yes.'

'You won't be sorry.' 'No.'

'Can I carry your bag as far as the bus?' 'Oh, thank you.'

Then we walked the fifty yards in complete silence and stood for five uneasy minutes waiting for the bus. I said: 'Soon I'll be leaving the home myself.'

'Is that so.' It wasn't a question. It was acquiescence growing out of indifference, not curiosity; but I wasn't discouraged because I knew my own kind. 'I shan't be crying when I go,' I said. 'The company can be exhausting.' She twisted her mouth wryly, the first twitch of life I had seen in her face. 'It can. Very exhausting indeed.' And then with an effort: 'It's not really such a good place to rest.'

'It isn't.' The bus came rocking around a corner. Her shabby clothes and pale worried face couldn't completely kill in me the suspicion that she had a shapely, lovely figure. But the thought didn't unsettle me, for I was more interested in her mind, more absorbed in my narcissistic fancy that she suffered like myself and shared my problems. I suggested: 'Perhaps we may meet again.' Her face darkened: 'Perhaps.' But when she climbed into the bus and I had safely deposited her blue bag she smiled down at me, a pleasant, warm smile, and said: 'Perhaps we may.' And we did meet again, under what the newspapers would call tragic circumstances.

Behind me Butler's large tan-shoed feet shuffled on the red tiles of the porch, came slowly into the kitchen, and I could hear him sigh with relaxation as he laid down his burden—probably on a brown plush couch in the corner between the range and a latticed window. The woman was whimpering softly as if she had been cruelly beaten. He said: 'Take it easy now, Mrs. Morgan. We'll soon have everything set right.' I could scarcely hear her answer. It sounded as if, awakening from her coma and wise with some awful enlightenment gained in the darkness, she said that nothing in this world would ever be right again, that there were devils walking abroad in bright daylight with the deceptive two-footed and one-headed appearance of ordinary men. I didn't rush out to meet Butler or to help him with the stricken woman because I wasn't able to take my eyes away from the body of the dead girl. I had been right about her figure. One naked thigh was still and shapely as a fragment of Greek marble found among ruins and death. Her face was blackening and the marks on her throat were less like murder than like sacrilege or barbarous vandalism. It didn't occur to me to find out whether or not she was still breathing, or to run right away for the police or the priest or the doctor. A man with presence of mind should under such circumstances do such things. He should also look around the room to see what objects are disarranged or broken or what windows open or curtains trailing or what fragments of letters half- burned on ashtrays. They do that—do nerveless men with presence of mind—in all the best books about girls found dead in boudoirs. But I couldn't see the room—only the girl, the shape of her bare lifeless thigh, her dark hair not now tightly plaited but broken loose and disordered in her struggle to escape from the tightening grip of the devil's hands. The marks on her throat seemed to beat like pulses. Her oriental child-princess face was neither pale nor brown, but some unpleasant colour between black and grey. Death held my eyes and paralysed my body, yet what I wanted to do was, not to run back to the light and warmth of the morning, but to touch her forehead, to kiss her lips, to assure myself that I was meeting for the second time a person who might have been my friend. Perhaps if I could have touched her she might have told me the secret of her lonely meditations between the rows of wet rhododendrons. Whoever the murderer was—the devil abroad in the daylight—he had done me a grievous personal wrong.

In the kitchen the woman cried: 'Lily. My poor Lily.' Butler's voice, mellowness restored to it, consoled her: 'Here now, Mrs. Morgan. Take a grip on yourself. Drink this until I see what is wrong.' Then he called to me: 'Where in hell are you? And What is it?'

'Here.' My voice was a curious dry croak, just loud enough to carry from the bedroom to the kitchen.

'Where's here?'

'Here in the bedroom.' Suddenly afraid, I wanted to be out of the house, walking with Butler the morning road to the station, all the screaming and dreadful discovery put away forcibly as if it were some nightmare fleetingly remembered from the hot, restless, drugged sleep of the previous night. Two of these tablets every night with a glass of milk, the doctor told me. But I couldn't take my glance away from the dead girl and my eyes, not my feet, kept me, as they say, rooted to the spot. Then I felt Butler's breath warm on the back of my neck and heard him say in a cracked whisper: 'Mother of Christ. This is a bad business.' With the warmth of his breath and the sound of his whisper reality returned. I saw the room. The eiderdown bundled at the foot of the bed was coloured a rich vermilion and one small right-angled rip in the covering cloth showed a patch of white lining and a curled grey feather. The wallpaper pattern showed impossible forests of cypress trees—all trunkless as if they also were murdered and mutilated. The furniture was a cheap imitation mahogany, well polished; and the open door of the wardrobe reflected in its interior mirror a portion of my shabby self and one of Butler's well-gaberdined legs. It wasn't for poverty or lack of taste that she had dressed shabbily, for the wardrobe overflowed with good clothes. There were no charred fragments of incriminating letters in the ashtray. There was, indeed, no ashtray. Her dressing-table was neatly and sparsely stocked with the things all women need on their dressing-tables. 'What'll we do?' I asked. The windows were closed, the white lace curtains undisturbed. Apart from the rumpled bed-clothes and the disordered black hair and, of course, the dead body sagging over the side of the bed, the room was quiet, tidy, unostentatious.

He stepped past me, gently touching my shoulder as he went, as if he was saying: Steady yourself; don't let it get you down. He slipped a hand inside her pyjama jacket, cupping it over her cold left breast, feeling in vain for heartbeats. My mind revolted. I wanted to be sick, not physical puking, but a cataclysmic mental revulsion. He touched the black marks with the tip of his right forefinger and bent his head down to her head until I thought he too wanted to kiss her and had the courage I lacked. But he was only searching for, hoping for the soft movement of breath. Then he stood erect so quickly I was startled. He said: 'The police. God rest poor Lily. This is a job for the police.'

'Did you know her?' I had almost known her.

'Everybody knows everybody here. She was a quiet girl. Jesus, what an end.' My palms were sweating. The woman in the kitchen still moaned. I was angry I hadn't had the courage to approach the girl's body, touch her breast and her bruised throat, put my face close to hers and wait for breath. He gripped my elbow and led me into the kitchen, bending down to my ear and whispering: 'Will you stay with her or go for the police?' Flat on her back on the couch, her hands joined over her body like the locked hands of a corpse, the poor woman lay half unconscious from shock, and moaning

11

pitifully. At any moment the moans might rise to shrill shrieks and she might rush again into the bedroom to make certain that her eyes had really seen the dreadful sight. 'When she wakens up it might be better if she sees somebody she knows.'

'It might,' he said. 'Lily had a bicycle. It's probably around somewhere.'

'I doubt if I could ride a bicycle at this moment.' And I really meant that, for my knees wobbled as I walked out into the sunshine.

'Better still,' he called from the porch, 'cross to the big house and borrow the use of their phone.' So I walked along the path between the beech trees, stepped stiffly over the stile, crossed the road, skirted the artificial lake on the avenue to the big house. Pampas grasses gracefully bowed feathery heads in the light wind. A waterhen, neck and head jigging like the neck and head of a child's toy, swam to shelter in green reeds. A uniformed maid doubtfully followed me across the wide polished hallway to the glossy redwood table on which the telephone rested, stood watchfully a few feet away while I rang the village police station. Swivelling around, I stared blankly at her and said in a clear voice: 'Sergeant, a girl has been found dead in a cottage on the road to the station. It looks like murder.' It gave me warm satisfaction to see the watchful little bitch gasp, turn pale and scuttle away across the hallway, caring no longer whether I did or didn't steal the rugs off the polished floor or the phoney antlers off the ancestral walls. Giving the remainder of my message to the sergeant, I looked vacantly out through the graceful doorway left open to the morning and, just as I returned the phone to the hook, running steps came up the gravel and Butler's big body blocked out the sunshine. 'Took a chance in leaving her for a few minutes,' he said breathlessly.

'Have a call to make myself. Oh, wait for me. Don't go.' I waited while he dialled his number, while he said: 'Hello. Hello. That you, Miss Jones. George Butler speaking. Well and hearty. Never better. Only tell Mr. Mac I won't be at work today. No. Well, perhaps late in the afternoon. Got mixed up in a murder. Yes. Murder. Really and truly. No. Not my own. Not yet, anyway. Too bad. Well, I suppose it is. Happens to all of us sooner or later. You do please be careful, Miss Jones, especially when you're on overtime with Mr. Mac. Good-bye, darling. Good-bye.' Such a man, I thought enviously, watching the swell of bicep and shoulder muscle straining the cloth of his coat, could lead a regiment to glory in a lost battle. 'Good-bye, dear. See you on the gallows.' Then he dropped the receiver and said: 'A nice girl that. But it'll never do her any good.' On the threshold he said sighingly: 'Murder or no murder, a man has to keep his job.'

The maid hadn't returned. Somewhere in a deep ancient basement she was whispering the terrible news and the village and the city would soon know all about it. Butler and I belonged now with that strange body of the chosen: the men who discover dead bodies. In a moment of arrogant pique I left two pennies on the polished redwood. Two policemen and a doctor came running behind us as we walked back between the beeches.

III

The inquest happened four days later. Butler talked sensibly to the police and with the aid of a doctor's certificate kept me away from that ceremony. I was grateful even if I was a little embarrassed, for I couldn't have faced the ordeal, the meaningless talk, the verdict that death was the result of something done by person or persons unknown.

The morning of the discovery, when we'd satisfied their curiosity and escaped from their questioning, he took me to a public-house in the village and for the first time in months I drank whiskey. Lacking congenial drinking company and not knowing how to find it or how to make friends, and afraid of becoming that pitiful perilous thing —a solitary drinker—I had for some time avoided even the thought of drink. But walking back to the village, the sun hot and high in the heavens, he crooked his right arm about my shoulder and said: 'Have some malt, Hartigan, old chap. Have a jar. By Jesus, we need it after what we've been through this morning.'

'I've no money. I was going into town to cash a cheque.'

'The drinks are on me this morning. Come on.' I went with him down a long passage to a semicircular private bar built and supplied with cushioned seats for the benefit of visitors from the city. At that time of the morning and of the week it was quiet and empty because the villagers drank in the public bar, generally after hours, and the city people were, most of them, at work. Green roughcast walls were hideous with futuristic decorations done by a very amateur artist. The grate was choked with cinders of a fire, bright some night when the room was full and faces red and singing loud. A slattern of a women chewing the bacon rinds of a late breakfast poured our whiskies. Her hands were grimy. She said: 'Missed your bus this morning, Mr. Butler?'

'No, missus, I've a free morning.'

'I hear there's some bad trouble at Morgan's cottage.'

In villages even the blue morning air can carry bad news. I'd have answered: Is that so?—and made the woman my enemy for life. But Butler had more wisdom. Everything he did and said increased my envious admiration for him. 'Aye God help us', he said, 'the world's full of trouble.' The woman, satisfied, returned to her cave, leaving us to drink in peace, interrupted only by fragments of talk wandering in through an arched opening from the public bar.

'The police and the doctor went out in a rush.' 'Is it that Lily girl?'

'The dark one.'

'She kept herself to herself.'

'Or so we all thought.'

'A disgrace to the locality.'

'Get us some publicity for the holiday season.'

They couldn't yet have heard that, after the girl and her mother and the unknown devil, we were the principal characters in the piece, the discoverers, the link between hell and the bright world of normal men. If they had known they'd certainly have swarmed around us. 'A ghastly morning,' Butler said. He nipped his lips around his second whisky. 'They get a real kick out of this.'

'Ghastly'.

Was the secret nursed between the wet rhododendrons, the knowledge of the devil, the thing that had killed her?

'Particularly ghastly for you. No addition at all to a rest cure.'

'None.'.

'I feel guilty. Only for me you wouldn't have set out to walk to the station.'

'Oh, don't be silly.'

'I must see more of you. Come to town with me now and again. Step out of yourself.'

'That's decent of you.'

14

'I don't mean it that way. After this morning we've something in common.' The dead girl held us together. Some day I could tell him when and how I had almost known her and what my dreams of her had been.

Afterwards, when we were warm with spirits, he walked with me to the foot of the fair-green, stood on the street watching me and waving his long right arm while I climbed homewards, stepping from stone to stone to avoid mud and slushy dung. My back to the village and my feet on the stile at the top of the slope, I could see my cottage, my hut, half a mile away across the fields. I went towards it along a field path with the feelings a criminal might have approaching and entering a condemned cell, fearing grisly unshapen thoughts about unalterable things.

My hut was one of six huts, all in a row. The ascent of the fair-green and the walk along the field path under overhanging hawthorns was the direct route from the village. The longest way round, which was the shortest way home if you were drunk and the night dark, was out of the village past two shops and a schoolhouse, a Protestant church and the rector's residence, a row of low white cottages, dishwater grey and clammily odorous in a cracked gutter, then along a tarred road for a hundred yards, then for fifty yards to the right along a winding lane. My hut was the first of the six huts on that lane. Except in the high holiday months of midsummer, and this was late August, four of the six were boarded up and un-inhabited, waiting for the city people who owned them to return with noisy children, golf-clubs and fishing-rods. The sixth hut was inhabited by a labourer and his wife, a fat, warm girl, not long enough married to be burdened with a family and so able to contain their lives and their love in a one-roomed board hut with a bunk nailed half-ways up the wall. By day she came to the doorway, hair blowing, sleeves rolled up, smelling, I imagined, of warm sudsy water and pleasures bouncingly enjoyed. By night their one window was coloured pink with the light, suggesting a homeliness that attracted me and at the same time revolted me. It was so easy for the crude and ignorant to find their fellows. When a branch creaked on a windy night in the ragged wood between our lane and the demesne wall I thought of their bunk creaking against their wooden house and was tempted at times to creep out and listen. Solely for the sake of company. I haven't, I hope, any of the malign instincts of the voyeur or whatever the French call a man who listens at thin walls as the next best thing to looking through keyholes.

She looked up laughing as I passed. The short cut came first to her cottage and there she was on the grass patch before the door, playing with a collie pup, holding her round bare arms above her head, the collie leaping up to paw her fine tight bosom. Her brown hair was like a wind-tossed blossoming exotic bush. A woman for couches and comfits, not for wooden huts and the washing and darning of a labourer's socks. But she seemed happy where she was. 'Good day, Mr. Hartigan,' she said. 'You're back early.'

'I missed the bus and set out to walk to the station.' 'Did you miss the train as well?' Her voice was flat and without the emotional sort of resonance the voice of such a woman should have. But her laugh was throaty and musical, and she laughed then at the leaping collie or perhaps at the spectacle of a thin-faced, dark-chinned man who hadn't the energy to catch trains and buses. Her husband energetically cycled to work and cycled home again—six miles each way. He was a quiet, sallow, wiry man with dungarees and brown brooding eyes. 'No,' I said. 'I met a man called Butler and the two of us walked into a bit of trouble.'

'Is it Mr. Butler from the hotel?' Again the laugh. She was bending down, her thighs under a tweed skirt widening to a tailor's squat, to quiet the collie and snuggle him against her bosom. What would the collie do when the first child came? Her brown hair tumbled forward to hide her round face.

'Do you know Mr. Butler?'

'Sure, everybody knows Mr. Butler.' The collie struggling and licking leaped free. The afternoon was pleasantly warm on my shoulders and on hers too, for she turned her back to me and grabbed teasingly at the belly of the dancing, delighted dog, and said suddenly: 'Was it serious trouble?'

'Just a murder.' Her husband had cycled away to work that morning leaving her kissed and contented. 'God protect us,' she said. She was up square on her feet again, tidying back her hair, and then, when it was tidied and under control, piously cutting the Sign of the Cross. 'Where did it happen? Who in God's name was it?' She was excited, yet her voice hadn't lost its curious emotionless flatness.

'In Morgan's cottage on the road to the station.' 'Jesus, Mary and

16

Joseph. Poor Lily Morgan.' It didn't strike me as odd that she should have known before I told her that Lily Morgan had been the victim. Nerveless men with presence of mind who frequently act as private detectives always notice such things, almost by instinct, and straightaway draw conclusions and find the answer to riddles— conclusions and answers to be revealed coyly by the author on the penultimate page of the book. It seemed somehow reasonable to suppose that if there was going to be a murder in Morgan's cottage then the victim would be Lily and not the old woman. More picturesque too. 'Strangled in her bed,' I said. 'A horrible sight.' Who, apart from big Butler, had a better right than myself to spread the glad news? The collie leaped unheeded and unheeded pawed at her motionless frozen bosom. The warmth of the sallow man was six miles away being wasted on unskilled work. She said in a husky whisper: 'Did the police catch him?'

'Catch who?'

'Whoever did it. It was a man, I suppose. Poor Lily had a weakness for the men. She wasn't too sound up here.' She tapped her forehead with a short, strong forefinger.

'Nobody knows who did it. Not yet, anyway.' I shuffled forward a few steps. She said: 'It'll bring a bad name to the whole place. The world's gone mad.' I agreed with her. There didn't seem to be anything else to do, or anything further to say except good afternoon and God help us all and what is the country coming to. So I walked on past the four empty huts, their windows uncurtained, their doors bolted on complete emptiness, but not, I imagined, from the nature of the thin impermanent buildings on any ghosts. When I turned round to look from my own doorstep she was standing quite still where I had left her, and the collie dog, weary of neglect, had grovelled at her feet.

IV

I closed my door behind me and stood for a while staring fixedly at my radio, my bunk, my four shelves of select books—Pascal, Papini, Sartre, Dostoevsky, Epictetus, Sir Thomas Malory, and others—at my small electric cooker, and also at the remainder of the afternoon. It appeared leaden and colourless like a stagnant lifeless sea. I looked ahead then and saw the coming night: a black man with an axe skulking around a dark corner.

Tomato soup poured from a tin and heated in a saucepan and slowly supped while I crumbled fragments of bread between my fingers and desultorily chewed. Then a cup of tea and some digestive biscuits. That was lunch. One of the worst things about being a nervous wrcck is that your appetite can go from you so completely that every bite of solid food, meat or vegetables or potatoes, sticks in your throat like sulphur mixed with grey glutinous office-paste. Dish-washing was a good pastime. No mental strain involved. Wash every dirty dish and spoon, and even some clean ones to pass more time, in pleasant warm water, then dry them until they glow and pack them away on low shelves behind a green-and-red flowered curtain. Tidy the place. Dust each ledge. The afternoon is eternity. Her body is now somewhere in a morgue, naked on a slab, doctors discovering the nature of wounds and when inflicted, policemen making notes. Sweep the floor carefully, methodically routing dust out from each corner to the centre. Dust every book on the four shelves, one after the other, take them out, fondle them, read a paragraph here and a line there—Kafka dismally writing diaries, Gorki studying gorilla-like murderers, Osbert Sitwell at opulent ease in Italy, Graham Greene with dysentery in a ditch in darkest, lawless Mexico—then replace each dusted, inspected volume and at the end of all that the afternoon is still eternity. Mix with crowds, one doctor said, and shake yourself out of yourself. So I mixed with crowds to find myself staggering among steady people, grabbing at elusive elbows, even at waists; and, once walking on a crowded street with a girl I knew, I staggered, put my arm around her redcoated waist and she laughed so that people looked at us. Laughing, she said: 'Not here, Donagh, not here. Neither the time nor the place.' Silence in my hut, the cooking, eating, washing, sweeping, dusting all done, while I listen again to the pain of her laughter. The square green glass clock above my bunk struck five. Malory and a rocking-chair out to the grass patch to sit in late afternoon sunshine, to read in closely printed columns, two to each thin page, how King Uther came disguised as her husband to the bed of Igraine and was welcomed by her as she would welcome her lord. No antidote for my black afternoon mood, for my dread of the blacker night. Go disguised as a sallow faced labouring man mounted, like a king of Arthurian legend, on a high bicycle, all the way gallantly to the sixth hut to find Igraine plump and brown-haired on her creaking couch. Suppose Uther had arrived to find Igraine dead in her high castle, black bruises on her swan throat. Queen Igraine, fond of the men, remembering them between convalescent rhododendrons—their differences, their devastating similarity.

The clock in the hut behind me struck six times. The sun dropped towards the tops of the tufted trees beyond the demesne wall. 'The trees are in their autumn beauty,' I quoted, 'the woodland paths are dry'—crisp underfoot for night-walking when my hut became, as it would, oppressive. Her husband cycled slowly along the curves of the lane, relaxing his sinewy yellow legs after his six-mile cycle run, waving a casual hand to me as he passed, but sending no word with the hand-wave. The door of the sixth hut slammed behind him—rest and steak and onions and other things before him.

Go out on your own, another doctor had said, and learn independence, learn to shake yourself out of yourself; and, because his advice was fairly close to what I wanted to do myself, I followed it. At least, shaking oneself out of oneself wasn't so humiliating when you were alone: the rocking-chair gently rocking, the wind fluttering the thin leaves of the book to the chapter where Sir Launcelot vanquished a foe and leaped into a bed, evening air losing its warmth, demesne trees blackly outlined against a pale-gold sky. In a big house among those trees and looking across park-land to the slow bends of the river above a salmon leap an eighteenth-century soldier had once lived. A business man lived there now, motored every morning to his shop in the city, and allowed his five daughters to risk their necks on galloping horses. On quiet mornings I could hear hoof-beats thundering along the taut flat land by the edge of the river.

A postman came free-wheeling down the lane with the evening delivery, dropped a letter into the green tin box fixed to my gate-post, shouted a greeting, and cycled away again. No news from the world outside to disturb the sallow man and the brown-haired woman at their steak and onions. The sky faded and the grass turned grey. The letter was from my mother, and a letter from that good woman always had, even before I read it, power to upset me; it is trying to be so different from one's own people and to be forced to listen, even through the mail, to so much good advice.

'My darling son Donagh,' she wrote....

(One or two uncharitable friends had not been above hinting that my nervous ailment could be partially explained by the fact that my mother had always singled me out among my brothers and sisters for special consideration. When I was a child I wasn't allowed to play with other children on our suburban avenue. When I was going to school and studying hard the rest of the family were forced to go about the house like mutes at a nineteenth-century funeral; but I could practise, vilely, at the piano even when my elder sister was stewing advanced mathematics.)

'. . . by time I sincerely trust that you have grown tired of your mountain solitude. I still can't help thinking that that young doctor who had little practical experience was extremely rash in advising you to go away and live in a cottage on your own. What you need more than anything else is home cooking and comfort and pleasant society around you all the time. . .'

(Pleasant society? My brothers and sisters. My mother enjoying herself whispering to the neighbours her solicitude about her nervous son. If I had sick leave with pay then I'd live for a few months just how and where I pleased.)

'. . . every moment of the day I expect to see you on the doorstep, sensible and glad to be home again. . . .'

(No, never shall sun or moon that moment see. Better the thin hut, the lonely roads at night, the casual nods of villagers no longer curious, than the cakes and comforts of home, the grand piano in the drawing-room, the patience of my mother, the odour of my sisters dressing for dances. Threats could not more effectively keep me away from home than the thought of her saintly waiting, the door always open, the fire glowing, the meal prepared-temptations, tentacles.)

20

'. . . your sister Sue has done very well indeed in her university examination. . . .'

My sister Sue would do well in anything. No purpose in reading any further. Shadows are rising out of the river valley somewhere between the village and the city, spreading out from the city's smoke or driven out by the radiance bursting from street lamps and sky-signs and shop windows. In a suburban road my mother switches on her light and waits for her wandering boy. I know what the news she sends will be and I know her normal exhortations. So crumple the letter into my pocket and carry the chair, Green Malory, master of Arthurian tales, resting on its gently rocking seat, back into the hut, to my two tablets and glass of hot milk and three golden biscuits, to an hour reading by lamplight—so much more restful than electric light—until the tablets burst inside me and their drowsy fumes rise to my brain. Turn down the lamp and climb into my bunk, chasing hungrily after rest, feeling the bunk straining slightly against the clamps that hold it to the wall, then sinking down into sleep as if some gentle unseen hand had pushed me over the rim of a deep, dark well.

Dreams came up around me as I sank. Dreams fumed up from dissolving fragments of the exploded tablets.

By the winding river in the demesne I walked with the wife of the sallow man. Springtime and lime leaves soft and long grasses leaning to touch sea-blue water, and my arm around her waist, not to support tottering steps, but the way a man's arm should be about a pretty woman's waist. Then without warning the staggering began, not myself, but the tall trees and the sky and the woman by my side. When I, the only erect and unshaken object in the whirl of an earthquake, gripped her more tightly to steady her she turned black and hirsute and crumbled under my touch.

I was seated upstairs in the last bus from town to my mother's suburb on a frosty, misty November night. The seats were cold and clammy, the windows patterned with ice so that passing street lights could only be seen as dim yellow blobs. Passenger after passenger arose and glided noiselessly, facelessly down the aisle between the seats, without bumping went down the stairs and, no bell ringing to stop the bus or start it again, faded away into frozen night. In the end only one passenger, excepting myself, remained. She sat a few seats ahead of me. By craning my neck I could just see her profile, smooth and clear, nose and chin gently rounded. Anyway, there was no mistaking her dark hair straining against the steel comb that held it in a knot above the nape of her neck. Several times I tried to attract her attention, craning forward, opening and then closing with a snap a book I held in my hands, coughing, shuffling my cold feet, making great play with a match-box and a cigarette case. She paid no attention; and once straining forward a little farther than I had previously managed to do, it seemed to me I could see her eyes dark with reserved, smiling, self-satisfied mockery.

The bus stopped suddenly in a cold silence. No conductor called cheerfully the name of some coy, cosy suburban road or park or avenue or drive or square or garden estate. No bell rang. She stood up and walked, not towards the stairs and myself, but away from me, never showing me her face, towards the wide windscreen. She wasn't shabby. She was dressed like a queen. She didn't hear or pretend to hear my shout of warning, and when I tried to rise and follow her I couldn't tear myself away from the chilly leather-covered chromium-framed seat; and shouting and shouting, I tried to warn her, until I woke myself to hear faintly my own shouts drifting away from me into sleep like the cries of a drowning man covered and extinguished by grey water.

The bed-clothes were damp with my perspiration. I dropped to the floor, towelled my shivering limbs, and dressed myself.

Men in prison cells probably pace their stone unimpressionable floors the way I then paced up and down my creaking straw-mat-covered planks. Between the planks and the ground on which these huts had grown like mushrooms there was a hollow space twelve or eighteen inches deep. That hollow echoed and magnified the noise of my restless feet until I feared the labourer and his wife would hear me, and even the people in the village over the hill. The neighbouring couple hadn't gone to bunk yet. Peeping out, I saw the light in their window, but, as I watched, the bright square abruptly went dark and my awful loneliness went over me like a high tide. How could one live alone and learn self- reliance when one was at intervals tormented with a sickening craving for company? Or how draw self-reliance from company when, the moment it was available, body and soul closed up like prickly shells? Up and down, up and down the booming floor. Let them hear. Let the sound of my feet burst in on their warm sleep or, if they're not sleeping, play metronome to their pleasures. Let the village hear me too: Butler in his hotel, laughing that high loud laugh of his and drinking whisky with normal men or making telephone calls to hot, attractive women; or the chewing woman with the grimy hands squeezing profits from car-loads of city drunks in her prosperous pub; or the hardware dealer with all his laughing shiny buckets safely stowed away for the night.

Up and down, up and down, faster and louder until a shout came to my lips and was choked down with an effort, a shout like those lost in my dream in futile pursuit of a ghost of a girl. Then I knew it was time to grip my sanity hard and hold on, and sit down sweating to try to read; and feel the thin walls close in on me and know that my only escape was the long walk over dark roads until I was so utterly exhausted that sleep would return with the speed of a stunning blow.

The woodland paths were certainly dry. I closed my gate behind me carefully—it was lopsided and took a deal of closing—then crossed the lane and followed a footpath through the ragged wood to the tarred road. Small things scuttled unseen in dark undergrowth. Fifty yards along the road there was a broken place in the demesne wall. My hands on the shattered stone, I thought: Am I awake or asleep? For two or three times in the last year I had actually dressed myself in my sleep, walked out of my mother's house, and awakened on suburban roads with a bewildered isolated feeling, a man exiled on a strange planet. The rasp of crumbling plaster against my palms convinced me I was now awake. Rub them there until they ache and you smell dry stone and until fragments of plaster drop like hail to patter on dead leaves under the darkness of the demesne trees. Then climb up and slither down into the darkness after the crumbling fragments.

Between high mysterious pillar-like oaks I waited motionless for a while, the life of the night woods stirring all around me. Poacher ancestors might thus have dropped, crouched, waited, while breaking in for illicit purposes on my lord's privileged land. The house was away beyond the river.

Forward cautiously for a while, hands feeling the darkness for leaning, grasping branches. Then finding the path, I walked furiously until the trees were behind me and the river by my side.

Oh, the solace, the peace of deep water. On along the river path, up and over at three different stiles, shapes of cattle dark on the rich grass, pale moonlight filtering through a cloud to silver the broken water at the salmon leap. One punt was moored above the fall. It looked like the exposed back of a sleeping whale. No galloping girls dared the night. Scenes and fancies from the urgent night walks of a neurotic. I had the world to myself. On and on over more stiles. I ran at two of them as a champion hurdler would run. In the night air I never staggered. Along the narrow, unkempt strip that greedy cultivators grudged to fishermen and to night-walkers by the river. Ripe golden oats rustled all around me. Then up a steep slope at a five-arched stone bridge and my feet again were on the hard metalled road, wires over my head humming messages from people to people: Good night, darling, and I wish you were with me, or, Yes, certainly, buy twenty more gross, or, Lily Morgan has been murdered and the police suspect a thin neurotic who lives in a hut and had amicable but possessive designs on the unfortunate girl.

The road went one way towards the village and the city, and the other way to plunge into dark country. Pacing quickly, my arms loosely swinging, I went back towards the village.

Most of the villagers went early to bed. Two lamps and four lighted windows, like navigation signs through darkness, marked the full course of the street; and in the grimy woman's pub the city drunks were singing, happy until midnight. My mother's letter was still in my pocket, so I smoothed the envelope and carried it in my hand, endeavouring to seem as if a real errand to the post-box at the far end of the street had taken me from the retirement of my hut. The effort wasn't necessary, because I met nobody all the way there and all the way back. The door of the hotel was closed and the ground-floor windows heavily curtained, but within, for certain, the doctor, the curate, the solicitor, the chemist, the school teacher, one or two grocers and other local aristocrats, perhaps even the man who owned the laughing buckets, were drinking with Butler. I stopped at the door, but turned away without knocking. Ten to one they wouldn't open or wouldn't admit me if they did. Late drinking in the hotel was not for the uninitiated or for car-loads of strangers from the city. If I asked for Butler I'd be admitted, but I couldn't expose my weakness to a man, however friendly, met only that morning. Inside now in the hotel bar he was probably the hero of the place, describing how he had found her and what he had done, holding all his listeners morbidly enthralled, telling nobody—naturally—that, after the murderer and her mother, Donagh Hartigan, the queer fellow in the hut, had been the first person to see her dead body.

So I walked for a while along the road towards the station. A horrible lonely road smothered in darkness by high hedges, and the pityful trying-hard moon smothered again in tumbling clouds. In the morning high bushes had waved like banners, and birds had whistled around the shell of the ruined mill. But if I walked on this road as far as the ill-fated cottage some watching, waiting policeman might accost me; and sweating with unreasonable terror, my limbs at last exhausted to the edge of sleep, I went back through the village and, splashing hopelessly in mud, up the slippery fair-green. Below, the village was in darkness, the two street lamps quenched, light gone from the windows. But with one tired foot on the wobbly stile on the grassless summit I looked down and saw three cars, loud with singing drunks, turn the sharp corner and take the road to the station and the city—past her cottage. Exactly at that moment I sensed the emptiness of my right hand. My mother's letter and its enclosing envelope were gone. They weren't in my pockets. I searched thoroughly, thought for a while of returning step by step over the way I had walked since I'd taken them from my pocket and smoothed them out to look like something ready for the post, a reason for being abroad approaching midnight.

Well, whoever finds my mother's letter won't be wiser or richer for the finding; and I crossed the stile to stumble wearily, oh, so wearily, along the footpath. The sky was ominous with great masses of dark cloud cracked here and there by struggling moonlight. The wind had switched around for rain. No light in their hut. Warm crushed sleep in the creaking bunk. Then light somewhere ahead affronted my weary eyes and I walked three tottering steps before I saw that it came from my own hut, from the uncurtained window which I had certainly left curtained, from the open door which I thought I had left closed. Fire, I thought, and, echoing Butler, cried: 'Mother of Jesus. The shack's ablaze and my precious books in black powder.' Tired as I was I ran like a hare past the four empty, lonely huts.

V

But it wasn't fire. It was a man, a big man crouched on a chair and nursing a full sealed bottle of whisky as if it were a delicate loved child. I stood and looked at him for several minutes, my blood chilled with panic, at his broad back, at the tails of a heavy navy-blue overcoat flowing out from the chair and trailing to the floor. He didn't apparently hear me, didn't at any rate turn to see me as with planned heavy-footedness I went up the three wooden steps and across the threshold. He slept the profound sleep that a drunken man could enjoy in a wet ditch or on an icy pavement or on the iron points of a harrow. Yet when I touched his shoulder he woke up like a shot and glanced at me, sideways, clutching the bottle by the neck as if he meant to make it into a weapon. He may have been a drunk man, but by the look in his eyes he was also a hunted man.

Odd as it may seem, the things I noticed first were the large gold-coloured shield-shaped label on the bottle and a smaller label showing three white swallows in swift ecstatic flight.

I said: 'Who are you? And what do you think you're doing here?' A lout who had never heard of Rilke or of Henry James could have said as much and said it probably, as I couldn't, without a coward's quiver in his voice. To conquer my fear I again touched his shoulder, and he stood up, stepping away from me, still gripping the bottle. 'A stranger,' he said, 'just passing through.' His voice was hoarse either with drink or with the exhaustion of being hunted.

'How did you get in here?'

'Is it your wee house?'

'It is. You've no right to be here.' That was jejune, but under the circumstances it was a brave thing to say. 'The door was open,' he growled. 'So in I walked. Any objections, Paddy?' I had objections, of course, but it wasn't easy to phrase them in a style the man would appreciate. Then in another way I hadn't any objections, for with his coming the tedium of the night had gone as if it had been blown from a gun.

'What's your name?' At that he began to laugh, bending down and leaning on the back of a chair and laughing silently until he coughed; and I realized he was the remains of a big handsome man, dark-headed and swarthy as a Spaniard, with a long straight nose and a pleasant wide mouth and piercing black eyes. To realize so much needed discernment, for he was ragged and a wreck and couldn't have shaved for four or five days. 'That's a good one,' he said through his laughing and coughing. 'You want to know my name.' Then he straightened up until his high head nearly touched the ceiling and I felt dwarfed and puny. He said: 'I used to be well known in these parts. But I've been moving around for some years.'

'I'm a stranger here myself. Living here for my health.' That was as banal as a remark could be, but somehow there didn't seem to be anything more pungent or more decisive to say. For when he straightened up the wreck of his great body and said he had once been well known in these parts he became both admirable and pitiable: a sailor home after decades in purple countries and searching in a land of green pastures and white cottages for the survivors of his companions and kindred, a man rich with experience but as lonely as a dying swan. I didn't want him to go. I wanted to be pleasant and friendly, patronizing even—perhaps to compensate myself for the support and offers of friendship given to me that morning by another big man, another stranger. Clumsily with his free hand he was buttoning his overcoat. One of the buttons was missing and a bright safety-pin, as big as the pins used to fasten babies' napkins, dangled from the dirty greasy cloth. 'I won't stay where I'm not wanted.' He slipped the yellow bottle into a gaping pocket. The shield-shaped label vanished first and then the white wild swallows. He said: 'Sorry for intruding', and made to walk around me to the door, but I kicked it shut behind me, proud of the decisive speed of my action, and said: 'No harm done. I'm going to have supper. You look hungry.'

The first great drops of the coming tempest of rain were cracking like hazel-nuts on the felt-covered roof. 'It's going to pour from the heavens,' I said. 'Sit and eat.' Nervously he sat down again as if he distrusted the chair and, tightening the lapels of his coat around his throat with his right hand, he turned his eyes upwards—swivelling eyeballs of negro minstrels—to the roof, seeing the night sky above and the dark gathering storm. Then he decided and relaxed. He swallowed, said thanks, placed the bottle of whisky gently on the floor and said: 'You're very good. I didn't mean to come in here. It was an accident. Wrong number.' From his other pocket he pulled a soft parcel wrapped in white paper blotched with spots of pale red and handed it to me. 'I won't be a burden on your supplies. I've food here and a wee drop as well.' 'What is this?' I touched the white parcel.

'That's bloody good mincemeat. Two pounds of it fresh from the mincing machine.' He stretched his legs and smiled with self-satisfaction, his face wrinkling and softening under black beard. His boots were cracked and gaping. 'A girl in a shop gave me that mincemeat this evening. She took pity on me, I reckon, out of the goodness of her heart. Christ, I'm a down-and-out, Paddy. I'm an object of pity.' There was no answer to that one. Turning away for a moment, I did some rattling business with cups and saucers. Stirring in his chair be belched, and the small room filled with the odours of stale porter. He said: 'I took the whisky, without asking for it, from a pub on the road from the city. You never saw a publican giving a bottle of whisky to a tramp out of the goodness of his heart.' I unwrapped the meat, shuffled it on to a plate, and carried it, a red crushed mass, towards the cooker. For the first time in days I felt like food. The result of my frenzied walk? Or the shock of finding a stranger in possession of my hut? Or just the mere presence of the man, for although he was a drunken wreck and a ragged tramp there was something about him, an inspiration, a secret of life, a mysterious vitality. 'That was the first time a woman ever offered me charity,' he said.

The first four slices of mince sizzled on the pan. Thank God he had had it in his pocket, for golden digestive biscuits and a half-loaf, and I had nothing else in the hut, wouldn't be provender for a man in his condition or even for myself with my surprisingly novel hunger. Above the sputter of frying and the increasing thunder of rain on the roof, I listened to his monologue. The hut was uncomfortably warm, but I didn't mind because I had known it when it was ice cold and at the same time suffocatingly close and small. 'Every time before today I was the one that did the charity. Even last night I did a good deed for a woman.' It was good rich mince. Watching it turn crisp and brown, my appetite strengthened.

'Are you interested in women, Paddy?'

'Not a lot,' I said. 'Not a lot.' There had only been my mother, and one or two girls tentatively kissed, and a dissolute street-creature one night after a college dance when I stupidly tried to act like my companions—a dark sweaty experience. Then there had been my dream of Lily Morgan.

'There's nothing else,' he mumbled. 'Just drink and women. Not even war. I was a soldier and I know.' The kettle boiled. Most of the mincemeat was ladled out carefully on to two plates. 'Have a drop, Paddy?'

'Afterwards.'

He lowered the bottle again to the floor. He said: 'I soldiered with the British and I deserted for drink and women. I lived for six weeks in a Norfolk inn, never showing my face in daylight, I swear to God, all because the woman who owned it was a lonely widow and gave me free whisky for keeping the bed warm. When she found out I preferred the whisky to herself she showed me the door.'

'Eat something.' Head tilted back, he looked up at me, his face under the beard softening with laughter. 'You never did a thing like that in all your mortal life, Paddy. You should break out and have a fling. It'd make your life worth living.' Advice from Butler, employee of an advertising agency by day, and by night a theatre and music critic for a fashion magazine, and then advice from a nameless derelict tramp, and from specialists and parents and priests and friends and brothers and sisters: Go on, Donagh, break out and have a fling, shake yourself out of yourself, mix with people, live alone and learn independence, dance a jig, break a window, seduce a woman. Some day, by God, I'd show them.

His left hand grabbed down towards the floor as if he was searching for something in the dark. His fingers closed around the neck of the bottle. 'If you won't have a drink, Paddy, I will.' He ripped off the yellow leaden seal, jerked out the cork with his teeth, spat it from him, and drank four fierce gulps of neat whisky. 'Nothing like it for giving a man an appetite. Here, try some, Paddy, for jay's sake.' And to humour him I put the bottle to my head and drank, not absolutely unwillingly. Oh, the warmth of it, the pungent memories of peat smoke by Connacht hearths. Oh, the world's best and most violent drink. Then we ate like animals and drank tea and whisky until the two pounds of mincemeat and the half-loaf and two large brown earthenware pots of tea and half the singing whisky were no more.

'Women,' he said, licking his lips and sucking his teeth and walking backwards and forwards, head and shoulders stooped, between my bookshelves and the one window. The timbers shook with the lurching weight of his stride. Once he stopped by the window and peered out at what the light showed of the stiff continuous spears of rain. 'I know the tart that lives over there,' he said. 'She's an old friend of mine. I did her a good turn last night.'

'Tart?' But he didn't notice or didn't heed the question in my voice. 'She married a queer boy,' he said, 'a craw thumping yellow-hammer,' and bending as he passed he lifted the bottle from the floor and gulped and coughed as the hot spirit hit the back of his throat.

'Fond of reading, Paddy.' He was staring at my books. 'Read me a bit. Go on, read me a bit of something.' Yawning, he dropped down into the rocking-chair at the foot of my bunk. The food and whisky and the heat had brought back and reinforced the drowsiness invoked by my walk on roads and woodland paths. But I took down the first book that came to my hand and, opening it at random, read a few sentences. 'And one has nothing and nobody, and one travels about the world with a trunk and a case of books, and really without curiosity. What sort of a life is it really: without a house, without inherited possessions, without dogs. If only one had one's memories! But who has them? If one could bring one's childhood to mind—but it is as though it had been buried.' The ghastly appropriateness made me stop reading and look at him—whisky pallor on his face, his head bowed and his eyes closed, his great body rocking gently to and fro.

'I slept in bloody ditches,' he muttered, 'until I've no more left lung than would cover a thruppenny bit. True bill, Paddy, I've only one lung between myself and Jesus.' Then later he said: 'That guy writes with style. I'm not an ignorant bastard, Paddy, no matter what I look like. I used to read books too. My poor mother sent me to a college to make me into a clergyman. That's a bloody good one, isn't it, Paddy?' Flicking the pages of the book, I listened to the rain and tried to think of something to say and, dumb before the man's desolation, felt frightened at my folly in playing host to a ragged tramp who stole whisky, deserted from armies, and breathed with difficulty through one lung. Suppose he died in his chair—or in my rocking-chair. Suppose he refused to leave the hut or burned it down or broke the furniture. The thoughts that should have troubled me when sober now jostled each other into my drunken mind. The bottle on the floor seemed to rock to the rhythm of the rain and the rhythm of the big one-lunged body in the rocking-chair. The world was a pendulum. 'Women,' he breathed. 'Women. Women.' Then abruptly he sat up, rescuing himself from the pit of sleep, and said: 'Lily Morgan's dead. Lily's dead. Did you hear the news?'

'I did.'

'That's what set me drunk. I didn't get drunk here in the village, though. You couldn't get drunk among all those pious bitches and yellow-hammers.' He closed his eyes as if his decayed lung had stabbed him with pain. 'Lily was a great friend of mine.'

'I was one of the two men who found her body.' In this place where everybody knew everybody, and everybody knew everything—it seemed—about Lily Morgan, finding her dead body was part of my tenous claim to her friendship. My words didn't register. He was looking at something held in the hollow of his hand. 'She had a ring from me once, but she gave it back to me. She'd never have me in her bed, although I slept with women that looked smarter than poor Lily, God rest her. Women, Paddy, with rumps as tight as kettledrums and as bouncy as golf balls. Poor Lily was thin, but she was different.'

As a private detective I'd be a complete humbug. Granted I was drunk, but drunk or sober I should have suspected that I might possibly have a murderer under my roof. Any company was better than my own company, even that of a twenty-foot devil—if he could have fitted into the hut—with the scalps of twenty murdered women dangling from his belt and the scalp of the twenty-first victim stuck like a silk handkerchief in his breast pocket. At least that was the way I'd thought when sober and conscious of the impossibility of removing such a man if he didn't want to go. Now, drink-stolen whisky-had inflated me, satisfied me with my own company, put an edge on my sense of proprietorship, given me a desire for proud privacy in my own hut, on my own bunk, with my own books. Anyhow, why the hell should he keep calling me Paddy when my name was Donagh, and why should I be compelled to hear him talk as he talked of the dead girl. So I pendulumed over to him and said: 'Look, I'm going to bed now. You'd better be on your way.' Rain danced on the roof. A rising wind lashed rain against the window. He'd slumped back in the chair and fallen asleep.

Listening to the rain and the wind, looking down at his pitiable unshaven face, red-rimmed eyes closed, mouth gaping open, my mood switched again. Oh, let him steal whisky, despoil women, dodge columns, burn the hut down if he feels that way.

Partially undressed on my bunk, I relished the slumber of the unneurotic. I was a healthy drunken man.

In the morning he was gone. Conscious of a headache, I lowered myself to the floor. The hut had been tidied, the greasy plates washed and dried. Looking out through the window, I saw the sallow man cycle away to work, caped and hatted against miserable drizzling rain.

VI

There was was a policeman seated at his ease in the red-tiled porch of the cottage. His shiny cape, still dripping from the morning mizzle, dangled from a miniature hallstand. His cap was pushed high on his forehead and, with his pipe going well, he filled his red bulbous cheeks with fragrant smoke. He had made himself at home. It wasn't a normal house any more.

Without welcome, without emotion he stared at me out of pale blue eyes and said: 'Can I do anything for you? The house isn't open to the public. You're not a reporter or a photographer, are you?'

'No. My name's Hartigan. I was wondering was the old lady at home.'

'Oh, Mr. Hartigan, is it?' His manner was straightway friendly. 'Sure I saw you here yesterday. You were along with Mr. Butler.'

'I was.' The walk from the village through the moist steaming air and along the wet path under the dripping beeches hadn't left me the power to laugh at that recurring image of myself and Butler—a small, dirty, insignificant dhow rocked in the wake of a sky-high snowy galleon. 'No, the old lady isn't here,' he said. 'Step in out of the rain.'

'No, thanks. I'll be heading back.'

'There's another shower on the way. Come in, Mr. Hartigan, and have a smoke.' He wanted company. It was depressing sitting there alone guarding a shell of a house in which life had been destroyed, listening to rain hissing down through beech leaves to flattened grass. Men who wanted company and men who shunned company were my friends, a minority in the world, brightly aloof or darkly aloof from the great majority who went on monotonously living. In the porch of Lily Morgan's house I sat with the red-faced policeman—with his cap off, his hair showed grey and short-cropped—and we smoked and watched the shower prancing and steaming past. 'My orders are to let nobody past the porch.' He was proud of his prohibiting position, the keeper of the dark-gate, the one hero on the bridge of danger.

'Sensible orders too,' I said. 'You couldn't have the whole village about the place.'

He stressed the point with the moist stem of his pipe. 'Lookit, Mr. Hartigan, it wouldn't be only the village but the whole city, young and old. There's no knowing the morbidity of the public in a case of murder, particularly when there's a girl in it. I know men, respectable business men, wouldn't look at a bad picture or read a bad book, and if they had the chance they'd be inside there fingering what the poor girl wore next to her skin.' Case-hardened against morbid things, he could sit and smoke, undisturbed by any desire to peer into the fatal room or to touch thin cloth once warmed by a body now eternally cold. 'Mercy of God,' he said, 'the morning's wet or we'd be inundated by trippers. By rights we should have a man down at the road to head people off. God only knows what clues are scattered there in the wood or round about the fields. But with the inquest on we can't afford another man.' 'Oh, yes, of course. The inquest.'

'Mr. Butler explained you'd just as soon not be present if it could be avoided. Sure, he'll be able to tell them anything they want to know.' Then after a pause, the shower galloping past in its last show of violence: 'It must have been a shock for you in your present state.'

'It certainly was.' Thanks to Butler's consideration and the strangling hands of the murderer of Lily Morgan, the whole village would soon know I was a nervous wreck. But about nervous ailments, unlike physical ailments, there's a certain distinction and my annoyance was not completely free from pride. 'I imagine, though,' he said, 'you'll have to show up for the depositions and the trial. When we get our man.'

Whether I had to show up or not I was already determined that I would show up, claim the place due to me as the first man, apart from the murderer, to see her dead body. 'Will you get your man?'

'Sure and certain. This country's too small for a man to get away with a job like that.' Watery sunlight followed the shower, fingered a cautious way from wet leaf to wet leaf. 'Between ourselves, Mr. Hartigan, we've our eye on the man already.' Only then for the first time was my mind stopped thinking by the black appalling realization that I had met the murderer. I said: 'That's good news. It'd be an awful thing if a strangler like that could go free.'

'The old lady went away to some relatives.' 'Is she taking it badly?'

'To go away was the best thing she could do.' I agreed easily with that quiet statement. Yet a morbid curiosity had made me wish to see and talk to the mother again, because yesterday when she had come screaming through the beechwood something familiar in her face or voice had attracted me, some hint of resemblance to a daughter otherwise so dissimilar; and I hoped perversely by looking again at and listening to the mother to brighten my tiny already fading memory of what the daughter had been. I suppose I should really have returned to the cottage filled with zeal to catch her murderer, intent on picking up the clue the police had passed over. But, honest as daylight, the thought never entered my head, and it seemed that the police, unlike those dear, stupid men in the best books, didn't pass over clues and evidence, didn't need the help of a private neurotic. They had their eyes on their man. At the moment he might be miles away and thinking himself secure, but quietly and patiently they were watching him.

'Nice place, this,' I said.

'They kept it well. The old woman was an engine of a worker. At it day and night.'

'Terrible to think of what happened in the room inside. Yet I suppose tragedy can happen anywhere.' He looked up at that. It was a stilted literary sort of thing to say. My weakness in conversation is that I'm always saying such things and then dissecting them immediately they're said. Once, in a room full of young men and women who were playing parlour games involving hands and knees and feet struggling under the table, I quoted something from Pascal and felt myself wither in the chill, uncomprehending silence.

'Dare say you're right, Mr. Hartigan,' he said. 'Still, it was an awful death to give any poor girl, even if she was a bit queer.'

'How queer was she?'

'Not daft or anything like that. Don't misunderstand me. Just quiet as a mouse. She dressed in dull clothes and never bothered dolling herself up.' That wasn't news to me and I could understand it. He breathed out smoke with slow satisfaction, a round-cheeked, red-cheeked image of some Greek personification of a gentle warm wind. 'She wouldn't look next or near a man. I think she was away a while to be a nun in one of those queer foreign convents. Now, my own opinion is that those places aren't right. If a girl wants to be a nun let her at least stay at home in her own country. In the heel of the hunt she gave it up and came home to her mother. And as sure as she did the boys round here nicknamed her the white sister after a book or a film or something.'

The boys would. I had seen them several times loafing at the bridge or around the entry to the hotel garage, and I could imagine their thoughts and their words, their scabrous stories and pimply desires. 'I suppose,' he said, staring meditatively at his pipe, 'the fact that she was in the convent made her feel for that scapegrace Jim Walsh. He was once in a college studying to be a priest. There couldn't be any other connexion between them.'

'Who's Jim Walsh?' He woke up suddenly from his halfdream and smiled wisely at me, his watery eyes again opaque. 'Oh, now begod, I'm talking out of my turn. We'll leave it so.' He was consciously proudly enigmatic. 'We'll leave it so.' Then looking up at the clearing sky, clouds scattering in wisps before wind and strengthening sun, he laughed loudly and said: 'The rain's gone, God be praised. It'll be a pet of a day for the inquest.' After that I divined, as the mystics like to say, that he didn't need my company any more. Loneliness and boredom went scattering like the clouds before the sunshine. So I stepped out on the clean gravel before the cottage, and he, either out of friendliness or watchfulness, walked by my side. Since the gravelled pathway went all the way around the place, green grass to the right and a colour-splotched flower-bed to the left, we automatically did the whole circuit once, smoking, chatting little. Birds in the beechwood felt, as the policeman felt, the change in mood when the rain passed. The branches were loud with movement and song. He pointed to one closed latticed window, a window right off a greetings postcard—virginia creeper and all. 'That's her window. But the boy who did it didn't enter that way. He knew his way about well enough to come and go by the front door.'

Peering through the small panes and across the neat dressing-table, I saw the bed as it had been yesterday, except, of course, that the body was gone. 'So it was a man did it.'

'What do you think? 'Twasn't her old mother for sure.'

'A sad business.' And still thinking of it vaguely as a sad, rather than a wicked or foul and horrible business, I tramped back between the drying brightening beeches and sat for a while on the little bridge. There were no cars parked before the big house. By the pear-shaped artificial lake the blonde delicate alien pampas grasses had been beaten and subdued by the night's whipping rain. The lone rook wasn't to be seen rising and falling, playing at exile, above the tree-tops as it had been yesterday. Off foraging in distant farms with black raucous companions. Sitting there, my hearing soothed by the chatter of the small stream, it was possible to feel little more than the casualness and unimportance of murder. A girl choked here or there and streams still went on flowing, flowers still growing up from fresh-turned flower-beds to fill unseen coloured moulds beneath latticed windows. Beech leaves and grass obstinately declined to blacken as a sign that God's wrath was abroad or that life had been outraged.

Two more minutes and I'd have been up to the neck in sententious meditations about the horrors of modern war: but with a flash of wheels and polished bonnet, scattering of gravel and gentle purring of well-tuned engine, the small blue car driven by the ash-blonde girl came from the direction of the station and the city, curved up the avenue towards the big house. I had a flicking glimpse of a clear-skinned babyish face, coil of hair like a crown around her head, scarf worn college-boy fashion, bright blue sweater to emphasize uplifted, pointed, prominent breasts.

To the stream and the almost responsive beech trees I quoted: I have firm breasts that are seated high. I was quietly proud that I could remember fragments from fourteenth-century songs. J'ay dur sein et hault assis. Tell me, tell me, am I, am I beautiful. I have a blue car capable of touching seventy-five on a good road and no fourteenth-century beauty ever had anything like that. Sui-je, sui-je, sui-je belle?

The car pulled up, the blue sweater showed for a moment as the girl mounted the steps to the door of the great house.

My father has the finest mansion in the locality and pots of money, and I cup my breasts in the most expensive uplifts the city can afford, so tell me, tell me, am I, am I beautiful. J'ay dur sein et hault assis.

The door of the house slammed and the morning was my own again.

There was an atmosphere in the village. After all, a murder was something. It brought distinction to the secretive huddle of houses between the bridge and the fair-green—generally so secretive because the city was near and much bigger and full of movement and talk. It brought distinction to a secretive man like myself. People I didn't know from Adam stopped me on the street and spoke to me. Overnight the world had found out about my nerves. In the tobacconist's and newsagent's, in the grocer's, in the butcher's and the greengrocer's, outside the drapery and hardware, they said to me: 'Mr. Hartigan, it must have been a terrible shock for you.'

Outside the police station the grey-headed scholarly-looking sergeant spoke to a rat-faced man in an ill-fitting brown suit. The whole village knew he was a detective from the city.

Outside the hotel there were seven parked cars. The inquest would be held there in the ballroom. I wouldn't call on Butler. I'd wait until he called on me.

The woman stood at the door of her hut, the sunshiny breeze coming from the river and the demesne to tumble her hair and flap her plaid skirt against her round pillars of thighs. She raised a bare arm and smiled, so that I thought she was beckoning me to come to her. But when I approached she extended her hands, palms towards me, with the gesture of pushing me away, and laughed and said: 'I only said good day, Mr. Hartigan.'

'Good day, Mrs. Kavanagh.' 'The rain's gone.'

'It's a beautiful day now.' I have thighs like young trees and a sallow husband who can cycle six miles, so tell me, tell me, am I, am I beautiful. 'Great excitement today.' 'No wonder.'

We laughed then as foolishly as if we had exchanged the first pecking kisses of a shy affair; and I went into my hut and had steak and onions for lunch and read Kafka's diaries with positive pleasure.

VII

Early the next morning Butler called to see me. The rising-and-falling vibration of the engine of his car, turning in the lane so as to be ready for a quick getaway to the city and his office, thrummed across the quietness. From the open door I watched him walking towards me, meeting as he came the sallow cycling man and casually nodding his handsome head. The nod wasn't returned. In tweed coat, white crimson-trimmed singlet, well-pressed grey flannels, the sunlight on his dark curls, Butler was a dashing figure; and I could understand the resentment that made the sallow man ignore the friendly casual nod. Perhaps I wasn't myself completely free from a similar resentment. His hand struggling with the hasp of my green lop-sided gate, he called: 'Come to a show tonight, Hartigan?'

'Glad to,' I said. 'Glad to.' There wasn't anything else I could say; and I moved to help him handle the gate, but, giving it up as a bad job, he vaulted over it and came to meet me. He walked with an easy swaggering stride. His pants flapped rhythmically around the necks of his shoes. 'This is a pretty place you have here.' We both looked at the hut as if it were a third party to our meeting. 'It's not too bad.'

'It's cosy and quiet. You're comfortably on your own. I live in a bloody hotel. I can't cook a damned thing for myself, so I have to stay where somebody does it for me.'

'Wouldn't it be more convenient for you to live in town?' He twisted his mouth and breathed the pure air deeply and said 'I'd suffocate. I'm country born and bred. The food's good here and the attention. And the prices aren't too steep.' He looked at his watch. 'Gee, I'll have to be hitting it. I've missed two days already over this unfortunate handling.'

Handling is the right word, I decided grimly, but because of the memory of the dead girl that wasn't the sort of thing I could say. 'Suppose we meet,' he suggested, 'in the Pyramid Bar at six. We could have a snack and a jar there and then go on to the show.'

'The Pyramid?'

'Know where it is?'

'I've an idea.'

'Just walk into the snack counter. I'll be there.'

I moved to reach around him to open the gate, but once again he was too quick for me. One hand on the green wood, he easily vaulted over, very light on his feet for such a big man. 'Good luck until we meet again. At six o'clock.' Almost as if I was intruding on something that didn't concern me, I said diffidently: 'How'd the inquest go?'

'The usual. Murder by person or persons unknown.'

'The police have something up their sleeves.'

'So I gathered. How'd you know?'

'I was talking to one of them yesterday. He let slip something about somebody called Jim Walsh. Who's he?'

'A poor unfortunate bastard. I'll tell you about him some time.' I thought: I could tell you something about Jim Walsh, but then, I wasn't absolutely certain that the man the police were looking for was the derelict creature who'd slept in my rocking-chair, who'd shared with me his charity mincemeat and stolen whisky. Even if he was the same man my information wouldn't make much difference to the story. They'd find him soon enough. It was a small country.

'Good luck again,' Butler said, walked away two steps, then turned towards me, fumbling in his pocket, bringing out something and handing it to me. 'This probably belongs to you. I'd almost forgotten it.' It was my mother's letter. Casually I took it and said thanks and said: 'It does indeed. Where did you find it?'

'Of all places in the world, in the hotel letter-box.' Covering my embarrassment, I laughed with a great deal of effort. The night before last, absorbed in my melancholy thoughts of Butler stealing my thunder as the discoverer of the dead body, I must have halted at the hotel door with some intention of knocking and, instead, dropped the letter, held stupidly in my hand, into the letter-box. No man enjoys being found out in folly. For a moment I wanted to snatch the letter out of Butler's hand, tell him to take his car and his free seat at a show with him to hell, turn and rush into my hut and lock the door. While I felt that way I fortunately went on laughing so that he didn't, I hope, notice anything odd in my eyes or in the way my hand trembled as I reached over the gate to catch the letter. Then sanity returned like bird-song after tempest. Good Christ, Butler wasn't to blame if I'd acted like the feckless unreckonable creature I was. 'Must have dropped it somewhere,' I said. 'Perhaps

some kid picked it up and dropped it into the letter-box for a joke.'
'That probably explains it.'
'It isn't important.' I hoped he hadn't read it: Come home, Donagh, my son, my son Donagh, come home, so that Mama can cook your rashers and wash your combinations. 'Just thought I'd bring it along, in case,' he said. 'Thanks a lot.'
'Six o'clock. Don't forget.' Did he, just because a letter of mine was found mysteriously in the hotel letter-box, think I was too scatter-brained to remember an appointment in a pub? 'The Pyramid,' I said.
'Sure. The snack bar.'
I stood by the gate puzzling out whether I hated him or liked him, whether I should or shouldn't meet him, until the sound of his car had died away. The Kavanagh woman was out on her doorstep too, shaking dust from coloured woollen mats, her arms bare, her hair for once restrained in a sort of turban. She waved and I waved. What would Butler do if he were in my place? Or Jim Walsh—if the ragged man was Jim Walsh—who had known her before she married the craw-thumping yellow-hammer? Some day I'd march to her hut and cuckold her husband, just to show her, to reassure myself, to show Butler and the ghost of Lily Morgan and the whole world.

After a month in solitude the city was a shock. News-boys were screaming with excitement, but I was too occupied dodging people on the pavements and traffic at the crossings to listen to what they were saying. Fumbling for coppers and stopping on a busy street to buy a newspaper is one of the many ordinary things I can't do. By God's grace I met no friends, relatives, or acquaintances; nobody to shake the hand and say with crushing jocularity: Where the hell've you been hiding, Hartigan; or, You're looking thin; or, Donagh, since you are in town, the least you might do is go out to see Mother. Of all the times in the day Butler had certainly picked the worst in which to ask me to make my way from the bus terminus to the Pyramid. People were rushing right and left, from offices and shops, into cinemas and restaurants, queuing for buses, cycling in droves, gladly escaping from work to table-tennis, card-parties, meetings, dances, theatres, devotions, copulations. The wet rhododendrons seemed to close around me again, shutting me off from the huddling and kissing of convalescent couples; but if any other person, man or woman, shared my solitude as Lily Morgan had once shared it, then I didn't see that person, because in the crowd the rushing faces were as meaningless as snowflakes. Hiding for sure somewhere in the city, running and dodging like a beast hunted in a forest, Jim Walsh might perhaps have shared my feelings. The chase should now be closing in on him, iron rods rooting in the earth around the sheltering rhododendrons, bloodhounds baying and sniffing for the scent of a man who had choked the life out of a girl.

Also, by God's grace the pavement stayed steady under my feet. The high houses didn't threaten to topple sideways and crush me. The quiet and peace of my hut seemed to be doing me good. Or perhaps my feet were steady and the houses and pavements steady because I had an objective, because I was marching past thousands of people to meet a man who had taken an interest in me, who might become a permanently valuable friend. All of a sudden I decided I did like Butler, and quickly I crossed the bridge, saw red lights from shops and cinemas and sky-signs reflected on black ebony water, felt the exhilaration of salt wind from the distant dock-lined estuary. Then to the right along the quays, stepping on and off the pavement to avoid passengers and luggage waiting for long-distance buses.

The Pyramid was a turreted red-brick building at the farther end of a maze of eighteenth-century lanes. In this part of the city, away from crowds and wide new thoroughfares, I was happily at home, knowing the short cuts, the most direct way through the maze: in one place across a patch of waste ground, under a low archway and, in the shadow of an ancient church, up a curving stone stairway. The great circle of the counter in the Pyramid's public bar was almost full. I bagged one high stool and with my hat staked Butler's claim on its neighbour. Brisk waiters carried steaming food and stout, white-topped with froth, to the men at the counter, and chatted and made jokes and knew intimately four out of five of the customers. A pretty cashier in a glass box presided over the ceremonies, one woman captured and caged in the middle of a world of men and interested only in her cash register, completely impervious to glad or ravenous glances. Dark oak panelling high on warm walls. Nineteenth-century carvings as gross as the customers' appetites. Mirrors inset between brown bellying whisky barrels.

41

Bright bottles on high shelves. A whole row of bottles with shield-shaped labels and white wild swallows to remind me of Jim Walsh, if my whisky-stealer had been Jim Walsh. All that—and five minutes to wait for the advent of Butler, and in one corner of the room the evening paper comfortably purchasable without fumbling. Leave your own money and collect your own change. All our customers are honest or, at least, too well off to bother about halfpennies.

Back safely on my perch, I sipped stout and loosened the paper from its folds and saw Jim Walsh, staring and startled and pale before a flashlight camera, looking at me reproachfully from the front page. His eyes said: They grabbed me and dragged me out from behind the sheltering bushes, and there you are, sure of food and drink, secure on a high stool among free men.

Beside me, two commercial men slappingly ate soup and glanced at the paper and talked.

'Villainous-looking boy, that.'

'He did it right enough. just look at his eyes.' 'They say you always know a murderer by his eyes.' 'The cops are hoors when you're drunk in charge, but in cases like that they seldom make a mistake.'

'The mounties always get their man.'

'They wouldn't want to make mistakes or we'd all be strangled in our beds. Our wives and daughters wouldn't be safe.'

'They say the women love it.'

'No accounting for what women like. It's the men that do it I can't fathom.'

'It takes all sorts to make a world.'

'God, it does.'

'Only twenty-seven years of age too.'

'A bad type, though. Take a look at the cut of his chin.'

And so on. I looked at the cut of his chin and Jim Walsh looked back at me. No doubt now, if I ever genuinely had had any, that he and the ragged man who liked Rilke were one and the same. Was he listening, as I was, to the soupy banalities of the two commercial men? It seemed as if his arrest, his imprisonment not behind bushes with red blown blossoms and smooth wet leaves, but in a box of stone and iron, had raised him aloft like a god to some cloudy place from which be could see, hear, and understand the nonsense of living. He didn't speak to me, but the evening paper spoke for him. Protecting bushes were down before bloodhounds and police and the manacles were on. The paper spoke simply and not at all as positively as the two commercial men. It said: 'In connexion with the death of Elizabeth Anne Morgan (23), found dead in bed in her mother's residence at such and such a place under circumstances which a coroner's inquest held pointed to wilful murder, the police have detained for questioning James Henry Walsh (27), of no occupation and no fixed address.

'Walsh, who was found by the police in a south-side lodging (it actually mentioned the name of the south-side slum lane and the number of the house), deserted twelve months ago from a British regiment stationed in the London area.

'He is also detained for questioning in connexion with some burglaries that have recently taken place in the vicinity of the north city.'

As simple as that. A sad record. Probably a clear case. They hadn't detained him for questioning in connexion with his left lung being rotten and his right lung, as likely as not, infected.

I looked up from the paper to my stout, from my stout to the girl in the glass box, from the girl and her cash register to the door at the far corner of the happy room, to see Butler making his triumphal entry. It lacked only the blare of trumpets tilted upwards. He was popular. He knew everybody and everybody was glad to know him. It appeared to be an honour to be one of those who saluted that swaggering, hastening man; and listening to the greetings, watching hands raising the tumblers as if for wassail, I was proud of him. Being in his royal company gave me status, even if it was something like the dubious status of a king's favourite or of a black-gowned medieval secretary with hands locked in wide sleeves and mind soaked with the secrets of state. The girl, the imperturbable girl in the glass case, raised her eyes from the cash register and smiled to welcome the seigneur. He took my hat off the empty stool and hung it as carefully on the rack on the oaken panels as if it had been a costly Christie and his own property, and not a frayed velour spotted by dust and rain and the only head-covering of an unsure shabby man. 'Thanks, Hartigan, for holding the throne. And apologies for the lateness of the hour. Had a bloody awful day at the office. Catching up for the last two days.'

43

Elbows on the marble counter and soup steaming, an acceptable sacrifice, before us, I said: 'I see they've got their man.' He frowned through the steam at the pale staring picture of Jim Walsh. 'The poor civil lout. So they caught him in a kip.'

'Was it a kip?'

'Oh, the true native Irish bordello. Fleas, disease, and fights in the backyard. Girls with all but leprosy. Trench mouth from the cups as well as everything else.' One of the two commercial men, ending his meal and sluicing his pipes with porter, said: 'A good spake, Butler, boy.' We all laughed together and the two commercials fought their way into their overcoats, tossed back a small whisky each, and went away home, possibly, to their waiting, wondering wives. 'Apparently Walsh was engaged to Lily Morgan,' Butler said, 'but she had no time for him.'

'Is that so?' For some neurotic reason of my own I didn't tell Butler that the murderer had spent a night in my hut. Maybe I felt that that night of mincemeat and whisky and readings from Rilke should, as the last time light had shone on the life of an abandoned, ruined man, remain a secret for ever. 'I suppose she gave him the run-around,' Butler said. 'She had the reputation for being a bit of a bitch.' So roughly he trampled on my imaginations of Lily Morgan. 'Let it be a warning to all of us, Hartigan. Keep clear of the women.' 'Never had much to do with them.'

'Let's forget it, anyway. We're away from the village for one night. Let's have fun.' To a waiter he said: 'Two large yellow men.'

'Certainly, sir. Coming, sir.' And at seven o'clock, swinging down off our stools, we were passably merry. In the hallway he halted by the public phone and dialled and spoke while I waited: 'Hallo. That you, Emily? Say, listen, will you be there tonight? In the bar. Certainly to God in the bar. And hallo. Could you root up a friend? Certainly, I'll let you think.' His hand over the mouthpiece, he said to me: 'That's Emily. A good kid. A smart piece. You must meet her.' While Butler the priest invoked the unseen Aphrodite, Hartigan the acolyte, wondering was he to be part of the sacrifice, waited morosely. 'Yes, Emily. You could. It's for a friend of mine, a very good friend. Who? That valiant woman. Tell her to bring her saddle and bridle. See you later, then. And thanks a million.'

Putting down the receiver, he said: 'Boy, you're in the swim. You're away on a hack.'

In the street he laughed loudly as we sat in his car and, because of the food, stout, and whisky, I also laughed.

The late-news box in the paper said that James Henry Walsh (27) had been charged by the police with the murder of Elizabeth Anne Morgan (23).

VIII

To my horror the show was variety of the poorest possible description. We sat near one of the doors of the dress circle and watched six girls attired to symbolize turkeys, very bare-legged turkeys, doing a routine movement plus gobbles around and around the stage. It was too ridiculous for words, so I kept my words to myself and sat in speechless paralysis. Then a girl crooner gave us a sobbing song and a heavy baritone gave us a hollowly jovial song and a sweet pale-faced tenor sang a ballad asking the audience to take him back to dear old Ireland, anywhere at all from the lakes of Connemara to the Hills of Donegal. Butler, moving restlessly in his seat, peered at his watch by the shy gleam from one of the spotlights inset to the terraced passage beside our seats. Realizing that he was as bored as I was did give him a lift in my estimation. A man had to work to eat and he wasn't to blame for the advertising agency or the fashion magazine.

A juggler with a trained dog, a collapsible ladder, and a flow of antique jokes, dry and fragile as autumn leaves, came nervously bowing on to the stage. He was an old man, probably conscious of coldness, intensifying with the years, between himself and his audience. Butler whispered: 'Have you had enough?'

'More or less.' Nerves or politeness kept me from saying exactly what I thought. As we tiptoed out I whispered: 'What'll you write about that?'

'Praise it to the clouds of heaven. Show-people adore praise. So do the advertisers. The magazine, they tell me, wants more advertisements and I want more money. Be sweet to everybody, Hartigan. It's the only game. Makes the world a nicer place.' The ushers and usherettes knew him and met him with smiles. The evening-dressed manager shook hands with him and with me and told me that any pal of Mr. Butler was welcome at almost any time

45

to the theatre. Going along a blue-carpeted corridor from the dress circle to the bar, Butler whispered with heavy welcome irony: 'Don't they all love me? Amn't I everybody's friend? And the little girls love to see their names in print. God, you've no idea how they like to read nice things about themselves. Season it with a word or two of harmless criticism and they'll swallow the craziest bloody compliment you could think of'. Then we were on the threshold of the warm, glittering theatre bar and waving his hands and excitedly calling: 'Emily, what'll you have?', he was gone from me through a phalanx of men with wigs and women with grease-painted masks of faces and eyes that seemed loose and jiggling in their sockets. Or so it seemed to me, bewildered by noise and smoke, by being left so suddenly shabbily alone on the fringe of a new unexplored planet.

Steady now, Donagh. I wanted to turn and run. The floor's steady. The house isn't on fire. The people aren't grotesques. You're imagining things. Step steadily forward. Pierce the dreadful phalanx. That girl there on the high stool hasn't a painted face. Her eyes are as soft and blue as pigeons. Her ash-blonde hair is twisted like a crown around her boyish, childish head. Her presence gives arrangement, design, and meaning to the whole geese-gabbling dazzling room. Then Butler said: 'This is Emily Rayel.' The heat of the room affecting the drink I'd taken so hurriedly in the Pyramid made me want to say: 'Sui-je, sui-je, sui-je belle?' But instead I said humbly: 'How are you?' and mumbled: 'I think I've seen you before,' and took her offered hand which was cool and small and soft as a child's hand. She wasn't wearing the blue sweater she had worn yesterday morning.

Butler said: 'Of course you've seen her before. She's a neighbour.'

Staring stupidly at the white blouse that had replaced the blue sweater and showed just the suggestion of a curve of white breast, marked with one tiny dark brown spot, I blushed like a boy caught peeping, and mumbled something—I can't remember what. Butler was reaching between jostling shoulders and rapping the counter with silver coins in an effort to call a barmaid. From one corner of his mouth he introduced me to the second enthroned young woman: 'This is Donagh Hartigan and Jill Kelly.' Jill's handshake was firm and her voice a fine contralto. She left me then and always afterwards with little more than an impression of something tall and dressed all the way in dark tartans, with red hair tied in a bun and a long freckled face. 'And I know you by sight, Mr. Hartigan. I'm a neighbour too.'

'Is that so?' The knowledge that some eyes somewhere—even if they looked out from an unattractive freckled face—had rested on me so as to remember me, gave me a brief glow of pleasure. 'Sure thing,' Jill said. 'I live across the river from you.'

'In a more palatial shack, though,' Butler said, handing round the drinks: two whiskies and two lemon-infested cocktails, rims of the cocktail glasses sickeningly crusted with sugar. Sipping my whisky, I knew that Jill must be one of the five galloping girls from the demesne house. 'We should have a table,' Emily said. 'It's so crowded here.' Those were the first words I'd heard her speak, and they left me startled because her voice was not unlike the voice I remembered from my one brief conversation with Lily Morgan. It was level, gentle, and unhurried, and just the smallest bit forbiddingly cold.

But Emily's voice had also the suspicion of a lisp, as if in the assortment and arrangement of creation a childish defect of speech, along with a childlike face, small nose, innocent eyes, had been mixed up with the vocal chords meant, after growth and development, for a cold woman.

We found a table in a corner. I listened while the others talked about people and places unknown to me. I wasn't a success, I felt, but then, I never expected to be a success at this or any other sort of gathering. Jill, who at first tried to be nice to me, revolted me. She was a prudish, easily embarrassed girl. When Emily whipped off the tweed costume jacket that partially concealed her white blouse and her striking bust, and a few men in our neighbourhood looked around with ill-concealed interest, Jill blushed herself into ugliness and said: 'Emily, for goodness sake. We'll have a following.'

Emily's voice attracted me, and the quiet limpid glance, shallow sandy pools under April willows, with which she silenced poor Jill's complaints. Odd how so much bounding horseflesh between gripping whipcorded thighs could still leave a girl a freckled blushing adolescent. Emily's bust attracted me—even me—as it plainly attracted Butler and any other male man who turned eyes in our direction. Above all, I was attracted by the conviction and the more I drank the stronger the conviction became that Eustache Deschamps, prolific man with the thirteen thousand lines of his mirror of marriage, had so many centuries ago thought of Emily when he wrote his sweet song of red rich mouth and gentle face, little eyebrows, round chin and comely nose, firm breasts high-seated and, tell me, am I, am I beautiful. Drinking red wine or green liqueur, I might have made a fool of myself by quoting as I had once quoted Pascal at a necking-party. But it wasn't the sort of song that went with Irish whisky, white wild swallows on every label and memories of pungent peat smoke in every sip; and, at any rate, Emily, absorbed by Butler's talk, didn't seem to know I was there.

So I confined myself to making the odd remark and paying for my share of the drink, becoming slowly and sullenly drunk and proud to rediscover my capacity for absorbing whisky. People came and went, frequently saluted Butler and effusively embraced him and embraced the girls, theatrical drunks or drunk theatricals; and I felt as much at home as a kangaroo. Once, at the bar buying a round, I heard two painted men discuss the murder of Lily Morgan.

'So they've got their man.'

'They wouldn't have much bother in a case like that.'

'Strangling and running's no way to do anything.'

'They have him now. He won't run any farther.'

They! In uniforms, buckles and peaked caps, they, twelve leagues high and slowly pacing, vigilantly walked the earth, saw and understood all things.

On the shelves behind the bar were two of the bottles that seemed, with flying swallows, to pursue me everywhere to remind me of Jim Walsh. How much more at home, I thought, I'd be with Jim Walsh and Lily Morgan, glad to warm myself at the fire of the love that must once have burned between them, than here with gallant Butler and horsey freckled Jill and that impossibly pretty thing from the fourteenth century. But Lily Morgan was dead, already decaying, blackness spreading from the marks on her throat all over her cold corrupting body; and Jim Walsh would be hanged for her murder.

Carefully balancing the drinks on a small tin tray, I zig-zagged back through the crowd to find Jill and Emily and Butler also talking about the murder. Their talk was heated, but it wasn't profound. Emily wondered did Jim Walsh do it, and if he didn't, then who did.

Butler said the case looked black against him. Jill said that Jim Walsh had once worked for her dad, that her dad had liked him, that he had been a fine horseman. Emily said that even good horsemen had been known to murder people. Then, scarcely seeing me as I put the drinks down on the table, they glared at each other, and I realized that they, my three gay, superior companions, were well on the way to being bulliphants drunk. Commend me, I congratulated myself, to your phlegmatic sullen man for genuine solid drinking. As far as I know that was the first time in my life I'd preened myself on being phlegmatic. It was a new experience, too, for me to stand securely on my feet and watch a solid man like Butler slip and stagger and fall as he did in the gents, his hands clawing at the damp cream and blue tiles on the wall. With the help of a stranger I fixed him up in a half-leaning, half-sitting position against one of the hand basins. 'Jesus, I'm drunk, Hartigan. Give me a while to steady.' I powdered my nose with great deliberation, swaying on my feet, but feeling as sober as, under the circumstances, a man could. 'It isn't the drink,' he said. 'I could drink twice that amount in different company. But Emily does that to me. She goes to my head like a keg of poteen. She's such a little self-assured china doll. Sometimes I'd like to choke her the way Jim Walsh choked Lily Morgan.' Laughing as if I was the strong man and Butler the weakling who needed advice and support, I said: 'I wouldn't do that. One strangling at a time's enough for one parish.'

'You've no idea, Hartigan.' He had straightened up, then bent again to the hand basin to cool his face with water. 'Women are queer. Times, to look at Emily you'd think she loved me. But there's an invisible wall between us.'

'Do you love her?' I honestly was anxious to hear his answer to that question.

'Do I what. I never knew a woman like her, and take it from me, boy. . . .' His face was beaded with water, his curls damp over his forehead, '. . . I know women inside out.' I handed him a towel. 'Once,' he said through the folds of the towel, 'I was as good as engaged to a girl, a black-haired girl, and I got sick of her. Then I was as good as engaged to a red-haired girl and she got sick of me.' With astonishing rapidity he recovered sobriety, or at least stability, so that without staggering or wobbling he went up the three terrazzo steps and out through the door of the gents. 'Then I said to myself,

Butler, I said, every night for twelve nights running you'll have a different Tivoli Starshine girl, rouge, grease-paint and all; and I had.' The show was over, the bar almost empty, the corridors mysterious with gloom. Through an open doorway I glimpsed rows of mute empty seats. 'Nowadays,' Butler said, 'my general rule of life is drink until I want a lay and take it if it's handy, and if it's not handy drink more and forget about it.'

'Not at all like Marcus Aurelius.' That was, if possible, worse than talking Pascal at the necking-party. He turned on me almost truculently. 'Who the hell's he? A jockey?' Then, his pockets clinking with baby bottles, he led the way, swaggering down the long sloping corridor towards the stage door. Half-way there he buttonholed me so fiercely that I thought for a while he was making the first movement of a fight. 'Hartigan you're a sound man. We found a corpse together, didn't we?'

'We certainly did.'

'You'll understand me when I say nothing of all this applies to Emily.'

'Yes, I do understand that.'

'She's different, you know. She registers in the soul. Emily.' He shook me gently, gripping the lapels of my coat, 'registers in the soul.' If he had only guessed how clearly I understood him when he said that Emily registered in the soul.

There she was waiting with Jill at the stage door. She wore a short fur coat, and tapped her feet, but not impatiently, on the semicircular concrete patch just within the threshold. It looked rather as if she was meditatively rehearsing the opening steps of some ancient Provençal dance, so ancient as to be forgotten everywhere except in the blood. Jill wore a brown tweed coat, long enough to cover even her long tartans; and in each hand she swung, as carefully, rhythmically, as if performing with bolas, a long-strapped over-the-shoulder handbag.

IX

The streets were still crowded, but the crowds and the very buildings were as irrelevant as good drink can make them. 'You'll tear the strap from my bag,' Emily said, as if she were escaping from meditation on that half-remembered dance to see for the first time Jill playing games with two handbags. With a slight swing of her body, emphasizing the jut of her firm round little hips, she shouldered the bag. 'Where's your car, George?'

'Somewhere, oh, somewhere. Where did I put it, Hartigan?'

'There.' It wasn't more than twenty yards away along a side-street, but it was attended by a policeman, who checked numbers in his notebook and patiently waited for erring owners to reclaim their property. Jill said sourly: 'Could none of you read the no-parking sign?' One felt that she was weighing our eyes and minds in the balance against the eyes and minds of wise instinctive horses and that the result was not in our favour. 'It won't matter,' Butler said, 'if he doesn't sniff my breath.' He swayed slightly.

Emily said: 'If he does you'll have more than a parking charge against you.' The policeman looked up from his notebook as if he hopefully expected to see parking offenders crouched in doorways waiting for a safe, surreptitious chance of removing their cars; and led by little Emily—oh, she was plainly a woman of resource in time of crisis—we retreated quickly around a sheltering corner. 'We'll all go in my car,' she said.

Breathing deeply, Butler leaned against the wall. Irrelevant crowds flowed past, a face now and again looking towards us and flashing white for a moment as if a floating dead fish had been whirled circling by a twist on the top of the water. 'You're probably delighted, Emily,' he said, and leaning towards me: 'She doesn't trust me driving while drunk.'

'Don't be absurd, George. Whoever said you were drunk?'

'You implied.'

'Oh nonsense. You know you can't possibly move your car with a policeman standing by.' Her voice was suddenly sharper, but her smile was all sweet curves. She knew, I thought with pride in my phlegmatic sobriety, how to handle drunks. Yet the big fellow was a man and had made himself my friend and I sympathized with him as he took correction mildly, following Emily along the pavement to the perfectly legal place where she had parked her blue car. Jill took my arm and we followed. She was two inches taller than me and bounced on her toes when she walked. Butler's dark head was twelve or more inches above the crowned blonde head.

Out of the city and into dark fields, a village or a roadside pub threatening us with light, then dipping and dropping behind. At every pub Butler, probably from habit, suggested a halt, and Emily said: 'No, George. We'll have a party in your place.' For two or three minutes I dozed, woke up again, and for some reason never since clear to me, I kissed Jill. She was as startled as I was, her lips cold and lifeless, tight perhaps with sapphic anger as she watched Butler's big head slip down sideways to rest on Emily's shoulder. Then sitting upright again, he sang in a sober tenor voice, with great life and leap, a Boston Irish song:

> *Good-bye, Molly Durcan,*
> *I'm sick and tired of workin'.*

In green tailed-coat, caubeen, knee-breeches, and knobbly shillelagh, I could see him, a new man, completely in his environment, making big money in New York music-halls or in Hollywood films about leprechauns, cottages, crocks of gold at rainbows' ends, and the old plaid shawl and silver hair of Mother Machree:

> *As sure as my name's Cooney*
> *I'm bound for Califoorney;*
> *And instead of digging mortar*
> *I'll be digging lumps of gold.*

Jill, applauding because, I suspected, she wanted to release her left hand from my right, said: 'The fun's beginning.' But the boisterous singing ceased as suddenly as it had commenced and, his head again slipping sideways, Butler went asleep mumbling. After a long silence Emily said: 'We're not such good company tonight, Mr. Hartigan.' It was a direct appeal to me. 'I'm not the brightest of company myself. And my name's Donagh.'

'Donagh. Donagh.' She repeated the name as if by repetition she had determined to remember it. The car bumped over a small bridge, turned a corner, and climbed a hill. We were at the top of the hill before the shape of that bridge and the adjoining beechwood, the pattern of lights from the windows of the big house set well back from the road, struck my consciously-sober drunken mind as familiar.

'None of my people in sight, Jill?' Emily asked.

'Not a sign of them.'

'If my good father saw me taking George Butler home this way.'

'You can handle your dad. Our dad is a raging lion.'

Butler groaned, resting an arm along the back of the seat behind Emily's shoulders. 'George is drunk,' she said. 'He must have been beering all day.'

'He told me he'd had a hard day in the office.'

'He always says that when he's been drinking more than usual.' I remembered then that, of course, advertising men could do a great deal of their work in public-houses. She said: 'It looks as if we'll have to help him to his room.'

'Glad to help.' And I did, too, want to help her and to see Butler's room and the inside of the hotel from the door of which I had a few nights ago turned away in envious discouragement. Was I now after this night a bigger, steadier man? The thought drove me back to chilly consideration of the trivial aid my flaccid muscles would be when we came to heave Butler, inert as a full sack, up the hotel stairs. Jill, the long plaid tamer of horses, would probably be worth seven neurotic, wobbly Hartigans. The drink was dying in me and corrupting by its death my temporary bravery and stability; and for the remainder of the journey to the hotel I dismally raked about in my mind to find the differences and similarities between my sudden attraction towards Lily Morgan and my equally sudden but certainly more senseless attraction towards Emily Rayel, Emily's breasts or the suspicion that Lily had a lovely figure or . . . the wind blowing the skirt about Mrs. Kavanagh's round strong legs? I didn't want to admit to myself that such things could attract me as they did attract more normal men. Lily's seclusion, her lonely quietness, or the feeling that Emily had come to life from the pages of a fourteenth-century romantic poet, or. . . ? There was no quality in Mrs. Kavanagh to compare with those aloof, unfleshly things in Lily and Emily. When Emily pulled up suddenly at the hotel door I had just realized with a shock that I was thinking of Lily Morgan as of a woman still living, walking somewhere in a quiet place where I, seeking solitude, might come upon her, discover her soul, know her for ever. 'Well, here we are,' Jill said.

Butler's room opened off a corridor that opened off the ballroom where the inquest had been held. He needed less help than Emily had imagined or myself feared, for once he had been shaken awake he staggered towards the door, fumbled for a while at the lock, then with a laughing good grace that made one love him, gave up the struggle to find the keyhole and handed the key to Jill. The tiled entrance hall was as narrow as a tea-chest. A door lay partly open showing white draped tables in the public dining-room. A glass sliding panel, now shut, said in square green letters the one word: OFFICE. Then at an oddly acute angle, so that you wondered how fat men ever made the turn without hurting themselves against the great terminal ball of the oaken banisters, a steep staircase dressed in red and black mottled ruberoid went up to the kitchen, the bar, the ballroom and bedrooms, the residents' dining-room. One single light burned at the head of the stairs, but Butler groped for a switchboard, found it, methodically turned on light after light. 'Stop it, George,' Emily said, 'the village will think the hotel's on fire.'

'Let it think what it damned well pleases.' We followed him up the stairs, Jill and then Emily and then myself. Her calves and ankles were exceptionally thin to support such a pleasantly plump body, but they were shapely even if they didn't correspond to those other shapelinesses of breasts and shoulders and sweet round face. They might have been the calves and ankles of some other girl equally attractive, but in a completely different way. That, I thought as I looked away from her ankles to concentrate on the mottled ruberoid, was the third anomaly I had noticed in her. There had been the startling contrast between her childlike face and her level mature voice, then between that voice and the lisp added, like an essence, drop by drop.

He found another switchboard. He said: 'One for sorrow', and clicked one switch, then: 'Two for joy,' and clicked a second. The corridor from the head of the stairs, past the closed door of the bar and into the ballroom, was illuminated before us. 'If I did that at home when I came in late,' Jill said, 'my furious father would pitch me out.'

After horse-whipping, I hope, I thought.

'They won't throw me out,' Butler said. 'In this place they eat out of my hands.' Staggering just a little, he led us down the corridor, and it was possible to feel that the hotel people did literally eat out of those large, long, lovely hands: one touching either wall by its fingertips to give him balance as he went. He stopped to rattle futilely at the knob of the barroom door. Had those long fingers ever fondled Emily's soft cheeks? Yet I felt then no twist of envy, not to speak of jealousy, for the best that Eustache Deschamps, five or six hundred years ago, could have imagined about a beloved desired woman wasn't too good for that big swaggering man, again radiating confidence, making hotel owners eat out of his hands, taking a different chorus girl every night for twelve consecutive nights. Momentarily I resented Emily for daring to build a wall between herself and the desires of such a man, and in her daring to do so considered I had discovered her fourth anomaly. Was she religious or frigid or innocent. Or ignorant or just afraid?

'Not a bloody sound,' he said. 'Closed like a shell and all in bed.' Then he turned away from the door to encounter the uniformed boots stepping suddenly from the ballroom into the corridor. We were startled. At least I was, for certain, and I know that Jill and Emily stopped dead and Jill said: 'Mother of God,' and Emily said: 'Bless us.' The abrupt appearance of the mild-faced, long-nosed, bald little man was as unsettling as an apparition. Our party didn't honestly look like a proper party to enter an hotel at that hour of the night: one man—a resident—a friend and two women, all reeking of drink and heading for the resident's bedroom. Such pleasant little parties have frequently been misunderstood even in the most liberally conducted hotels, and in hell's kitchen itself the management may have reasonable objections to noise after midnight and blazing lights in the corridors. But Butler wasn't worried. With simple sober dignity he said, and how admirably big he seemed as he said it: 'What cheer, Jerry? Bring a bottle of ten-year-old up to my room.'

His face creased in a smile of genuine welcome, Jerry said: 'Certainly, Mr. Butler. With hot water and lemon?'

'And sugar, Jerry, God bless you, and a jug and four tumblers and four spoons.'

'And a tray too, sir?' Jerry and Butler laughed together, the laughter of friends performing a ritual grown comic through repetition. God guard the sleep, I thought, of the other quiet denizens of this hotel.

'Glad to see you home safe, Mr. Butler.'

'And sober, Jerry. Never knew the old firm to fail yet.' Another laugh in which Emily, Jill, and myself, even myself, joined. Were angry respectable people sitting erect, buttocks on wrinkled sheets, to listen to us?

Turning, showing us the shiny back of his waistcoat and two inches of crumpled white shirt between waistcoat and trouser buttons, Jerry went before us, Butler's obedient slave, soft-footed, obsequious. As we crossed the ballroom towards one door he disappeared through another that opened back into the bar. On the brown floor of this room, waxed for the benefit of warm people joyfully dancing, the witnesses, the police, the crowner, and his merry men had made up their minds about the manner of Lily Morgan's death. But in Butler's bright room no man could remember for five minutes death or wilful murder by person or persons unknown. The bright fire was the first thing you saw and you thought of the loving hands—Jerry's, perhaps, or perhaps the hands of some worshipping chambermaid—that had tended it carefully for Butler's return. Two huge walnut beds, steads curved and ornamented like prows and sterns of ancient ships that might have sailed purple, glassy seas from Athens to Aulis, did seem superfluous in a room inhabited by one bachelor man. Oddly enough, they didn't crowd or encumber the room, for it was long, oh, amazingly long, going away from the door past the two beds and a wardrobe, dressing-table, antique wash-stand with an incongruous white enamelled basin, past the fireplace and three arm-chairs, to end at a low deep-walled window surrounded by shelved books and pinned-up ranks of glossy pictures supplied for publicity purposes by the best film companies. Carmen Miranda on high-patterned shoes showed a knee; Ann Miller tiptoed with impossibly glistening grace; a dozen well-known actresses, more or less dressed according to the public taste, stood and smiled or sat and smiled or were fondled and kissed and smiled. An extraordinary gallery. The books too, when I had a chance unobtrusively to look at them, I found intellectually unimpressive, gaudily new, the choice of this club for readers and that club for book-lovers, not a name among them.

But peace to his pictures of unattainable women and his shelves stuffed with best-sellers, for he was a splendid generous host. He knew how to live, how to help others to live, how to make magnificent punch. The bottle wasn't one of those that for me were for ever associated with Jim Walsh. In delusive warm colours the label showed a map of our wet, cold western island. Looking down into the whisky's amber depths, when it had been poured into a high narrow jug, where slices of lemon were sunken fragrant islands and cloves circled like shoals of morose dolphins, Jill said: 'I'm warm already,' and I thought: How glorious to drown. The semicircle of the fire's goodness went round the four of us and made us one. Emily balanced on a buttock soft as a peach on the rim of Butler's chair and he slipped his left arm around her, his hand cupping over her left breast, firm and seated high. She didn't move away. But I looked away, angry with myself because I'd no right in the world to be angry with Emily or Butler. Staring at Jill's abnormally long plaid thighs, at the fire, at the books and pictures, at the swimming slices of lemon, at my own portion of hot drink, my heart was cut between admiration for Butler and desire for Emily. Then I thought, consoling myself: What is she but some quaint thing found between the pages of an old book?

'Drink up,' said Butler.

'Cheers,' said Emily, sipping her drink, staring in a strange abstracted way at the hand cupped over her heart. Jill said: 'Down the hatch and plenty of them.'

'Good luck,' I said at the end of a minute or two. 'Now that we've time to listen,' Butler said. 'Tell us all about Marcus Aurelius.'

'The jockey.'

'No, honest, I want to know.' He had a habit of stretching his neck forward until his collar seemed too large for him and of looking at you half-mockingly out of round brown eyes. 'He was a man,' I said, 'who indulged in meditations and had an unfaithful wife.' Emily said: 'That gave him something to meditate about.'

'He didn't know she was unfaithful, or at least nobody knows if he knew she was unfaithful.'

'Poor dope,' Jill said.

'Sounds complicated,' Butler said.

'When he spoke of her he always praised her faithfulness. I think that was his evil way of laughing at the world and the flesh.'

'And the devil,' Jill added.

'I think he himself had the devil in his heart.'

'You puzzle me,' Butler said as he filled his tumbler brimful from the steaming jug. A steady, greedy drinker, he was coping gloriously with the larger part of the punch. 'There must have been somebody,' Emily said slowly, 'to whom he told the truth. Doesn't every man need a shadow or a stooge.' But I was no longer interested in telling the world about Marcus the meditative cuckold, or in the unknown, unremembered confidant who must have seen now and again how hot hell burned in the holy emperor's heart, or in the emperor's spoiled son who could have been another bitter joke at the world and the flesh—with his gladiatorial sports and his two hundred concubines and as many boys. Were all the concubines faithful, and all the boys? The heat, the steam from the punch, the desire for sleep made my mind careless of all things, except Emily: and as soft as velvet. Gently she had extricated herself from the crook of Butler's arm. The fingers of his cupped caressing hand had relaxed and the big handsome man was undeniably unsnoringly asleep in his chair. The jug was almost empty.

'One for the road Donagh,' she said, 'and do please help me into my coat.' My hand trembling because she had called me by my name, I divided the remainder of the punch between us. Jill stared indifferently at her empty tumbler. Then I assisted Emily into her short fur coat; how soft it was and how nerve-racking the moment when I settled her scarf and my fingertips touched the nape of her neck. My voice was quivering exactly as if I was frozen cold when I asked her: 'What about George?'

'He'll be all right. He's happy.' She bent over him and from his pockets as he lay sleeping extracted with nimble fingers the baby bottles that had clinked in his clothes in the darkening corridors of the theatre. 'These are of no use to him,' she said. 'If he needs a cure in the morning Jerry'll provide it. The servants aren't so considerate in my dad's house.'

'Love's joys,' I quoted, 'are for the living.'

'Nobody mentioned love,' Jill sombrely said.

Since Jerry didn't answer our ringing we tiptoed cautiously down the dark stairs and let ourselves out to the street.

X

Although I pride myself on my exact memory I find I cannot trace back in any sequence that makes sense over the things done and said for the rest of that night. Every moment was so important and I was more than a little drunk, so my head, pardonably, got muddled. Yet

I must for the sake of clarity force a pattern and an arrangement on my scattered wisps of memories.

Some time during the night we disposed of Jill. This was how we did it.

Because Jill had said: 'If they hear the noise of the car approaching the house they're sure to suspect something and my furious father'll be waiting on the doorstep,' Emily drove round the wide circle of the crumbling demesne wall and parked finally on a damp boggy road shut in deeper darkness by scrubby bushes. We walked with Jill along a rutted path raised above the bogland and came through a wood of tall slim trees almost to the back of her father's house. Were all the other galloping girls law-abidingly asleep? Not a light showed. Up the sloping park-land the sound of the water at the salmon leap came distinctly. Standing there in the shadow of the trees, I found myself casually holding Emily's hand and was surprised at myself and even more surprised at Emily. This was one night-walk on which I was blessed with pleasant company. Jill didn't seem to notice our hand-holding. She was watching the bulk of the great sleeping house. She said: 'Tiptoe with me as far as the courtyard gate. Not a sound, for God's sake. My sisters have the key of the side door hidden in the usual place.' There was, apparently, honour among galloping girls.

Our shoes soaking with dew, we crossed grass, avoiding the crunching gravel of the paths, until we came to a high enormous iron gate, last closed and bolted, by the look of it, in the days of the eighteenth-century soldier. Then Emily and myself hid, standing close together in the shadows, while Jill tiptoed away from us down a sloping cobbled courtyard, the house soaring blackly threateningly above her. She had said: 'Good night, Emily,' ignoring myself, and lightly brushed Emily's forehead with her lips—a cross lonely girl in spite of her quivering horses and cooperative sisters. Half-way down the courtyard she stopped and fumbled around the base of a stone pillar, then straightened up and triumphantly waved her right arm. 'She has the key,' Emily said. Standing close to her in the shadows it seemed the most natural thing in the world that I should slip my arm around Emily's waist and rejoice rhythmically in the rise and fall of her sweet, warm breath. She didn't move away and we stayed like that until Jill also melted into shadows and the faint click of a closing door warned us that the house had swallowed her. 'You're a quiet man, Donagh,' Emily said suddenly, 'and quiet men are such a change. I meet so few of them.'

Conscience-pricked for a moment, I can't pretend that I felt particularly happy, remembering the big noisy man now quietly asleep in his chair while I, awake in the darkness, fondled the girl he loved. He had, after all, gone out of his way to be kind to me. But going silently, my hand clasped in her hand, back across the grass, through the wood, along the rutted causeway raised above the bogland, my scruples perished at the thought of her moving warm and alive at my side, a poet's dream from another, more beautiful century. When at the car she said: 'Donagh, my feet are soaking,' it followed like a movement in a game of draughts or a further line of proof in a Euclidean theorem that I should say: 'Come to my place and dry and warm them, then.' What disloyalty to a friend could lie in simply holding a girl's hand, putting a supporting arm around her waist, helping her to dry her soaking, sopping shoes and warm her feet?

These are some of the things that happened and didn't happen in the hut.

I plugged in the electric fire and modestly turned my eyes away while she slipped off her shoes and stockings. What had the poet Deschamps said about thighs? My head was buzzing and I couldn't remember.

I boiled water and made tea.

From her handbag Emily took Butler's baby bottles and we drank whisky and tea in alternate sips. Ideas and hopes came rushing down to me like wild mad-winged diving birds. Under my roof she was, and her legs bare, and the warm fire, and the bunk there invitingly.

I said nothing about the remainder of the stolen whisky or about Jim Walsh.

After some pleasant drowsy talk (about what, I can't remember), I put my hands on her shoulders and, bending down, kissed her lips gently. Drowsily she accepted my kiss and liked it and told me so. Irrelevantly, almost, she said: 'You know, sometimes I'm afraid of George.'

'Because why?' It wasn't pleasant to be reminded of that sleeping, unsuspecting man.

'You know we're engaged. Unofficially.'

'That's not a reason for being afraid. Not always or even frequently.'

'But I haven't made up my mind.'

'Why not? He's a fine fellow.' That tribute was the penitential whipcord on my bare and bleeding and would-be sinful shoulders. She said: 'My mother would kick up hell. Not that I'd mind. The real reason is . . .' There she stopped dead and wouldn't say another word about her real reason; and since I didn't relish discussion on the unofficial engagement between herself and Butler, I didn't press the matter any further.

But later in the night, or in the morning, I kissed her several times, always quietly and gently, since quietude and gentleness appeared to be assets, and we drank all the whisky. Her speech softening and thickening, she said once by mistake: 'Whicksi,' and we were always to remember that word.

Later still, feeling as faithless to Butler, my friend, as Faustina had been to her husband, Marcus the Meditator, and also something flabbergasted at the shrieking degree of my importunity, I cupped my hand over her left breast. She leaned against me and murmured something incoherent. But when I tugged clumsily at a button of her white blouse she said sharply: 'No, Donagh. No further, Donagh.'

'Sorry. It was the whisky. Or Eustache Deschamps.'

'Who's he? Another jockey?'

'A man I know,' I said wearily. 'He lived centuries ago and wrote poems.' Unexpectedly she touched my forehead with her right hand, smoothed my hair with a soft palm. Shc asked, her small forehead wrinkling: 'I'm a queer girl, amn't I?'

'You're a beautiful girl.'

'Anybody could say beautiful. But I'm queer too. You're queer yourself, aren't you, Donagh? You're all nerves or something.'

'I'll keep saying beautiful.' Tonight I had almost forgotten about my nerves and, suddenly reminded, I felt as if I had been disloyal to my own dark shadow, a wizard neglecting his familiar's obscene nourishment.

She bent down and kissed me lightly and laughed. 'I like to hear you saying that. But, Donagh, there is a reason for my queerness. I think I could tell it to you.' She plainly thought it over for a moment and I silently pressed her small hands to my lips. 'I couldn't tell George. He'd laugh at me. He's too tough and too normal.'

'Normal?'

'Yes. I'm not really normal, Donagh. And some day I must tell George the truth.' Even though for the moment I was preferred to George as a confidant, the breathing of his name between us still caused me trouble. But whispering closely to my right ear she gave me the story of the origins of her crowning anomaly: how she who could stir desire in a stock or a stone, or in a half-dead creature like myself, remained always as cold and unmoved as a marble pillar in a cathedral vault.

In Brighton one day, she told me, when she was nine years of age and holidaying with her mother and nurse she wandered away from mother and nurse, lost herself and was found by a tall, strange man. He patted her head, promised her a mamma doll, and enticed her up a quiet side-street where flowering bushes billowed out over high blank garden walls. 'I can still see those bushes and their pink flowers,' she said, 'as clearly as if it had happened yesterday.'

I said: 'It isn't so long since you were nine.'

'But you mustn't think,' she assured me with burning earnestness, 'that anything dreadful happened.'

The man had, she told me, done no more than untie the ribbon from her hair when footsteps approached and he fled, holding the bright trailing ribbon.

'All you lost,' I said, 'was a ribbon. It doesn't seem too serious.' But with more earnestness than ever she assured me that the memory came between her and the things most girls of her acquaintance did without a second thought. Her mother had always been careful, too careful perhaps, to suppress all talk that might give life to that memory. 'Kissing's all right,' she said. 'But anything beyond that. Even the idea.' And she shuddered.

'You're cold, Emily. The whicksi's dying.'

'No, Donagh. I'm glad I told you. You're nervy yourself. You'll understand.'

'Tonight I was as solid as a rock.' Was it Butler I had to thank for that or was it whisky or just the wine of her company? If it hadn't been for Butler I'd never have experienced the ecstasy of her company, a queer ecstasy breaking off now for tonight with such a joyful agonizing abruptness.

When she drove home I went with her and stood at the gate until the light died in her window. Even in my haunted mind Lily Morgan was now dead, for most unexpectedly I had found someone like myself walking along secluded paths, hiding oddity behind wet hedges, searching for someone who without laughter or good advice would quietly understand.

XI

The depositions were taken on a damp dark day in a cold courthouse in a seaside town several miles from the village. Narrow streets climbed a steep hill above the courthouse, the harbour, the three hotels, and a pale blue block of boarding houses. The first chill of winter was in the September air. Little boats lay motionless on grey water and from the south pier where trawlers, smelling of fish and silver with scales, were lined, came the groaning of a strained crane and the casual slow-motion talk of working men. Nobody seemed to bother about the few car-loads of people entering the courthouse. Depositions had no finality about them, no sense of struggle and something at stake. They didn't matter. They weren't exciting. They were merely the prolegomena, the argument, the stale trite sentences before the epic cantos began. After a murder and Butler and Emily and the story of the ribbon raped in a Brighton lane, the whole thing, I thought, was a whimpering, whinging anti-climax.

For the second time I saw Lily Morgan's mother, not now in a nightdress and screaming, but subdued in sober mourning black, her hair tucked away in an old-fashioned black bonnet, her face as pale as Lily's face had been when I first saw her in the grounds of the convalescent home. The sight didn't touch me, didn't mean a thing to me. I kept remembering Emily, who wasn't there because she had nothing to do with the murder. For the second time, too, I saw Jim Walsh, cleanshaven and wearing a dark suit. His tanned face was hawk-like, ascetic, the face of a Spanish monk, except that the lower lip was curved and full not with sensuality but with a suggestion of geniality. His mouth was slightly opened and his eyes, recognizing nobody, looked with resignation at the cold room, and with contempt. He didn't seem to mind standing there for a while between two policemen.

Several people, strangers to me, who seemed at first sight to have no earthly connexion with the murder, had all their own part of the story to tell, and with such an accumulation of detail that Butler and myself shrank into insignificance. But from their several angles here's the story of the way Lily Morgan died, made as lucid as, from memory and the garbling of newspaper clippings, I can make it.

Mrs. Morgan, the sorrowing mother, had known Jim Walsh for several years. So her statement said. She had never approved of him coming about her house because he was only a casual labourer and he was spoken of in the village as a wild sort and a reckless horse-jockey. (An odd thing, I thought, to call a man of his size a horse-jockey, but later I discovered that the good villagers used the name to describe a combination of corner boy, odd-job man, poacher, vagabond, and whoremaster.) He was an orphan when she first met him and had a few years previously returned from a college where he had been studying.

(I looked at his brown ascetic face. The ingrained tan didn't stand for good health. What would it matter to him, his lungs rotting, if he were hanged in the morning? I could still hear him saying: I'm not an ignorant bastard, Paddy, no matter what I look like. I used to read books too. My poor mother sent me to a college to make me into a clergyman. That's a bloody good one, isn't it, Paddy?)

It was true that her daughter Lily had accepted an engagement ring from Jim Walsh, but in doing so she had been acting against her mother's wishes.

(Soft and sobby, as she was, I decided I didn't like Mrs. Morgan and then, remorseful, considered that by disliking the mother I'd spat on my remembrance of her daughter.)

As long as that Walsh boy had stayed about the village she had kept urging her daughter to have nothing to do with him, but the girl was stubborn and wouldn't pay any attention to her urging. Then Jim Walsh went away to work in England and Mrs. Morgan thanked God and hoped she'd have no more trouble with him coming about her house and making claims on her daughter.

(At this point in the story and here and there in other places the white-faced fat woman wept bitterly. But in my mood at that moment my sympathies were with the dead mother of the doomed

Jim Walsh and her pitiful wrecked ambition to see her son priested.)

After his departure for England it was quite true to say that Lily pined and failed in health. She had had to spend some time in a sanatorium and some time in a convalescent home, but she had recovered completely and had never suffered from any disease of the heart. There had never been any disease of the heart in her family or in her late husband's family.

(Except, I thought, that hindered by natural or unnatural causes the hearts of many Morgans and of many other men and women had stopped beating and they'd died. The irrelevance of it all sickened me. What did it matter about heart disease among the Morgans or about Lily having pined herself into a sanatorium when the man who was to murder her was working, or soldiering, in England? When she had spoken to me on the way from the convalescent home to the bus-stop she had still, perhaps, been pining for her absent lover. That realization—in a general way and not solely because of Lily Morgan—made me envious of the man, in peril as he was, because some woman had once for his sake fretted the health from her body.)

Then after her return from the sanatorium, said her mother in a sworn statement supervised by lawyers and by police, she seemed to forget about Jim Walsh. One day about three months before her tragic death she had told her mother she was finished with him for ever. Her exact words had been: 'Mother, you needn't worry any more. It's all over between myself and Jim Walsh. I'm writing to him to tell him so.' She wrote a letter and posted it and afterwards seemed to be in the best of good humour. From that moment until a few hours before her death his name never crossed her lips. She was a quiet girl by nature and sometimes went for days without saying more than a few words.

(How much her quietness, I thought, would have meant to me, as listening to her story she came for me slowly glimmering back to life, oddly confused with Emily, the ice-cold provoker of desire. How little, beyond vexation, could her quietness have meant for her babbling mother.)

Mrs. Morgan could give no reason for her daughter's decision to throw over the man from whom she had accepted an engagement ring. But she always had in her heart been a good girl and an obedient daughter, and in the sanatorium she must have had time sensibly to think things over. As far as Mrs. Morgan knew there never had been another man in her daughter's life. She had never mentioned any other man.

(Never even mentioned Donagh Hartigan, who had once carried her luggage and hoped to see her again.)

Two months later the girl was back at her brooding worse than ever. She had certainly received two letters with English stamps and postmarks, and although Mrs. Morgan had guessed that those letters came from Jim Walsh, and had asked to see them, they had not been shown to her. (How clever of her the prying, meddlesome old bitch.) Then about dusk of the evening that preceded Lily's death (violent tears), a knock came to the door and, when it was opened by Mrs. Morgan, there stood Jim Walsh as ragged as a scarecrow and his eyes so like the eyes of a madman that she was terrified and tried to slam the door in his face. But he blocked it with his foot. His exact words had been: 'Mrs. Morgan, is your daughter Lily at home? I want to see her.' Her exact answer had been: 'She is not at home, Jim Walsh, and even if she was she wouldn't want to see you.' Then he said: 'Why wouldn't she? Aren't we engaged to be married? Didn't she accept a ring from me?'

Mrs. Morgan denied that she then said: 'A fine sketch of a man you are, to think of marrying any decent woman's daughter.' Her exact words had been: 'She wrote to tell you that she had decided to break off the engagement.' She had not said: 'It never was an engagement, since I never gave my consent.'

He was quiet for a while and she tried again to close the door, but he prevented that. Then he said: 'She did right enough send me a letter to England, but I didn't get it until recently. I was changing addresses.' Mrs. Morgan had not said: 'By the look of you, you must have changed your address once a day, from one ditch to the next.' But Jim Walsh had said: 'Will you tell her I called? Will you let me see her?' She had said: 'My daughter is old enough to make up her own mind about the people she will and will not see; I don't think she wants to have anything to do with you.' (What a porcelain-cheeked old madam she must have been when confronted merely with the ruin of another woman's son. What a mass of whimpering putty when ruin had had its moment on the wrong side of her own threshold.) All that time her daughter Lily had been sitting in the kitchen and hearing every word. She had made no move to come to the door and speak to Walsh, although there was nothing to stop her from doing so. He had finally taken his foot away and Mrs. Morgan had closed the door, but through the closed door—he had actually bent down and put his lips to the letter-box—she had distinctly heard him say: 'If she won't see me or marry me, tell her I'll come back to collect my ring. I could sell it and buy food.'

He went away then. The clock said between seven and eight. That was the last time Mrs. Morgan had seen Jim Walsh. Later she and Lily had securely fastened the doors and windows and gone peacefully to bed.

An irrelevant man—irrelevant to the story as I saw it—swore that he had bought Jim Walsh two pints and two small whiskies in a public-house on the road between the village and the city. This irrelevant man also swore, unnecessarily, that he made his living and, incidentally, the money to buy porter and whisky for Jim Walsh, by driving truck-loads of vegetables to the city market. He had bought Jim Walsh the drinks for old time's sake and because he seemed down on his luck. Walsh had told him he was wanted in England for breaking and entering, and for deserting from the army. There was a great hullaballoo about that part of the statement, which was finally, to somebody's satisfaction, proved clearly inadmissible.

Walsh had then talked to the vegetable man about Lily Morgan, saying she had done the dirty on him and ditched him, but that he'd be even with her yet. Those were his exact words: 'She did the dirty on me and ditched me, but I'll be even with her yet.' He said also that Lily Morgan was holding on to a valuable ring that belonged to him and he knew a Jew man in the city who'd give him fifty pounds for that ring. The vegetable man gave Walsh a lift almost as far as the village and warned him to have sense and to forget about the girl. But Walsh was in a wicked humour and said that he'd forget about the girl when he had his hands again on his own property, the ring. He was slightly intoxicated. The time then was about nine-thirty. The vegetable man had not seen Walsh after that.

A neighbour woman, a thin, angular creature who looked like a whist-fiend and a member of many pious sodalities, swore that on the night of the murder she had gone late to pay a visit to the Morgans. The time was about eleven o'clock. The reason for her going so late to the house was to borrow some tea for her husband's breakfast the following morning, as the shops in the village were all long closed when she remembered that the tea-caddy was empty. (Thin, pious women and squat, empty, gaping tea-caddies ringed like monoliths the pool of blood.) She knocked for some time at the door of the cottage, but received no answer. The door was ajar and she would have slipped in and helped herself, only Mrs. Morgan was not the sort of woman in whose house one could take such neighbourly liberties. She didn't slam the door shut because she was afraid the noise might awaken the people in the house; she assumed they must have been very tired to go to bed and get soundly asleep by eleven o'clock.

But going back through the wood she heard somebody's footsteps approaching and, being alone, and frightened in the dark, she hid behind the trunk of a tree until the somebody passed. It was a man. She had known Jim Walsh well when he worked around the village and she was positive the man who walked through the wood was Jim Walsh. From her hiding-place she could see the door of the cottage and the man definitely walked to the door, pushed it open, and entered. She had gone over the next morning to tell Mrs. Morgan about the scandalous fact, but when she arrived at the cottage it was in the possession of the police.

A medical statement said that Lily Morgan had been strangled between twelve midnight and one in the morning.

A police statement said that when Jim Walsh had been detained he had in his possession the engagement ring he had once given to Lily Morgan. (I could have told them that myself.)

Jim Walsh admitted that he had gone back to the cottage for the ring. He found the door unlatched, unlocked, and unbolted, and walked right in. Lily Morgan was sitting in the kitchen. The lamp was not lighted. She was startled to see him. He said: 'What have I done to you, Lily?'

She said: 'Nothing, Jim, but it's impossible to think of our getting married. Please go away immediately and leave me alone.' He hadn't argued with her. You never could argue with Lily. He hadn't raised his voice because he was afraid of waking the old woman. He had been angry when approaching the cottage, but when he saw Lily all his anger went away. He told her he was down on his luck and that the ring would be useful to him, and she gave it to him immediately. He shook hands with her and left the cottage. Apart from the handshake he didn't lay a finger on her or in any way attempt to molest her.

A further medical statement said that Lily Morgan was not a virgin, and that she had had, shortly before her death, sexual relations.

There were other irrelevant people with their irrelevant statements, providing between them enough evidence to hang Julius Caesar. So, I felt, everybody coldly thought in that cold room, distemper peeling off sodden walls, a robin bravely singing somewhere outside, the tide filling the grey harbour, the crane straining and creaking, workmen talking on the south pier. The prisoner was put back for trial, to bite his nails and spit blood and wait in a cell for inevitable and merited condemnation. Butler drove me home to my hut, stopping twice on the way at public-houses and forgetting in whisky how Jim Walsh had strangled Lily Morgan.

XII

In the deep green jungle I sat down to read the latest letter from my mother. For several days it had been unopened in my pocket because I had had other things to think of, and all those things were about Emily Rayel. There was the sheen on the blue sides of her motor-car when one forenoon she drove round to my hut. My mother's notepaper was blue too, but what a different blue. There was a glimpse of ankles, calves, and knees, and a flutter of skirt and slip as she slithered sideways out of the driving seat, and the way her quiet, quick eyes noticed my hand trembling as I opened the lop-sided gate to let her pass into the hut. Mrs. Kavanagh, a second time turbaned, watched from her doorstep. Was it my quavery imagination, or was there actually a threatening silence, a sinister motionlessness in the right hand that so often waved to me, as she watched the lovely girl walking into the parlour of the gaunt delicate man? Then afterwards, after tea and pleasant casual talk about nothing, not a word about Butler or about our experiences at the taking of the depositions, there were on my hearth three cigarette butts sacredly marked by her lips and her lipstick. With the deft intention of treasuring them I picked them up, arranged them on the table on the page of an open book to mark the points of the three angles of a triangle. But an hour later, rational once more or almost rational, I set them afire as reverently as if I'd been burning incense before a shrine. No doubt in the world about it, I was in a bad way.

A boldly printed notice at the door of the glasshouse said that in this jungle explorers were forbidden to smoke, to scratch or in any way clip or injure the plants, and forbidden also, even if they were non-smokers, to carry lighted cigarettes, pipes, or cigars.

But what had she said or why had she called or what had happened between us to make me act like a lovesick fool? I wasn't quite certain. Yet, idiot as I was, it became clear to me-she took pains, quietly and curvingly and lispingly, to make it clear-that she had called for some real pleasure that talking to me gave her. She had put in my way, so plainly that I couldn't ignore it even if I'd wanted to, the chance to make an appointment to meet her somewhere away from the hut and her house and—first cold shadow of betrayal—away from the hotel and George Butler. There were times, remember, when she was afraid of Butler and she was so little afraid of me that she could tell me her secret.

Beside the Schomburakia Undulata, a visitor from Venezuela, I opened my mother's letter and gave it a fragment of my mind. For, looking less at the letter than at the rows of purple and pink bell-shaped blossoms drooping languidly over plashy green leaves, I remembered how, my heart inanely fluttering, I'd said to Emily: 'Perhaps some day we could have a drink together in town.' For a staggering man to make such a statement needed the nerves and courage of a tight-rope walker or a steeplejack doing jigs on the wind-swayed topmost girders of the Eiffel tower.

Not looking at me and probably feeling too that first cold shadow of betrayal, she said slowly, precisely, without a trace of a lisp: 'Not a drink. George is everywhere, in all the spots where one could drink in comfort.' George was to drinking places as God to the universe. Then she thought for a long while and said: 'Do you know the gardens in the North City?'

'Who doesn't?'

'Lots and lots of people. If they do they don't go there. There's never anybody there who's really alive.'

'Like George.' Then I stopped abruptly because it was bad for both of us to hear his name too frequently mentioned. She thought for a short while and said: 'Yes. Like George. Or you or me. Or Jill. Or any of the gang one meets around. There's never anybody there except students and children and nursemaids and old retired gentlemen whose hobby is botany. They're not real people.'

'I suppose not.' Some raving wicked demon inside me wanted to scream: Why do we have to hide? But I cornered him, chained him, choked the words in his sulphurous throat because better than he did I knew why we should hide. Our guilt was not yet even conceived or shaped in thought, but it was as real as our oddnesses or the air unseen around us. She said: 'I love the hot-houses in the gardens. They're right out of this world.' They were, too, and so was she, or at least, I thought breathlessly, out of this period of the world's story.

Side by side with the Lady Chesham variety of the Mexican Laelia Anceps, with pods like small evil bananas, and the Eria Velutina, a stranger from Malaya, I stood still in the jungle and made this time a determined effort on my mother's letter. Coming to this queer place of appointment I could, cutting my way through suburban afternoon have called to see my mother. She sat waiting for me not half a mile off the bus route. But when I stepped down from the bus I had resolutely turned my back on her part of the suburb: pulling up the collar of my rainproof against the chance of recognizing eyes, hearing as if they were far away the shrill sounds of children streaking by me on roller-skates—their balance, their bird-like freedom, seeing out of lowered secretive eyes the boxes of clean red carrots in the greengrocer's shop at a corner, and a black and white dog timidly nosing his way in at a green gateway, and children splashing around a drinking fountain inside the garden turnstiles, and white iron hoops coldly saying keep your feet off the precious public-owned grass. Escaping to the jungle, I had skimmed suburbia as a bather on a harsh day might skim with his toes or fingertips the dark unwelcoming pool and, wiser from the touch, go dryly home again. Yet I couldn't forget that half a mile away my mother had written this letter and now likely sat waiting an answer.

She had been reading the papers. She wrote: 'I see that yourself and a Mr. Butler have found your way into the news columns. My dear son, how did (twice underlined) you in your delicate state of health stand the shock? It should show you, if anything could, the danger of living alone like a hermit in a place where such awful things are liable to happen.'

There had never been a murder in my mother's suburb. In all her life she had known of murder only as matter for clever mathematically contrived books by brilliant bloodless lady authors, or as matter for sensational Sunday newspaper stories about acid baths and strangled children. 'Do come home,' she cried. 'I entreat you.' In the jungle, listening for a second, I feared I heard her voice. But it was nothing, not even Emily's footsteps bringing her to meet me in the hushed, gaudy hot-house. 'I'd go out to see you,' my mother wrote, 'if I wasn't so crippled with arthritis I can scarcely move except to go as far as the church, and your sisters won't go because they say that as likely as not you wouldn't open the door to them.' How right my healthy sisters were. 'The strain of giving evidence at the trial will be much too much for you. Get excused from it, I beg of you, if you possibly can. If that isn't possible come home directly, so that during the ordeal you'll have at least the comforts of home cooking.' Then Emily Rayel looked over my shoulder and standing on her tiptoes breathed pleasantly around my left ear. I wasn't as high in the heavens above her as Butler was. 'Oh, Donagh,' she said, 'had you forgotten I was coming? Reading letters from other women.'

'From my mother.' In her suburb that waiting woman didn't know—how could she?—how deeply I was involved in the murder, and how real it was to me and how unreal she, her arthritis, her suburb, my sisters, all seemed; and how real and how near to me was Emily Rayel.

'You weren't watching for me, Donagh.'

'I was listening.'

'But my shoes have crepe soles. Quite new too. Like springs.' Giving her soft plump body, I thought, a maddening resilience, bearing her quietly into this warm-coloured place where, as easily as the coy little Sclaginella Serpens from the remotely riding West Indies, she fitted into the background. She took my arm and slowly we stepped along the tiled passage, our sleeves touched gently by green leaves from the rivery places of pear-shaped Latin America.

'Were you long waiting?'

'Years.'

'No, honestly?'

'Honestly, years.'

'I'm so sorry.' Almost tearfully she looked sideways and up at me. In the narrow passage I felt the pressure of her left breast.

'I'm so glad you came. Waiting was a pleasure.' Never before had I spoken like that to anyone, or even imagined myself saying such things; and I had in my time imagined myself saying and doing almost everything, including spirit-rousing speeches and several of the comically posed actions of love.

Somewhere behind tall palms an engine throbbed, keeping the jungle warm. The red tiles under our feet were wet from the moist air. Among dense delicately fronded ferns the heat increased and the silence was deeper, dulling even the sound of the throbbing engine. 'Donagh,' she said, 'what are we doing here?'

'Walking. Arm in arm. In a hot-house. In a botanical garden.'

'We're not dreaming.' She said 'dweaming'; and mimicking her, I answered: 'No. Not dweaming.' Yet I wasn't certain if it was or wasn't a dweam: the warmth, the dully throbbing silence, the high-domed glass roofs, the mute jungle growths cultured for show like wild animals sullen in cages. I had had so many strange dreams, and the ground now being steady under my feet made me more than ever suspicious of the reality of our meeting. How was one to know? Was the earth steady only because I walked arm-in-arm with this most desirable girl, dropped as startlingly into my life as if she had come sword-bearing and radiant from the opening heavens? Or was she herself a dream or part of a dream? Yet how could one dream that we stood in the shelter of a South Caledonian tree called the Kentiopis Macrocarpa, or that, like an octopus from the high glass roof, dangled the Otochilus Fusca from northern India? Or were the names just nightmare names, delirious distortions of real words? 'Jesus,' I said aloud, 'Jesus, don't let it be a dream.' For if it was all a night's imaginings and if I was doomed to awake and discover she had never been, then for ever the world would be a desolate unstable madhouse.

'Amen,' she said.

'You like being here, Emily. No matter why.'

'I love being here. I was so excited coming to meet you.'

'Why?'

'You've just said: no matter why.'

'That was about something else.'

'I'm not positive why I was excited. Because I liked you that night in the theatre bar.' She thought that over for a while. She had a delicious habit of pausing with her lips parted and half- smiling, her eyes very wide and blue, and obviously thinking over the words that had escaped from her as sweetly and unreflectively as her breath did. 'Perhaps that was the reason,' she said. 'You were so quiet. I told you something I never told any other man or woman.' Not even tall plaid more-than-sisterly Jill. 'Once I was able to tell you, it made me easier with you than I've ever been with another man. Not being able to tell it put a gulf between myself and any other man I've ever known.' A gulf, she said, with her memory of an incident in a lane in Brighton. In his big brash ignorance Butler had said a wall. 'So after that night,' she said to me, 'I decided I must make a friend of you.'

Just a friend, I thought, but didn't say; for to speak my mind out plain might too swiffly shatter the dream, shatter the glass dome, dissolve into nothingness the plants, the palms, her fair body.

In the central glasshouse, the highest roofed part of the jungle, heat came belching out around my legs, and around her legs. Tall palms and mushy-leaved growths went climbing up along red iron girders towards the high dome and the muted, excluded alien Irish sun. 'Mexico,' I said, groping for something to say, 'sends us the Acanthorrhiza Aculeata.'

She said: 'I went to your hut and practically forced you into an appointment. That was shameless of me.'

'Don't be silly, Emily.' It wasn't easy for me to believe my ears. I could only stammer: 'I was gasping to see you again, but I'd hardly the courage to ask you. Or the cheek.' Since there were no keepers or gardeners at hand to spy on us we kissed, beside the pinkness of the blossom called Gloire de Lorraine, a dry, tight-lipped, dis-appointing kiss desiccating into adolescent laughter. The name and the pinkness of the blossom was too horribly appropriate and, besides, the long ranks of begonias smelled unwholesomely like unwashed old ladies crouched close to radiators in the corners of crowded churches. What she thought I couldn't guess, but I was anxious to be out again in the native sunshine and air before any suggestion of incongruity could touch her. 'How lovely you look.' I said, conscious of and trying to defy absurdity, 'among all these blossoms.' Beauty among the begonias; and to my alarm she laughed, but for compensation kissed me again, opening her lips and pressing fiercely against me so that I hoped she was for the first time feeling real passion. She whispered: 'Donagh, you're a darling.'

'Shall we go outside?'

'I'm in such trouble,' she said. 'I'm so worried.' The cactus-house, green bodies and brown spikes, stretched before us.

'Tell me about it. You can trust me. We'll walk down by the river. Unless you want to look at the cacti.'

'Oh, those horrible prickly things. Not those. Let's go out.' Shuddering away from the prickly horrors, she caught my hand and pulled me towards the nearest door; and I went easily, casting perhaps an eye in passing at the phallic Esposita Lanata from Peru or averting an eye from the lumpy diseased appearance of the variety monstrosus of the Cereus Peruvianus. 'My trouble is . . .' she said. We walked, my arm around her waist, between rockeries blazing with purple and white and crimson. 'I like you, Donagh. Not love but liking. You know how I feel about those things.'

'I do.' Then I said: 'Perhaps . . .' and said no more. To hope in words that the days to come might change liking into something else would disturb the balance of things between us, and I wasn't convinced that I wanted her to do anything more burning than to like me. For I had taken the measure of her liking, or thought I had, and supposed I could cope with it, but love would be a new, unmeasured, more powerful antagonist. 'I like walking here with you, Donagh. Walking this way and talking this way.' The noise of the river came filtered to us through a clump of warm aromatic cedars, and I said—could anything be more tasteless? 'I like being here with you, Emily.' The paths were soft under our feet. Graceful arms of the cedars extended above us in eastern blessing. The noise of the river increased. Voices of playing children and the far hum of the city died away behind us. Was I a sultan walking in his palace gardens with the fairest and most unattainable of women? No, I thought, I probably wasn't, for as far as I knew sultans didn't work that way and didn't, surely to Allah, dress as I dressed. Had there ever been a neurotic sultan with a harem full of frigid women or had Commodus, the wicked emperor, ever among his three hundred concubines, not to mention the boys, come up against beauty as cold as spring water? 'What can I do, Donagh?' she asked me. 'George has loved me for a long time.'

'I couldn't blame him for that.'

'He tells me so and he doesn't tell lies.' Big, forthright, hearty, honest he was; and already half betrayed by the girl he loved and the weakling he had befriended.

The river went past speedily under leaning trees. Every few yards it danced down over small hand-made cataracts—a little river tamed like a sultan's dancing girl. Oh, to be a sultan and have the power to subdue. 'But the thought of marriage with George,' she said, shivering in spite of the sun on the grass and on the hopping controlled water, 'terrifies me, makes me shiver.' 'Then you don't love him.'

'He's so big and vital.'

'What harm in that? They say women get to like it.'

'Oh, Donagh.' Ashamed not so much of what I had said as of the bitterness and envy that came out like dark vinegar through the cracks between my words, I leaned on the slanted railings of a narrow wooden foot-bridge, looked down at a cataract, and said: 'Sorry, Emily. I didn't mean to include you. just women in general.' Emily was different. She affected the soul, even big Butler's soul. My penitent look set her laughing, but she straightened her face with an effort and on the bridge I kissed her several quiet times, even though a keeper, spiked stick in hand to arm him against falling leaves, went past whistling a jig tune. Smiling up at me she swayed her body to the thin jigging whistle. 'I like him too,' I said. 'He's been a good friend to me.'

'Who? The whistler?' Laughing, she put her arms low around my waist and hid her face somewhere about my lapels. I said: 'You know well who I mean.'

'Of course I do. Let's forget about it now, Donagh. We're on our holidays.' As Butler felt, she seemed to feel that once away from the village she was moving in a tinkling, more carefree world. She said: 'Let's talk about you.'

'Not interested,' I stubbornly lied. The distant whistling, as a prelude to dying away, changed to a slow march tune. On the gravel path by the bouncing river we kissed again and talked of waterhens and trout. Seated on grass, not here guarded and forbidden by cold white iron hoops, we talked generally about nervous diseases. Above us swung in the musical wind the branches of a labelled and docketed monster: Aesculus Hippocastanum, a high horse-chestnut, native of some mountainy place in southern Europe. From a column in the morning's paper I read how a newspaper-man had talked with a fashionable, frightening hypnotist.

'You, of course,' said the hypnotist, 'realize the power of mind over matter. Feel my pulse.'

So the columnist and his companions fingered the pulse of the man with the compelling eyes and after a while the pulse stopped ticking.

'Isn't it extraordinary,' Emily said, her blue eyes wide with real wonder; and it occurred to me that more than most people, more than most women, twentieth century or fourteenth century, she would be helpless before the shadowy and the unseen. That thought drew me closer to her, in spirit and there and then in the flesh, and we kissed again as if we both meant it. Hail to Aesculus Hippocastanum, Balkan patriarch, who spread his arms above us and blessed our warming kisses.

Said the columnist and his companions: 'Let's feel your heart while you're stopping the pulse.' And they felt it—all at once or one at a time?—and, lo! the heart of the wizard also stopped.

'At that stage,' said Emily, 'I'd have made for the door.'

I said: 'Did they unshirt and unwaistcoat him in order to feel his heart?' But what I was suddenly and painfully remembering was Butler courageously bending down to feel the cold breast of Lily Morgan. Remembering that, I had a flashing accurate vision of her pale face as if she, alive, had looked at me from the chestnut branches or from the shrubs on the far bank of the river. Her pitiable horrible death had brought me here to these gardens, to kiss Emily Rayel.

'Or else,' wrote the columnist, 'we were all rooted to the spot,' and the hypnotist blandly assured them: 'It just shows the power of mind over matter. The heart can be stopped and started by the will.'

Folding the paper and rising from the grass, I said that hypnotism had been used to heal nerves.

'I know a hypnotist, Donagh. You must meet him some time.'

To meet her hypnotist would once again mean meeting her; so I agreed, and again we kissed, and again and again as we walked, between high trees and low dark shrubs, away from the river. Above us on a hill the ripe jungle grew in glasshouses. In that labelled world where nothing was anonymous I could have been for ever content only to walk with her and kiss her lips. For kisses in such a place couldn't lead to the goatish madnesses native to whinny yellow hills in midsummer or to the tangled corners, warm as boudoirs, of glossy grass meadows.

XIII

There can be nothing quite so terrifyingly silent as the lull and lack of interest between the end of the depositions and the commencement of the trial: like the hushed few seconds before the starting whistle blows, or before the pistol cracks that sets the runners away, or like the sickening moments of waiting between the shelling and the infantry advance. The story of Jim Walsh diminished and dropped out of the newspapers. It would come back to prominence again when he stepped into the dock; but for the moment there were parliamentary questions about whether or not the country's fuel supply was ensured for the coming winter, and speculations about international football prospects and the possibility of another war, and flowery speeches about our historic link with some country whose new ambassador had recently presented his credentials. There was, also, another case of murder in a distant western mountainy place—the result of injuries inflicted by pen-knives, blackthorn sticks, and limestone ammunition from the nearest, handiest mearing—and somewhere else a case of infanticide with complications enough to make it deserving of newspaper space, and in a northern city a spectacular robbery with violence. Jim Walsh was in prison and Lily Morgan in the grave, and the rest of us, in the wings and the dressing-rooms, walked around in circles and prepared for the next act.

In pubs, buses, and trains you'd never hear the murder mentioned and in the shops in the village you felt, or were made to feel, that to talk about it was a breach of etiquette. Having once indecently exposed itself and enjoyed the abominable nakedness, the village was now reacting sternly in favour of a secretive wordless modesty. To be absolutely honest I almost forgot about the business myself, for I was thinking of Emily and seeing a great deal of her and rapidly becoming her chosen confidant. She came frequently to the hut, no longer with any efforts after secrecy, sometimes taking the short cut from the village, over the fair-green, past Kavanagh's hut and the four empty huts to my welcoming door. Butler was at work in the city and couldn't know about the frequency of her visits and, even if he did know, it had occurred to us, he couldn't sensibly feel resentful because two friends of his were getting to know each other better and better. That was what I soothingly said to my conscience. Probably Emily told herself something similar. And we did get to know each other very well, all in the space of a few weeks, and I found myself happy in her company in a way I'd never before been happy with any other woman, or with any man.

That happiness must have brightened my face one raw evening— an advance guard for winter, grey rapidly revolving sky, cold dry wind, tree branches rattling like bones—as I walked back along the short cut from the village. Emily, leaving her car for cleaning in the village garage, had been to see me and I had walked back with her as far as the hotel for a drink. The remainder of Jim Walsh's stolen whisky was still untouched in a locked cupboard above my bunk. As we passed Kavanagh's hut we nodded to the woman who stood in the doorway awaiting her husband's return. We held hands as we walked up the sloping field path and as we picked our steps down the muddy slope of the fair- green, always damp from wasted, untapped springs even though it faced the bitter chilling north-east. We too facing the wind and the winter felt warmly content because the spontaneous way in which our hands found each other out meant contact and comfort for the dark days.

Mrs. Kavanagh still stood in the doorway as I returned, walking briskly, swinging my arms, smiling at the dying world. Her husband, bent and pushing against the wind, came cycling up the lane as I approached, dismounted beside me as I reached their gate. 'Evenings,' he said, 'are shortening.' That was the most words I'd heard him speak at one time. His sallow unshaven face had taken a faint flush from work and exercise and the buffeting wind. I said: 'It's cold enough for snow.' It wasn't, but I had to say something.

He leaned on his handle-bars. He said: 'Suppose you'll be off back to the city for the winter.' Was his unusual eloquence intended to make me understand that he'd be happier if all the neighbouring huts were empty for the winter? 'Hardly,' I said. 'I like it here.'

'Why should Mr. Hartigan go away when he's so popular with the local girls?' That was the voice of the woman speaking laughingly to us as she opened the gate to admit her husband. She had come, soft-footed in blue carpet slippers, from the door of the hut while the man and myself were exchanging greetings. Unturbaned now, the day's dusting done, her heavy brown hair was stirred only slightly by the chill wind that whipped my dark rats' tails about my forehead. In brown woollen sweater and skirt that sagged at the hem and buttonless cardigan and, obviously, no brassiere, she looked a sloven as she had never, to my knowledge, looked previously. For being an ample woman she needed bracing and tightening in plenty. Opening the gate wide, she said, as if sharing a joke with the green wooden paling posts: 'Mr. Hartigan never lets Miss Rayel out of his sight these days.' There was something in the smile she showed when she looked up from the gate and the paling posts to her husband and myself that made me feel her heart wasn't in the joke and that she didn't like Emily Rayel. And I felt so in spite of the truth that a smile couldn't but look pleasant on her fresh handsome face. Unable to think of anything to say—coy talk was never my talk—I smiled and stayed silent and her husband said sharply enough: 'Mr. Hartigan knows his own business best.'

'Does any man know his own business?' Her voice sharpened to balance the voice of her husband. Compelled to speak then to break an awkward silence, I said: 'She's just an acquaintance. I met her through Mr.Butler.'

'Is it Mr. Butler of the hotel? Sure, he knows all the girls.' She was working hard to recapture her smile. I wasn't, I felt, included in her anger. The man said: 'He has that reputation.' That was rude, since Butler was my friend, but it was interesting and it made me curious to know why the woman disliked Emily Rayel and why the husband disliked George Butler; and anxious to keep the conversation going, I said: 'I met him on the morning of the murder at Morgan's cottage. He's a lively fellow.' Irrelevantly the Kavanagh woman said: 'How do you like the cold weather?'

'Not at all. It's getting too chilly to sit out reading in the fresh air.'

'You read a lot.' The man moved awkwardly through the gateway as if conscious of his own rudeness, and ashamed, and ashamed of his shame. His black hair came to a pigtail point at the back of his yellow neck and the collar of his coat was greasy and unclean. He wasn't as well looked after as you'd think when looking at him and at all her cleaning, dusting, mat-beating, from a distance. 'Reading,' I said to her, 'passes the time pleasantly.' A profound remark, God help us.

'Were you very ill before you came to live here?'

Still trying to keep the talk going, I mentioned nerves and the things they could do to you, from head-staggers to blindness and persecution mania. I began to enjoy myself. I hadn't really wished to talk about nerves since the morning I'd met Butler. Murder and friendship and fourteenth-century romance and burning Irish whisky and love, I suppose, had all come between me and my favourite theme. But there was something about this strong, ignorant woman that gave every man—I mean me—a chance to be himself. She listened with obvious attentive sympathy. 'It all comes, I'm sure, from doing too much work crouched over a desk in an office.'

'But I'm better now. Three months rest has done me all the good in the world. And I've still three months to go.'

'Take as long a rest as you can.' She might have been my mother or an elder sister advising me for my own good, except that she had qualities I'd never noticed in my mother or sisters. She was novelty. She was another man's wife. 'I certainly intend to,' I said. 'Rest and books and fresh air and whisky and the best of company.' She looked over her shoulder at her departing husband, and the wind as she turned her head caught her heavy brown hair and had a brief ruffling triumph. Smoothing it down again with short, square-fingered, capable hands, she said: 'That wind. It's so cold, step inside and shelter for a moment.'

'I'd be upsetting you.'

'Not at all. Have a cup of tea, or there might be a drop in the house.'

'Mr. Kavanagh. . . .

'Oh, Joe won't mind. Joe minds nothing.' And she called to him as he went up the wooden steps to the raised threshold: 'Joe, is there a drop at all left in that bottle?'

'You should know better than me.'

'He doesn't touch it himself,' she explained as I closed the gate behind us, wondering as I did so if it wouldn't be more prudent to leave it open so as to allow for an expeditious retreat. Curiosity and the suddenness of the hospitable invitation after weeks of distant hand-waving and casual nodding and speaking, drove me on. In country places a man should know and visit his neighbours. So, resolutely I closed the gate and asked: 'Where's the collie dog?'

'Off hunting somewhere. He takes wandering notions.'

'We all do.' I was thinking of my own dark night-walks, but behind her husband's back she looked at me with such meaning that I felt as if I had just daringly parted her heavy chignon and kissed the nape of her neck.

Their hut was larger than mine, the floor covered with straw matting as bright with peacock and peony design as a Lurçat tapestry. The woman, or the man—now washing himself behind a red screen fixed firmly in one corner—had taste. There were two bunks, a few feet from the floor in diagonally opposite corners. Had I known that, six weeks or a month ago, my night imaginings might not have been so hard to live with. No books to be seen. The walls were lined with sacred pictures, so antique and violently hideous that they could have come only in the trunk of some nineteenth-century exile returning from Buenos Aires: a white fearfully battered Christ hung on a cross against a sable background, and two fat, yellow-haired, female angels, bent in soaring semicircles, came flying with refreshments; saints with incredibly emaciated faces strained eyes upwards at grim skies or contemplated grinning skulls. A red lamp burned on a bracket before a conventionally quiet picture of the Sacred Hcart. The man, I felt then, was responsible for the gallery on the walls, but the woman for the radiance of the straw-covered floor. There was a green horn-gramophone on a shelf above one bunk. As far as I remembered, I had never heard it play. One arm-chair, four hard chairs, white unpainted presses, a countryhouse dresser so large that it seemed as if the hut must have been built around it, and on that dresser a proud display of alternated willow pattern and plain white delph, bowls and cups and saucers and plates of all sizes—those things, with a fireplace and a real fire, completed the scene. In every way it was a superior dwelling to mine.

'You're very comfortable here.'

'It's so small,' she said, her face wrinkled with distaste and possibly with envy of wealthier women who lived in proud houses of stone: Emily, the bosomy blonde, or Jill, the longlegged hunter. 'But it was the best we could get when we married. Houses are so scarce around here. And the war put an end to the building.' The man hidden behind the red screen had ceased splashing and spluttering. Was he towelling his yellow face or listening to the woman making little of their home? 'You keep it lovely,' I said—nervously. 'You should see my place. Compared with this it's like a prison cell. It needs a woman's hand.' She lowered a kettle on an adjustable crook to the licking heat of the flame. 'It doesn't matter for a man. You don't always have to go keeping up appearances.'

'Thanks be to God.'

'People don't expect it of you. But a woman needs a real house with rooms.' She was momentarily pathetic. Muffled now by audible towelling, the man's voice came over the screen: 'Morgan's cottage will be vacant from this out.,

She said: 'The people won't be biting themselves to get living in it, after what happened there.' He came out, clean but still unshaven, jacketless, fixing his collar stud. 'Why not,' I said, 'the poor dead girl won't haunt the place.' though, I felt, for me she easily might. 'Lily was queer enough,' the woman said, 'to do anything. She was always praying.'

'No harm in that,' her husband said. 'Get the priest to bless the place and it'd be as right as rain. If the people don't want to live in it, more fools they. It'll go the cheaper.'

'The priest blessed it once for Mrs. Morgan. And that, and all Lily's prayers, didn't keep her from driving men to murder.'

'That ruffian didn't need much driving.' The sallow face was as bleak as a November moor. 'It's more likely, indeed, that his wicked soul would haunt the place when the rope separates it from the body.' Oh, Mr. Kavanagh, I thought, what a fine inquisitor you'd have made, handing over heretics for burning; or what an excellent

Salem elder witnessing against witchy hags. But the woman was subdued. She said no more about murder or Morgan's cottage and, as uneasy as if my buttocks had broken out in an agonizing bumpy rash, I sat and sipped tea. She made fine tea, too. We talked about painless topics: the differences between life in the city and life in the country, about a football match to be played next Sunday in the village in aid of the local fife and drum band. But once, in the middle of desultory chat about horse-racing, the man stopped munching bread and said, as if his mind had all the time been absorbed by the thought: 'He was a bad egg, that Jim Walsh. I always knew he'd come to no good. There's a few more like him going the roads.' Yet although his voice sounded hoarse with hate his dark eyes, when I quickly glanced at them, were soft as if bleeding with the consciousness of misery.

For a neurotic it was all excessively nerve-racking. But I was stubbornly determined,to sit there as long as I could, even though, after my departure, the husband might thoroughly flay his buxom wife. Before those grimacing tortured pictures that would be pleasantly appropriate, and it could be that they'd both enjoy it.

From the small round tea-table we turned our chairs and sat facing the fire. The brace was painted red, and lined, to simulate the pointing between great square stones, with narrow white lines. Out of the last few inches in a bottle, again the shield-shaped label and the three white swallows, she poured me some whisky. Like a peevish child he looked away, picking at a nostril with his left forefinger, when she rinsed her tea-cup and poured a drop for herself. 'I suppose you won't touch it Joe, dear,'and he replied miserably: 'You know I never do.' Seven extra lashes, I feared, for her effrontery in daring to share whisky with a strange man in the presence of her temperate, pious husband; and I permitted myself to marvel at how inaccurate it was possible to be when judging character on a distant view. From behind a cushion on the sagging cane arm-chair he picked up a tattered copy of some religious magazine and flicked the pages in a way that said: go home to your own cold hut. But the wind was loud outside and Kavanagh's hearth was warm; and the devil was strong in me, making me exult in the thought that here was a man who, in some ways, was weaker than myself. I went on talking to the woman, politely ignoring her yellow man. I said: 'Those are striking.' They were two huge pine cones, the largest I had ever seen, and their knobbly patterned surfaces shone with careful polishing. They stood poised carefully, one on either end of the mantelpiece. 'One of them's opening with the heat of the fire,' she said, and, turning it upside down, she shook it gently until two winged seeds escaped and fluttered circling down towards the flame. Shelley's wild west wind was outside the hut sending winged seeds off on their life-carrying journeys. A remote Asian voice talked of the seed falling and dying and by death making life. She said: 'I picked them up in the wood beyond and brought them home and polished them with brown polish. Aren't they lovely?'

'They are.'

Still flicking his pious pages, he said: 'When they open wide you won't look at them.'

'Then they'll burn well.' I was glad of the chance to contradict him.

'I cut a walking-stick too,' she said. 'I love the smell of pine.' From a corner behind one of the white wooden presses she lifted, as gently as if it was a child and she loved it, a pine bludgeon at least an inch in diameter. Green needles dropped from it like quills from a moulting porcupine. When my fingers circled around the handle I felt the stickiness of yellow oozing resin. 'A fine stick,' I said. 'You could strike a good blow with it.'

'One day over in the wood I cut it. It was a part of a big branch in the wind.'

'You must walk a good deal in the wood.'

'The days do be long when himself's away at work.' Himself was on his feet. 'It'll be no heavier than a straw,' he said, 'when the wood dries. Blackthorn's the only stick worth cutting. Or an ash plant.' Plainly proud of his knowledge of different timbers, he moved past me and, without an apology, went out through the doorway. I sat silent, looking at the green hairs of the pine, painfully realizing that not for a Jew's ransom could I think of anything important to say in this hut to this woman. With such people social intercourse went just so far and then ended as if in black night one had walked bang against a brick wall. She'd have made an excellent maid-servant or a better concubine, but not, for me, a feasible permanent companion. His steps went slowly round the hut on the gravelled walk that I knew led to the corrugated-iron dry closet. Six of them stood at a distance from the six huts like shadowing

Scotland Yard men with their eyes on suspects. The thought of him and where he was going embarrassed the two of us. For a moment she sat in his chair, looking vacuously at the fire, and then, from the depth of her humiliation, said: 'My husband's poor company.'

'He's probably tired after his day's work. I know well what that feels like.'

'Joe's always tired. He's the best in the world, but he's not lively.' Then she sighed and hid one hand between the nape of her neck and her brown descending hair and said: 'I hope you didn't mind my mentioning Miss Rayel. It was only in fun.'

We were friendly, abruptly, surprisingly, in an odd tongue-tied unexpected way.

'I hope himself didn't mind me stepping in.'

'Oh, him,' she said, and her soul was at last unpleasantly revealed and all my ideas of their warm, intimate happiness went before her words like smoke before the wind.

When I heard his steps returning along the gravel I stood up and prepared to depart. On the threshold we met, and he said: 'Good evening now,' not so much as if he was glad to see me go, but as if he hadn't noticed I had been there and was wondering where in blazes I'd dropped from. That night for the first time I heard the gramophone play. Perhaps it had played before, but not to my ears because, until I visited their hut, I hadn't noticed it: gallant green horn blowing tunes towards the roof. Do the eyes follow the ears or the ears follow the eyes? But assuredly it played that night and, in the lulls of the boisterous wind, I tried to listen to it until Butler came knocking to my door to bring me down to drink in the hotel. It played slow, solemn tunes like Gregorian chant, but with the way the wind blew it wasn't possible to make out what exactly the chants were or if they were or were not played to drown the sound of fighting and screams.

'The winter's with us,' Butler said as we drove to the hotel.

'It was cold today.'

'Jay, I was frozen in town. No bloody heating in the office. God, I want to get drunk.' In the course of the night and with the good help of hot rum he succeeded so well that I had to assist him from the bar to his bedroom. Who, I wondered, in this friendship was helping and encouraging whom? But with his amazing facility for recovering sobriety he steadied up again before the fire in his own room, became again genial and hospitable and strong. His fits of drunkenness came less from the effect of drink than from his deliberately releasing within himself something that made for riot or something else that made for stupefaction. Over hot buttered rum he said to me: 'Come to the races some day, Harty. Make some money. Take the fresh air. See the horses.' Tipsy to the extent of being conscious of intellectual superiority, I said: 'The Chinaman remarked that it has long been established that one horse can run faster than another, so why should I waste time and money going to see what everybody knows.'

'Ballsology,' Butler said. 'The point is which horse. And you're forgetting about the thrill.' His long powerful hands were gesturing in front of him, gripping invisible reins; he was rising and falling in his arm-chair like a gentleman rider—not a horse jockey, not Jim Walsh—seated high on a steaming steeplechaser. 'Emily and Jill will come,' he said. 'I've asked them.' Cold with jealousy, I agreed to go. He was still seeing Emily and she was still seeing him. But when the first jealous shock wore off I realized there were at least a dozen good reasons why they should go on seeing each other. He loved her. She liked him, probably as much or more than she liked me. She had known him longer than she had known me. Even if she didn't want to see him it would be foolish and unkind, by avoiding him, to draw too much attention to her friendship with me. And so on and so on. I drank rum and turned the knife in my jagged wound and felt also like a hound of a traitor sitting in a friend's room, drinking his drink, and at the same time thinking such thoughts of him and the girl he loved. When he passed across to me a clipping of the columnist's chat with the fashionable hypnotist and said: 'Thought you might be interested, Harty, old boy,' my agony was excruciating. Reading the newspaper, he had been thinking of my welfare. I read it solemnly as if I'd never seen it before, and said: 'That's damned interesting.' Then from remorse I swung back to cold jealousy because he said: 'I know a hypnotist chap in town. You should meet him.' He knew a hypnotist, and so did Emily, and ten to one they both knew the same man. Who was I or what was I to come butting in on all the days of friendship or something that had been between them? I mumbled: 'No, I can't go to the races. I can't,' and went out to the bathroom and, aided by Butler's kind hands, was gloriously and cataclysmically ill.

Later I walked home by a circuitous route. The rum and jealousy had so unsettled me that I knew it would be useless for hours yet to seek refuge in sleep. Muttering phrases from Renaissance poets who had written about beautiful women and faithless friends, I finally passed the Kavanagh hut. The windows were dark, the gramophone silent. I hadn't night-walked since the time I had met Jim Walsh and I was lonely and disappointed to find my hut closed and silent, no strange man, tramp or murderer or devil, to help me through the length and loneliness of the darkness. Unlocking the cupboard, I sniffed at the remnants of the stolen whisky, but the smell made me ill again, and dry-retching out at the back of the hut I heard, as if it were away on the moon, Kavanagh's collie lazily and resoundingly barking from its kennel. The wind was cold. The night was black, no moon nor reflection from a moon-touched cloud, not a star. The world outside was even more horrible than the confinement of my hut, so I fled back to my books and searched for a line in which some Shakespearian pansy king had wailed that he was sworn brother sweet to grim necessity. Sworn brother sweet to irrational nervous fears. Sworn brother sweet to big George Butler, if I hadn't in my heart betrayed him, as soon as I'd known him, for a cold girl's useless kisses. Then I turned the pages and read about Valentine and Proteus, gentlemen of Verona, about love and betrayed friendship; and in my shack, Silvia, daughter of the Duke of Milan and beloved of Valentine, spoke to the base Proteus, and to poor old shaky Hartigan, her shattering high-minded lines of reproach:

> *Thou hast no faith left now, unless thou hadst two,*
> *And that's far worse than none; better have none*
> *Than plural faith, which is too much by one:*
> *Thou counterfeit to thy true friend.*

And Proteus perkily replied, how I envied him his hard neck:

> *In love, who respects friends?*

But in four words Silvia squelched him:

All men but Proteus.

So that Proteus, beaten in argument, had recourse to the threat of rape and roared, in my hut, how he'd woo the duke's daughter like a soldier would, 'at arm's end', how he'd love her against the nature of love and force her to yield to his desire. At which Silvia naturally cried: Oh, heaven! and said also: 'Ruffian, let go that rude uncivil touch.' It was all too ridiculous; and with rebellion in my marrow against the claims of friendship and the barriers of coldness, I closed the book and climbed into my bunk. My mind was at ease, accepting the necessity of betrayal, not accepting the negation that cut off Emily from life—meaning me.

XIV

There were spots of frozen snow like a leprous rash on the footpath at the corner of the great building where the law did most of its business. Stamping my feet to keep warm, I waited until big Butler had parked his car. Barristers dressed in black and carrying bulging bags passed quickly through the guarded gates that led to their library. I regretted the peace of the village in this autumn weather, blustery leaf-dancing days alternating with calm frosty grey and blue days, and the quietness that had come last night with the first premature skiff of a fall of snow. The snow still lay pure on the fields around my hut. The woods on the demesne of Jill's father were a vivid black and silver. Yesterday in the newsagent's shop the little woman with the Scots accent had asked about my health with more than her normal solicitude, as if she regarded me as a victim cleansed, trussed, and ready for legal sacrifice, for the lawyer's knife. A short sharp note had come from my mother more or less ordering me to return home. But when her entreaties hadn't touched me her commands couldn't, and I'd resolved that even on the day of the trial I wouldn't visit her, or her house, or my sisters. Yesterday, too, in the door of the greengrocer's place a farm labourer had stood, hands in pockets, eyes on the cold blue sky, and plaintively and melodiously whistling the tune of an old country ballad. He was just such a man as Jim Walsh might have been before tuberculosis and the demons whisky and lechery had got into him, before he became an outcast, before he gripped his fingers around a girl's throat and murdered his love.

Yesterday, beyond the low green ridge behind the hotel, the men of that part of the country held their annual coursing. Butler was at work, so Jill and Emily and myself went up through a muddy sloping farmyard, stepped carefully through guttery gateways, saw sleek rumps of stall-fed cattle in shadowy, cobwebby byres. Jill went bravely in wellingtons and jodhpurs that made her look all legs: a sandy-headed, freckled, two-tailed, disappointed tadpole. Emily wore a silvery shower-proof that rustled as she walked and shone like a new sixpence over the curves of her hips. I went delicately from stone to stone because my shoes were light and as thin as paper in their unmended soles. Come back to me, Donagh, my son, and have home comforts for the duration of the murder trial.

From the top of the ridge we saw the whole horror of the coursing: twinkling tail of the tiny hunted thing as it twisted and turned and raced for life, the stretched necks of the pursuing hounds, the beaters lined everywhere like soldiers to make the hellery last longer. We heard the raucous shouts of big smelly red-faced men whose cars were parked in a double row on the village street. The clean crisp air was suddenly poisonous with cruelty, and Emily felt it as I did, and at that moment I knew that what I felt for her was love, the real thing, strong enough to destroy honesty and the claims of friendship. 'I'm near enough,' she said. 'I don't want to see any more.'

'Oh, for goodness sake, Emily,' Jill snorted, 'don't be absurd. It's sport.' What wickedness must go on behind that elongated, unattractive face; what horrible unnatural thrills under the sweater and jodhpurs when the hare screamed its pathetic ghastly scream. 'Bullfighting,' I said, 'is decent. At least, when you hit a bull you hit your match.'

Contemptuously Jill said: 'Did you ever hit a bull? You two are absurd.' She derived some twisted painful pleasure from lumping Emily together with another unloved person. We stood where we were while the next hare was released. 'Jim Walsh,' Jill said, 'was a marvellous man at a coursing. He had the best dogs hereabouts and he knew where and how to find the best hares.'

Emily said: 'No wonder he ended the way he did.'

'He's not ended yet. They haven't tried him yet. My dad says he's certain Jim Walsh never had hand, act, or part in it. He wouldn't have hurt a fly.'

'He hurt hares.'

'The evidence doesn't look good for him,' I ventured timidly, for I was never quite certain about the wisdom and safety of arguing with Jill.

'My dad says Jim Walsh would never lift his hand to a woman.'

'There's a first time for everybody,' Emily said. She turned her shapely silvery back on yelping dogs and bull-bellowing men. Two hairpins were coming unstuck, as her hairpins often did, from her blonde crown of hair, and heedless of the hurt and deprivation Jill might feel, I tapped them back softly into place with the tip of a forefinger. From the ridge we looked down on the roofs of the village, awry and irregular but dressed out in two roughly parallel lines, and wisps of smoke loitering over chimneys, and the bending river beyond, loving the flat open fields, losing itself in the demesne woods. 'This bores me,' Emily said. 'I'm going back for a gin. Coming, you two?'

'No,' Jill said, and I said yes and: 'We'll wait for you in the hotel, Jill.'

'See that you don't catch cold.' She strode away down the other slope of the ridge towards the blood fun in the flat land. 'Jim Walsh,' Emily said, 'is a bit of a hare himself at the moment. I wonder how he likes it.' For her honesty in saying those cruel words I loved her still more, because the same trite thought had been running in my head and Jim Walsh seemed now as remote as my mother, so that I could forget how once on a dark desperate night I'd met and liked him.

In the small dark room behind the public bar of the hotel Emily drank gin, I drank ale and ate a sandwich. Automatically abandoning Jill on the green ridge had taught us how close together we had grown. We didn't need to speak, and once, when our hands touched, Emily blushed and looked down to the table as if she was a soft shy country girl kissed for the first time. We couldn't hold hands because people were coming and going, coursing men in big boots and members of the hotel staff who all knew, I suspected and feared, that Butler was in love with Miss Rayel. The walls were lined with coloured prints of coursing scenes, given away in the eighteen-eighties as supplements to some sporting magazine; and in a corner of the room one bearded veteran told another about the great coursing he'd seen there beyond the hill in the year of the Titanic.

Jill didn't come to join us. That made us catch our breath a little, not because we wanted her company or because we were even sorry for her, trudging home indignant and alone. But that was the first time we had openly allied ourselves against a third person. We didn't know when the next time would be, but we recognized its inevitability and guessed the identity of the next person to be rejected.

Emily's car was in a garage for repairs. I walked with her as far as the small bridge where Butler and myself had leaned on the morning of the murder. The roadside grass was clotted and clinkered with fallen leaves and the wind in the beech branches had a sound of rasping and cutting, blades on whetstones, jagged wood scraping on walls of rough brick. I stood at the bridge, as once before I had stood, until she had mounted the steps and gone with a last silvery flash into the house. But this time she turned and waved a hand because she knew me and knew I was waiting, and why. There was no autumn in the world I was then living in; and when, moved by morbid curiosity, one with the respectable business men desiring to paw a murdered girl's panties, I walked between the chilling beeches to look at Morgan's cottage, I was idiotically surprised by the blank shuttered windows boarded against cattle, tramps, and souvenir-hunters, by the air of desolation, the flower-stalks rotting where they'd withered in the beds around the walls. Even the round ornamental shore stones were blemished with the first touches of a green glar. The house was dying. Round and round the cottage I walked, several times trying as a sort of scholastic exercise, angels on the point of a medieval needle, to see could I forget Emily Rayel and remember my dream of Lily Morgan. But poor waif, poor cold whisper, she was less than a dream, a pale ghost, a blur curdling the air before awakening eyes; and the very dying beechwood had been full of and alive with Emily, the sound of her smooth adult voice, the silky revolt of her hair always inclining to reject restraining hairpins, the sheen of that silver coat around her firm buttocks, her thin neat ankles-and her spirit that in some way beyond definition had grappled to mine as firmly as if it were something with hands that gripped, or claws, or muscular embracing arms. Like a man following a vision—blonde hair at last released and falling down, a corn-coloured cataract over white naked marble—I short-cutted back to the village across the fields, finding a fairly well-defined cattle path. Hard macadam under my feet would have jarred disturbingly on the softness of my imaginings. I passed another cottage, untidily thatched and needing whitewash, chickens picking hungrily around a sloppy doorstep. Farther along, two small ragged boys came gaily whistling from shopping in the village. One of them embraced a broken-handled basket of groceries. The other nursed a steaming fresh loaf and a quarter-stone packet of flaked oatmeal. Bread and porridge. Healthy food. Build them up. Jim Walsh was once a boy like that.

Then I hated the sloppy cottage and the two passing boys, and Jim Walsh as well, because between them they had for a moment taken my mind away from Emily Rayel.

As I came to my hut the first snowflakes began to pepper the grass.

Butler said: 'Sorry for keeping you waiting, Harty. A bloody old fool with a Dodge as long as a liner got in my way at the car park.'

'Probably the judge.'

He was white with rage. 'I wish this effin thing was over.'

'I don't like it myself. Still, I suppose if somebody was murdered they must have a trial. It hurts Jim Walsh more than it hurts us.'

'How the hell do we know who killed her? Ten to one they won't convict him.'

'Seems a clear case.'

'All we did was find the body. They could leave us out of this show. They know she's dead and that somebody killed her. What does it matter who had the misfortune to find her?' 'The twelve good men and true must have the whole story, footnotes and all.' Were we all just footnotes to the text dealing with Lily Morgan and Jim Walsh? Were murderers, the murdered, and suicides—the onanistic murderers, the only truly very important persons? 'Anyway, it wasn't a misfortune, Butler.'

'Except for Lily Morgan.'

'And Jim Walsh.'

'And everybody connected with her.'

'It was a most extraordinary experience,' I said, not quite seriously, somewhat conscious of pose. 'I never found a dead body before.' He stopped and turned and looked at me, and breathed out slowly. His long handsome face was still pale with fury from his encounter with the old fool and the liner-long Dodge. Against the pallor, tiny blue stubbles that would elude any razor showed on his firm jaws and chin. For his part in the trial he wore a dark suit and dark overcoat, a dark blue silk scarf. Although everything was perfectly and expensively tailored the get-up did still convey something of incongruity. For he was a man made to wear good tweed jackets and flannels to flap rhythmically when he walked swaggering, or else to go spur-clinking in decorated uniform, eyes half-hidden under a shiny acute-angled cap-peak. Behind him, adding to the incongruity, passed the procession of busy bag-bearing barristers on the way to fame and fortune, big briefs, politics, undergraduatish wit in the warm library. Then the grey sky, that had threatened more snow, shifted abruptly, gave out sunlight that shone on the shiny toes of the passing barristers, on Butler's dark oiled curls, on his pale face softening into a smile. He said: 'I declare to my Jesus there are times when you make me shudder.' I bowed.

'You're really serious?' he said.

'As serious as the judge we'll see in a few minutes.' 'You enjoy this, Harty, you microbe.' I bowed again, and we laughed. 'You get a kick out of it. An inhuman intelluctual pleasure. Where's your pity? That bastard in the dock? That girl on the bed?' We were walking ahead, away from the main law buildings to the ancient criminal court where in the middle of a maze of twisty streets as complicated as the capturing net of the law, great criminals had stood on trial for two hundred years. 'How do we know,' he said, as if he was asking himself questions, 'how much compassion she deserves? She had a bad reputation.'

'Some say that and some say otherwise. She seemed inoffensive enough to me.' In the quiet lane between the main buildings and the bridewell he turned and looked at me again. 'Did you know her?'

'Met her once in a convalescent home.'

'Jesus, you're a deep one. And you never breathed a word. It's just as well you're above suspicion. From what they say, any man ever knew her might have croaked her.'

'I didn't know her well enough for that.' That truth made her for one moment alive for me again because I remembered the agonized nights between our first meeting and her murder when I'd lain awake or walked endless roads wondering would I ever see her again, ever discover the secret behind her quietness. She had flicked past me like a picture glimpsed in some huge, clumsy book, searched for again painstakingly, and finally discovered to be something completely different from what the tantalizing glimpse had suggested. 'I spoke only a few words to her the day she left the convalescent home.'

'I suppose,' he said, 'you do, as a rule, have to know a girl well before you can murder her in her bed.'

'As a rule you do.' Then he was laughing uproariously his high, strident laugh, tossing his head back, unsettling his curls, saying: 'Jesus God, Harty, you're a liberal education. You're a deep one.' His loud laughter went unheeded amid the flurry of the fruit, fish, and flower market crowding one area of the narrow streets between the main law buildings and the ancient criminal court: fish on cold slabs, discarded fragments of fish in choked vennels, pyramids of curly kail and apples and oranges, great clusters of bananas, lorries loaded with hot-house flowers. 'We'll have a drink,' he said. 'We'll need one.' Around the markets the pubs opened early, so we drank hot whisky beside a sizzling barrel-shaped stove. The atmosphere was pungent with the smell of charcoal fuming coke, a furnace-room smell. The room was crazy with the voices of marketing men and women, bringing business in with them from the cold crowded streets. The court was round the corner, Jim Walsh without hot whisky, waiting in his underground cell, and we had a few minutes to spare. 'Well, here's to here's to,' Butler said, tossing back the remnants of his first and edging his teeth on a sodden fragrant slice of lemon. 'Here's to the hunt,' I said. 'May the hare run fast.' I was glad to see Butler back again in a good mood, recovered from his irritation with the dodderer and his long Dodge.

The policeman on duty checked our names and showed us the way in. Threshold stones gone concave from centuries of shuffling feet. Old brown wood. Modern radiators as incongruous as electric heaters in hell. Silence, made more complete by contrast with the noise of buying and selling around the corner.

XV

A courtroom is a stage. Don't tell me now that all the world's a stage and all the men and women, and so on. A courtroom is a most carefully constructed wooden stage, high here and low there, thoughtfully built so as to get the most out of an elaborate dramatic performance. That was the first thing I was conscious of. I'd never seen a murder trial before.

We entered from the left wing, tiptoeing breathlessly, moving with added care when we ascended the hollow curving wooden stairs from the flagged floor to the raised row of seats where the witnesses sat waiting. Diagonally across from us and nearer the roof than anybody else except the galleried public, the jury sat, faces as inhumanly composed as if they were the collected figureheads of twelve ships. Only the strained attention in and around their eyes showed that they were alive. The judge fiddled with a long fountain-pen and looked down over the clerks to the counsel, to the row of expert witnesses, to the scribbling reporters. The prosecuting senior counsel was on his feet, not upright and stiff with dignity, but bending sickle-backed over the table hands in trousers pockets, as if the courtroom was too cramped to allow him to stand straight and spread himself He mumbled. No pretence at oratory. There was much more excitement in the fruit market.

On the table before the judge, and above the heads of the clerks and court officials, stood a dainty doll's-house, a plaything for a child; and I was settled in my seat for five minutes before I knew it for a model of Morgan's cottage. They should, I thought, have included the beechwood and the bridge and the high house where Emily lived, and carefully fashioned puppets to show the borrowing woman hiding behind a tree and Jim Walsh walking towards murder, or Mrs. Morgan running out screaming, startling Butler and myself from our rest at the bridge.

The case for the State will be, said the bending prosecutor, that some time after midnight on the morning of the twenty-ninth of August the accused, having found his way into the house where Lily Morgan lived with her mother, did there strangle her in her bedroom until she was dead.

He straightened up for a minute or so, took off his spectacles, looked at the jury, then hunched again over the table. He didn't, as

I had expected him to do, groan with backache. Then in great detail he mumbled who the accused was, when and where he was born, where and under what circumstances he was reared, when he left the village but not what he was doing while he was away, when he returned, when he first met Lily Morgan, how their engagement had been broken off. We knew all that already; but this detailed biography reminded me to swivel around and look for the first time for Jim Walsh, hereinafter known as the accused, and the spike-guarded dock, the most unimpressive, inconspicuous portion of the courtroom's timbered ups and downs. I couldn't see him very well. The head, shoulders, and cap of one of the two guarding policemen—a man as tall as the accused—came between my eyes and his face. But once, when he leaned forward to rest against the edge of the dock and to listen more intently, I saw his sharp eagle profile, hair thinning over the temples, the terrifying paleness of his high forehead.

They would hear evidence, said the prosecutor to the twelve figureheads, to the effect that the accused had returned to the vicinity of the village some days before the murder of Lily Morgan, that he had been sleeping by night in various lodging- houses in the city, that he had been drinking heavily, that on the afternoon of the twenty-eighth of August he had been refused admission to her home by the girl's mother and told by Mrs. Morgan that her daughter no longer wished to see him or to continue in her engagement to him. The testimony of other witnesses would trace his movements for the remainder of that ill-fated day during which he had been heard to utter threats against the girl and to state his intention of returning to the cottage to reclaim an engagement ring. A neighbour woman would testify that she had seen the accused entering Morgan's house shortly before the murder was committed. The prisoner himself would say that he had reclaimed the ring peaceably and left the girl alive in her own home, but that claim would have to be balanced against a heavy weight of contradictory evidence and against the fact that the prisoner ncither would nor could give a satisfactory account of his movements after the time at which he said he left the house. Medical evidence would show that the dead girl had had relations with a man shortly before her murder and from the nature of the evidence they would see that the probability of force was not ruled out. . . .

At that stage I shut my ears, my eyes, and my mind, and thought of the sun brightening and melting the thin crust of snow on the fields around the village, and of the demesne woods losing their streaks of silver; and of the pleasant truth that in the afternoon, when Butler and myself expected to be called, Emily would be sitting, so precious and so near, in the public gallery. The thought of her presence would give me the courage, or the gall, to descend the steps, cross the stone floor, ascend the three or four steps to the brown eminence of the witness-box, take the oath, speak my evidence clearly—no phlegm balls around my Adam's apple. Only great lawyers were allowed to mumble. I would tell the world how I had found the body of Lily Morgan, and then forget for ever the whole accursed, interesting business. Points of evidence were for the judge and jury. I knew more of the real story than any of them and nothing that I knew could do a dammed bit of good to the man in the dock, the accused.

And in the afternoon, the sun on the windows behind the public gallery, Emily visible in one corner where a comfortable place had been made for her by a respectful policeman, the junior prosecuting council, a perky man who squeaked but didn't mumble,said: 'What is your name?'

'Donagh Hartigan.'

'You are a civil servant?'

'Yes.'

'When this event took place you were on sick leave and living in the village?'

'Yes.'

'You are still there on sick leave?'

'Yes. For another eleven weeks.'

Since that wasn't exactly a routine answer, little perky, squeaky Proteus raised his eyebrows and the judge looked at me as if I'd just coughed and spat phlegm as far as the reporter's table.

'Would you tell the court what you saw on the morning of the twenty-ninth of August?'

I told the court. I didn't mention my thoughts, or the sunshine like honey or yellow wine spilling through the despoiled windows of the old mill, or the lonely ragged rook above the beech trees, or the fact that ever before that morning had I laid eyes on Lily Morgan.

'And the body,' said the judge, 'was, you say, half in and half out of the bed?'

'Yes, my lord.'

'The black marks on the throat were distinctly visible?'

'Yes, my lord.'

'Was the room much disturbed?'

'No, my lord. Except that the bed was rumpled.' Judge nodded to prosecutor and prosecutor smiled gratefully at judge as if they had found out something from those three dam-fool questions; and I had a nauseating horror of the law as of a dangerous machine run by men, who, for their money, had to try to look and act wise.

The perky prosecutor bent down to whisper to his mumbling senior, who sat slumped over the table as if he had just been knocked unconscious. Then he surfaced again to ask me: 'Did you touch the body?'

'No.' What fun in court if I'd said: No, but I wanted to. Wouldn't you under similar circumstances?

'Are you quite certain?'

I told him I was quite certain, and he sat down looking as satisfied as Proteus would have looked if the duke's daughter, without argument, had sweetly said yes. That, thought I, is the sum-total and essence of the thrill of being a witness. But just as, dismissed, I was about to descend, the senior counsel for the defence, a tall bulbous-eyed man with a lean, scraggy throat, was on his feet saying something to the judge. The judge, by his grace of state enabled to interpret all legal mumbles, was pleasantly nodding assent and asking me to stay where I was for a moment. 'Have you ever seen the accused before?' asked the tall man, trying to earn his pay by the chance question.

I could have said no. Then I thought: Perhaps Jim Walsh has told his lawyers about the night in my hut; and anyway, I'll let them know that I did once talk to him and found him, all things considered, a decent poor sod, not at all like a murderer. 'Yes,' I said, and from the new angle of vision from the witness-box I looked across the well of the court at the guarded prisoner, but there was no recognition in his cold, pale face. He might have been a statue. He was a man who had had everything, good and bad, that his limited life could give him, and he no longer wanted to live, was interested no longer in people he had met or in lawyers' questions or witnesses' answers. Yet if it hadn't been for Emily, bright above the listening public, I'd have envied Jim Walsh.

'When?' asked the tall lean man.

I told him when and how. But I made no mention of the reading of Rilke or the stealing of the bottle of whisky. 'Did the accused mention the deceased?'

'Yes.'

'Did it occur to you that you might have in your house the man the police were looking for?' Shuffling movements and protests from the senior prosecutor. I didn't even listen to the argument that followed, and even had I listened I couldn't have heard or understood it too expertly. The judge allowed me to answer and I said no.

'One last question.' The courtroom was breathlessly silent. What in hell or high heaven could they expect to prove by cross-examining me? 'Why did you not mention to the police at the time that you had seen the accused?'

'I didn't know he was the accused and . . . .' I intended to say that I didn't see how his being in my hut could have any bearing on the Morgan murder, but further shuffles and protests interrupted me. This time the judge accepted the protests and I stepped down. My legs, to my annoyance, felt wobbly as I walked back across the stone floor. A mist with black spots like drifting blobs of soot dropped between me and the world. There was a buzzing in my ears. Butler was in the box before I could again see or hear with complete clarity.

'You are an advertising agent?'

'Yes, sir.' I hadn't thought of calling the creature sir.

'And your name?'

'George Butler.'

'You were with the previous witness when the body was found?'

'I was.'

'Tell us what you saw on that morning.' He told them. He carried it off well, as straight as a major, his voice clear and unhesitant; and the dark suit did, there in the witness box, give him dignity. Was Emily, up over my head—I couldn't see her now—unfavourably comparing the previous to the present witness? He told them he had touched the body to find out if the girl were dead. He told them he had been acquainted with the dead girl.

'Did you know her well?'

'Just slightly. To nod to.'

'For how long?'

'Off and on for four or five years.'

'As long as you've lived in the village?'

'Yes, sir.'

He had also known the accused, but hadn't seen him for eighteen months. Then I sneezed loudly, twice. The court was cold when you were more than half an hour sitting in it, and the place where the witnesses sat was caught between two draughty doors. But two policemen looked at me sternly and the judge started as if a pistol-shot had been fired. Purple with embarrassment, I shifted uneasily on my hard bench and watched Butler walk back confidently across the floor.

When the fun was over for that day, Butler and Emily and myself met Jill and had dinner in a hotel on the quays. In the crowd outside the court I saw one of my sisters, standing on tiptoe, straining her neck to glimpse her distinguished brother whose name was in the evening papers for getting into the bedroom of a dead girl. 'Trust dear Donagh,' one sister would say to the other—they were healthy, liberated, modern women—'to wait until the girl was dead.' She was looking too high, over my head, Spanish galleon guns blasting the air over England's low-to-the-water ships; and humbly and silently I slipped past.

At dinner Jill didn't mention the way we had deserted her on the day of the coursing, but she made no special effort to be civil to myself, and to Emily she spoke slowly, with difficulty and an unnaturally clear enunciation, as if they had just met each other for the first time.

The foolery went on for four days. Butler whispered: 'It looks to me as if that fellow doesn't want to get away with it.'

'Why should he?'

'Why not?'

'Dying on his feet. Lungs.'

'I forgot you know him better than I do. You dark horse, Harty. You deep one. The things you keep to yourself.'

The jury were absent for four hours and twenty minutes. They took their time about coming to a verdict that nobody in the court seemed to have any doubts about. Butler, looking pale and tired as we sat for change of air and altitude in the public gallery, said: 'Jesus, I've had enough of this. It's ghoulish. I'll never catch up on my work.' From the landing outside the public gallery we peeped through a doorway and saw the room into which the twelve good men and true would be shepherded for their next meal. Plain white delph on a bare scrubbed table. 'They might as well be in jail,' Butler said.

'Secluded like ancient Gaelic poets in their dark cells.'

'Bull,' Butler said. He was oddly aggressively impolite.

Secluded somewhere in another room the chosen twelve tried to make up their minds about Jim Walsh who, cold in his basement cell, waited for the end. 'What'll it be?' Butler thought aloud.

'He hasn't a hope.' The buyers and sellers had gone for the day. Piles of rubbish here and there, papers blowing tattered in the wind, fragments of packing-cases, wisps of straw, damaged fruit, discarded fish, marked where the market had been. Around a corner came a clanking corporation lorry flanked by two single files of cleaners. 'We should have waited for the bitter end,' I said; 'for the black cap.' 'That would have been fun.'

'They say the custom goes back to the days when clerics acting as judges used to cover their tonsure when they pronounced sentence.'

'How fascinating!'

Around the great main buildings all was quiet. One policeman stood at the gates as if he had forgotten to go home. 'That was to show,' I said, 'that they were acting in their civil capacity.' I didn't mean to sound so inhuman. But the whole thing had honestly been a ghastly strain and when anything touched me too close to the bone I found the only relief lay in being damnably, deliberately academic. 'You're a mine of information,' Butler said, his voice still sharp with irony, forcible with rudeness. Perhaps rudeness and irony at my expense constituted his relief from strain. The wind blew fresh and free down the quayside from a red west. We were out again from the quiet narrow streets in the city's full rush, death behind us, life around us. 'You're a fish, Harty, he said. 'A bloodless inhuman fish.' He put a strong hand on my shoulder and gripped and roughly shook me.

The late-news box in the evening papers told us Jim Walsh was guilty and ready for the rope. There was no mention of appeal, no recommendation to mercy from the twelve. 'If I could go to see him,' I said, 'I would.'

'You could tell him that little bit about the black cap. He'd love it.'

We stayed late in the city, drank a lot, talked little, took the last train home, and walked from the station to the village, past Emily's house and the bridge where the path went sideways through the beechwood to Morgan's murdered cottage.

Two

My mother wrote me the sharpest letter she had yet written.

'All the time you spent in town during the trial you couldn't afford, even once, to come to see me. And you knew I was too crippled to go as far as the criminal court, even if it was the sort of place a mother could enter in order to see her son.'

Mother, I thought, I was a witness, not the murderer, not the accused who was now the condemned.

'What sort of a son are you, in God's name?'

In God's or the devil's name, I didn't know what sort of a son I was.

'After all, you are my son and I did rear you and suffer for you.'

Tears could have been shed copiously over that letter, and for half a day it did make me feel as mean as a mule. But I cured myself by realizing that to go home even for a visit might be to risk the healthy reality of the life I was now living. Or was my existence in this hut, and everything that went with that existence just a mesmerized moment lost from real time? I remembered a play, seen once in a city theatre, about heaven and hell all happening around a big house in one stray hour while two servants doctored a grandfather clock. I remembered a Gaelic folk-tale that showed how the idea of a vagrant magic moment went back and back to the cold misty forest-surrounded first flutterings of life on this island.

There were one time, said the folk-tale, two warring clans. For convenience call one of them the Bradys and the other the Brennans.

And the Bradys, a black-headed people, deciding to make peace with the red-headed Brennans, invited the chief and his eldest son to a banquet in their castle. How the old story-tellers always said castle or palace when they meant a thatched, whitewashed cabin.

The two Brennans approached the Brady cabin, heard in the distance the noise of jollity. 'Take your skian from your leather

104

belt,' said the father to the son, 'and put it out of sight in the thatch. 'Tisn't wholesome to walk with a bare blade showing into a house of peace.'

The son drew slowly from his belt of Spanish leather his long, sharp knife. As the father stepped over the welcoming threshold the son reached up and buried the knife in the thatch above the door, stabbing it in until nothing showed but the brass-studded end of the heft. Then he also crossed the threshold to see his father wounded and bleeding on the floor and the Bradys crouched in a corner, hate in their faces, their backs to the wall, their weapons in their hands.

And after the hell and all of a battle the young man, who was strong and a hero and a match for a haggard full of Bradys, rescued his father, carried him away across fields and a deep river to the house of a leech who bound and healed the wounds. Fording the river, he slipped on a round stone and came near to drowning, but by a great effort he survived, and after many terrors saved his father's life. Then red hot for vengeance he turned back to the Brady cabin, reached up again, pulled his knife out of the thatch, stepped murderously across the threshold to finish the whole family—and saw the Bradys laughing and drinking, and his father among them as happy and unmarked as a man could be.

His father said to him: 'What delayed you, boy, and what are you doing with the skian?'

The Bradys said: 'Welcome, son of a good father. Drink some poteen.' Or words to that effect.

That was the all of the old story. No explanations, no moral: except perhaps that an honest bare blade is better than a blade hidden in the body of a neighbour's house, or that a man may live a whole life of dream in the moment of stabbing and pulling the blade out again, or in the moment of strangling a girl. For the young Brennan boy a gesture had stopped the world dead and given wonderful things the opportunity to happen. When and where had been the gesture that had liberated me from my mother's house and the proximity of my sisters? Was it when I closed a suburban door, or boarded a train, or first raised my eyes to look at my hut, or first met Butler, or when the lone rook went rising and falling above the beech trees, or when Butler's hand curved over the dead breast of Lily Morgan, or when the bright wheels of Emily's car spurted gravel at the gate of her father's house? When that moment circled again inexorably towards me would the dream be ending? Would I find myself entering my mother's house, waking up from a mesmerized moment in which a girl had been murdered and a man sentenced to death, in which I'd found a friend and a lovely girl who made me free of, at least, her lips?

To end the dream might save Jim Waish and restore Lily Morgan to life, but those things, desirable as they might be, would for me be no recompense for the loss of Emily Rayel.

In spite of my drunken refusal to Butler's invitation, they called for me one morning to go to the races. We drove to the city, had an early lunch in the Pyramid, not at the circular snack bar, but in the dining-room upstairs where women could go. Pleasantly warmed by drink and food, we went, Butler driving, out of the city along the sea road. Leaving the Pyramid, Emily laughingly said: 'I'll sit beside no man who threatens to grow a moustache.' With one finger she tapped lightly Butler's upper lip which had clearly not known the razor for three or four days. The excrescence didn't really improve his appearance. 'It's part of his winter woollens,' Jill said, wriggling her long body into the seat beside Butler while Emily sat, silver-coated again, in the seat beside me. He didn't respond to the gentle jeering. He never did respond genially to jokes levelled against himself; and leaving the city he drove the car as if he hated its guts, while I also stayed quiet, embarrassed by Emily's nearness, by the way our bodies touched when the car swung round a corner, by the thought that Butler's jealous eyes would now and again look at our reflections in the driving mirror.

Great grey clouds, silvered at the edges by a hidden sun, turned like mill-wheels across a cold blue sky, dropping sharp showers as mill-wheels scatter cold spray. Twice as we went along the sea road the weak sunshine was extinguished and heavy hail battered the car, Butler's car and all the cars speeding from the city to the races. Suburbia at intervals stretched out brick claws to cool them in the sea, to make our way more dangerous with concealed corners and the possibility of running children, to set the long line of cars hooting and honking like wild geese in flight. Butler remained silent, grimly attentive to the road and the business of speedily passing-out other cars. Once, to beat out a rapid Adler, he swung out and in again so violently that Emily was thrown against my knees, and I had to grasp her and help her back to her seat. 'George, George,' she said breathlessly, 'you'll get us killed.'

'Would you like to drive instead?' He didn't look around. His eyes were probably on the mirror. He flung the words crisply back, not only, I felt, at Emily, but at Hartigan who had the effrontery to sit beside her, to steady her with his hands as the rash Israelite had steadied the holy ark. 'If we don't get there quickly,' he said, 'we'll have to park half a mile away.'

Emily said: 'I'd rather park half a mile away than figure at an inquest.'

'Inquests,' I said, with a lightness that cost me a tremendous effort, 'are nothing to us.'

Butler said nastily: 'You dodged one.'

'Oh, quit it,' Jill screamed. 'Why's everybody in bad humour all of a sudden?'

'They're not in bad humour.' Butler meant Emily and myself. 'They're just plain frightened I'll hit something.' This was a new aspect of the big and genial George Butler. I swallowed my anger and laughed, not very convincingly. Emily said quietly: 'We're not frightened. But there's no harm in being prudent.'

'But George's driving well,' Jill said. 'I'm in the front seat and I should know.' It didn't, I'm certain, occur to poor Jill that her being instead of Emily in the front scat accounted for the big man's childish temper and for his reckless driving. Then the road swung inland from the sea, the hailstones hit us again more heavily than ever and, listening to their wicked rattle, watching them snipping the last poor leaves from the passing hedges, we mercifully managed to forget, or to pretend we forgot, that idiotic quarrel.

We passed through a village of drab, concreted and slated houses, brief sunshine glistening on wet pavements, the vennels running full with dissolved hailstones. Every door was closed. The two blank-windowed public-houses were uninvitingly silent. The village seemed, snail-like, to have gone into its shell for the day of the races. The sea met us again at the corner of one narrow steaming lane up which Butler resolutely, knowingly short-cutted to escape from the long continuous line of cars crawling funeral-wise through the impassive main street. I said: 'They don't seem to like horses here,' but Butler corrected me. 'They're horse mad. The whole place has closed up and gone out to the course.' Around another corner. The sea again. A dirty shore. Discarded tins and cabbages and chamber-pots half embedded in mud. 'What,' I asked, 'are the wild waves saying?' But nobody paid any attention to my mild irony. They were all, even Emily, looking forward to the speed, the challenge, the stretched muscles, the tiny toy-like bouncing men, the shouting of the odds, the fun and thrill of winning and losing; and I couldn't even try to share their enthusiasm. I couldn't look forward to a happy day or feel that we were going to the races as one homo-geneous party of race-lovers should go. Perhaps it was the weather, the hailstones and the cold wind that depressed me; or perhaps it was the memory of the recent past, a body rotting in the grave, a man waiting in the condemned cell.

Along for fifty yards in the shadow of a high grey monastery wall and we were free of the village and its soiled rotten shore. Across a vast plain the wind came at us somersaulting thunderously. The sky was darkening with the advance of the next shower, already lacing down along the horizon. But half a mile away was the long white-railed oval marked here and there by the jumps—and the stands and the crowds of people, and wet- roofed cars already rowed in hundreds in the cindery car park. 'We left it too bloody late,' Butler groused. 'We'll have to fight our way in.'

'Don't fuss, George, don't fuss. The first race hasn't started yet.' That was Emily talking; and the coolness of her voice must have been maddening, deliberately so, to a violent big man already, for pettish reasons, in a poisonous mood. 'It'll be started and over,' he growled, 'before we get there.' He was right, too. The wheels crunched slowly to their place in the car park. The hailstones madly attacked. I'd gladly have stayed where I was until the shower had passed on, and so, I thought, would Emily, but Jill and Butler were out with frantic speed and trotting away across the cinders. Short of going out of my way to make trouble with Butler, I couldn't very well go on sitting in the back seat of a car with the girl he loved; and as Emily and myself, averting our faces as much as possible from the steely whipping of the hailstones, followed the hurrying pair, the first race came in a huddle around a bend and went on slushing towards the west. It was a woebegone sight: those poor little men in their flimsy coloured jackets exposed to the pelting of the pitiless storm-and their wretched silly borses.

I don't have to go out of my way to prove to anybody that I'm not a racing man, not by any means a man for gatherings or public places, and that I shouldn't have been there that day. And such a day. Cold wet hands, fingers all thumbs, fumbled money from my wallet to pay for admission for Emily and myself. Jill and Butler had already passed through into the enclosure. The cost was excessive. My budget hadn't been balancing so well since I'd met Butler and Emily and taken to drinking whisky in the village hotel. Beyond the barrier the cold and misery merely increased. Even the women who came in good clothes to have their smirking photographs taken for the fashionable papers had on that day backed a gigantic loser: and wrapped in raincoats, and gabbling behind umbrellas, they tried to look happy, to pretend they came to the place for the sheer exultation of betting money on the running, jumping horses. Noses were red and sniffly. Hair-styles were coming unstuck. There wasn't a woman there among the fashionable ones who, to my eyes, looked a patch on Emily; and the horsey ones had, to a mare, visages like saddle leather. But neither cold wind nor hailstones could disturb the lovely rose-petal composure of her face.

When we had both lost money on the same horse in the second race—for the horse and jockey I felt almost affection because their inaptitude had given us an experience in common—I said: 'Emily, you don't really enjoy it, do you?'

'Now and again I honestly do, Donagh. But today's a dead loss.'

'I prefer to win money. I'm afraid I'm not a real gambler.' I looked around at the crowd suddenly bright in one of the brief fits of sunshine and parading in groups on the sloping concrete before the main terrace. 'Where's George?'

'He was there a moment ago placing a bet. He's in one of his moods today.'

'Why?' I didn't expect an answer. I knew she knew that big, volatile, masterly George was childish enough to be angry because she and Jill had joked about his incipient moustache, because she hadn't sat beside him on the way from town. She took my arm and drew me with her towards the nearest bar. 'You see now how difficult George can be, Don. And all about nothing.'

'It was foolish.'

'Could one face that for a lifetime, especially with my peculiarities?'

One couldn't and shouldn't, I thought, and told her so as we walked into a long-pillared bar to find Butler, red-faced, wet-haired, drink in hand, wandering about looking for us. Crowded as it was, the air choky with cigarette smoke and the steam from wet clothes, the bar was the only habitable place on that bleak plain. 'Where in hell have you two been?'

'Losing money,' I said.

'Poor saps. I lifted a fiver on the second race.' He showed it to us: the winnings of the strong, wise man.

'Lucky you,' I said, and Emily said coolly: 'Let's have a drink so.' Jill was in the ladies, but we had our drinks and she was back for the second round which I bought, even if I had dropped money on a horse and if my budget wasn't balancing. She had from her dad, said Jill, a good thing for the third race, in fact her dad had owned the horse's sire, so we drank a third round hurriedly and rushed out through the struggling, steaming crowd to—as it proved-lose more money. Then, our bets placed, we climbed up the terrace and the sun came out again with a bang. The great plain was all before us, fresh and green, the white posts spotless with the washing of the rain, the sky as blue as in early summer and no clouds for the moment to be seen, the horses and jockeys coming glisteningly away from the starting-post, racing past us, mud flying, going away and away across the plain.

One man with binoculars said: 'The best damned course in Ireland.'

His companion, also with binoculars, said: 'You can see their goddamned feet all the way round.'

I stood on my tiptoes, but, having only my naked eyes, still couldn't see the feet of the distant horses. Hooves were chopping hell out of the hail-softened ground. But it was, I can't deny, exciting, and when one horse took a flying lead as they cleared the last jump and another horse went down and sent its rider rolling in mud, I bellowed with the thrill, not yet knowing that the fallen horse had carried a fragment of my diminishing money. Everybody was shouting the names of horses, or, familiarly as if they'd known them since their stunted infancy, the names of little hoppity horse jockeys. 'In no time, Don,' Emily said, 'you'd be a fanatic,' and we went back to the bar for another gargle.

In the bar there was pandemonium. Excitement had parched the world with thirst. Led by Butler we pushed our way to a corner near the fire, managed by adroitness and disregard for the social law to grab two stools for Jill and Emily. 'Another fiver up,' Butler said. 'Drinks on me.' Then, loudly laughing, he slipped his arm around Jill's waist, pulled her close to him, and said: 'I didn't take your tip, Jill.'

She said calmly, turning away her face, keeping her cheek from his cheek, shunning contact with all men: 'You're crooked as a ram's horn.'

'Get the drinks,' Emily sighed. 'We're waiting.' The huge fire blazed like a furnace. 'Help me out of my coat,' she implored. 'I'll melt.'

Butler held the high stool steady, his hands against her buttocks, and I held the silver coat while she wriggled free of it. Jill, her elbows compressed against her sides, sipped gin and orange. 'That's better,' Emily said. I folded her coat, lining out, over my arm, and felt the delicious warmth of that lining go through me like an injection of hot rum. The crowd swayed towards us and swayed away again. Corks popped and somewhere a tumbler went smashing and the pieces were audibly and immediately crushed into powder by milling feet. In a white open-work sweater Emily's bust caught the eyes of all the men in the neighbourhood whose interest was not completely absorbed by drink and horses. 'Boy, oh, boy,' I heard somebody say, and an acquaintance of Emily hollered: 'Emily Rayel, you look terrific.'

'Who the hell's that?' Butler asked.

'A fellow from the art school.'

'He has a neck.'

'Can't a fellow compliment a girl?'

'Compliment my ass.'

'George,' Jill reproved.

His left arm along Emily's shoulder, probably to show the art school fellow who owned whom and who was boss around here, Butler began to sing, to do another of his Boston-Irish acts. But vexation made his voice quiver. He sang:

> *Off she went, off she went,*
> *Begod I wasn't worth a cent.*
> *The devil himself was in the cart*
> *Behind M'Carthy's mare.*

'My round, I think,' I said. He sang:

I held on with the rest
As we went racing to the west.
I'll never forget the fright I got
Behind MacCarthy's mare.

I'd turned to push my way through the mob to the bar, one hand on my pocket on my dwindling cash, my half-muzzy mind wondering how this thing would end, when behind me a drunken voice said: 'Sweater girl, you're sitting on my stool.' Emily said: 'Sorry,' and somebody laughed, and weak with anger I wheeled around with effort, for I was caught between two beefy, tweedy bodies, grain between the grinding stones. Struggling to free myself, I heard a fist crack horribly on a face, saw a big red-faced man go down like a log, bursting with his falling body a gap in the crowd, sending men and women staggering perilously back against the fireplace. Butler stood closing and unclosing his fist. His knuckles were bleeding. Emily screamed: 'George, what've you done?'

'Hit him,' Butler said. 'He asked for it.' Then he snatched back his drink from Emily's shaking hand and said: 'Don't mind him. He'll grow up. He'll learn manners the hard way. Go on, Harty. Buy us a drink. Make a noise like a man ordering a round.'

He had found the safety-valve and the way to loosen it, to blow off his anger like hot, scalding steam. On the floor the suffering safety-valve spat teeth, curses, and blood. Three burly friends gathered around him to help him to his feet. They glanced gloweringly at Butler the destroyer. It was Jill, the despised Cassandra, the disregarded tipper who saved the day, averting a brawl and police intervention. She knew one of the burly men. To him she spoke stiff, straight words and he and his two hefty friends dragged the wounded cursing creature from the field of battle. To the two stumpy old ladies who presided behind the bar, she, being her father's daughter, spoke soft soothery words, and they said: 'Yes, miss,' and, 'of course, miss,' and finally smiled in the general direction of George Butler. Jill's father owned horses and was one of the directors of that race-course.

Emily's face had lost its petal-bloom composure, was for once as pale as a ghost, but whether from fear of the sort of thing Butler might do or from simple vexation at being made the centre of such a scene, I couldn't say.

For myself—I felt more miserable than the ejected bloody, broken-toothed drunk. I couldn't have hit him the way Butler had hit him. The whole thing had been over and done with while I was still struggling to escape from the millstone pressure of two fat men in tweeds. Even had I been within arm's reach and had mastered enough decision to hit the lout I'd, ninety to one, only have hurt my knuckles and left myself open to a retaliating, crushing, flattening, humiliating blow.

I was no knight, no hero. I couldn't look Emily straight between the eyes.

'Drink up,' Butler said, 'we'll have large ones all round. This is my lucky day.'

II

The sixth race, casual and unexciting as a murder trial, was slogging along halfway round the course when we met the two women in black, the tall man in the duffle coat, and the French student who wore American infantry boots. One of the women in black was tall, dressed like a mannequin. She was a model for several of the best shops and her face appeared in the papers on an advertisement for lipstick or vanishing cream or something. The advertisement said she was a typical Irish beauty. She held her head high, had dark fuzzy hair and a sharply cut Roman profile. She talked a great deal, but never looked at the person she was talking to, never bothered to see where her words were going to or how they were being received. Her name was Angela.

The other woman in black was a small roly-poly jewess, still as sun-tanned from the summer that had ended as if she had lived all her life in southern Spain. Her name was Catherine.

The man in the duffle coat was taller than Butler, but even the slack empty folds of his sack of a garment couldn't conceal the truth that he was thin and fleshless as the handle of a spade. Black hair was oiled and plastered flat to his skull until it looked like a tight-fitting rubber cap. His nose had once been broken and reset a little off-plumb. His eyes glittered and his voice was an amazingly deep bass made for verse speaking, to the accompaniment of solemn occasional drums, about Pocahontas in the tombs, the cool tombs, or about the fallen works of Ozymandias, king of kings. His toes turned in when he walked and his long bony hands were the hairiest hands I had ever seen. His name was Oliver.

The French student with the American infantry boots was, to me, just a French student who wore American infantry boots, had his hair close-cropped, and spoke, when he spoke at all, a scatterment of words half-English and half-French. His name was Jacques.

Handshakes all round. Introductions for myself. (Circles were widening about me, a black stone flung into a mesmeric pool: first striking Lily Morgan and murder, then Butler and friendship, then Emily and love, and Jill, and now Angela, and Catherine, and lean beady-eyed Oliver, and bald-headed Jacques. The Kavanagh woman and her husband must then be a blossoming bush and a stunted thorn growing on the edge of the pool, and Jim Walsh a branchless tree leaning ominously over the water and ripe for the woodsman's final axe.) Comparing of experiences at the races; who were winners and who were losers. Butler said: 'I had a fight.'

'Don't talk about it, please,' Emily said.

'I hit one of Emily's many admirers.' He spoke rollingly to the whole world, but he meant his words mostly for me. He could, when he wanted to, be a crude, cruel bastard.

Jill, hands in the waistband of her jodhpurs, dangled one long leg to scuffle a heel against a lower step of the terrace. She stayed silent, claimed no credit for her share in the post-war negotiations. I began to like Jill even though I knew she hated me, perhaps a little less than she hated Butler. 'Tell us about it,' Angela said to Butler. She looked at the farthest away point of the white-railed oval, then brought her eyes slowly home again, or almost home, as far as the crowds streaming along the concrete below us and towards the exits from the enclosure. The races were over. Butler walked with Oliver and Angela towards one of the exits, and as he walked he loudly told them all about the battle and his conquering blow. Jill walked with the French student and I went between Emily and the brown little Jewess. They weren't tall women and I could be at ease beside them, as I never could be beside that tall mannequin with the false distracted eyes. Emily said: 'We'll never hear the end of this.'

I didn't know what to say. I chanced: 'It was a decisive action.'

'I don't like decisive actions.'

'The lout he hit was bad-mannered.'

'He was drunk.'

The Jewess said: 'George is a bit of a brute.' I defended him: 'He's a strong man.'

Emily said: 'Who wants strong men?'

'George,' said the Jewess, 'should go to Africa and persecute the blacks.' Because she had a good heart and a fair mind and a lover who was a student from Fernando Po, Catherine was, I discovered, a champion of the rights of coloured people. 'Let's not argue about him,' Emily said. 'I hate scenes. I hate violence. I hate strong men. I'll never forget that ghastly scene as long as I live.' That, I thought, with a glow of joy, is the way I want to have you. The hailstones were gone, the sky quiet, the evening sun going gently down on the rim of the wide plain. 'No woman,' she said, 'wants to be the centre of a pub brawl.' I saw again in my memory a doxy once seen in a bar in a dance-hall, joy on her face while two fools battered each other for the doubtful pleasure of leading her home to her papa's garden gate. But I kept the memory austerely, unargumentatively to myself. Emily Rayel wasn't that sort of woman.

Out on the gravel, cars were twisting and crunching from their parking-places in the long rows. People talked at the tops of their voices so as to be heard above the noise of engines and wheels slowly revolving on cinders. People heartily shook hands with each other, and waved at each other from varying distances; and in the back seat of a black Rolls an elderly drunken man was contorting himself to place his lips on the lips of a well-dressed uncooperative girl. 'Emily,' Butler bellowed, 'will you go into town in Oliver's car? I've something private to chat to Angela about.' His air of proprietorship was most offensive: he'd show her which car she'd travel in and which man she'd sit beside.

'Business, is it?' Jill called. Although she had to scream to make herself heard she didn't lose from her voice a quiet cynical disapproval of men and their ways, particularly of George Butler. Angela said: 'George says his boss would like me to do some outdoor modelling with new cars.' She may have been looking towards Antananarivo, hidden round the corner of the world or towards the moon not yet visible in the pale blue sky, but she was speaking directly and only to Emily. For a second the artificiality cracked and through mascara and eye-shadow and the smear of shiny lotions I saw sincerity, and embarrassment. She knew she was being used in order to annoy Emily. The French boy blurted: 'Not, let us hope, posing of that nature in automobiles,' and he nodded his cropped head at the absurd pair in the back seat of the Rolls Royce. Everybody laughed immoderately except Emily, who had already turned away, her arm linked in mine, and Jill and myself, and Catherine who was tugging at the stiff-handled door of Oliver's car.

We went back to the city, back to the Pyramid, to the expensive bar where ladies could go. Oh, the gallant variety of the lives of the splendid people who go to races in big cars.

Catherine sat beside Oliver, a careful, steady driver; Emily and myself sat unashamedly close together, my left hand locked in her left, my right arm around her waist. 'Do we or don't we,' Oliver asked, 'sample that cognac?' For the benefit of Emily and myself he explained: 'Catherine has some wonderful cognac. She has it sent to her by her people in France. That's one of the advantages of belonging to a persecuted race.'

'Whoever said I was persecuted?'

'You don't look it, my sweet, my pretty.'

'I'm not your sweet, Oliver.'

'Alas, no. I've no claims to suffering, no dark skin and pathetic pleading eyes.'

'Your eyes are your fortune.'

'Fortune.' He was dryly amused. I envied him his ability to talk to people as if he was insulting them and still to show them how much he liked them and, incidentally—almost—how fine a fellow he himself was. He was a fine fellow and he knew it. Right down to the black hairs on his hands he was organized, directed, under control. Then I could have stabbed myself for once again envying another man for doing what I couldn't do, and I clutched at reassurance by tightening my arm around Emily's waist and closing my right hand on her right breast. She moved towards me, not away from me, and for two minutes I was high in the air above the car. I was Pegasus. I was a winged race-horse hurdling through heaven, everybody's favourite, backed by all the angels. When the orgiastic exultation passed and I planed down again to earth Emily was talking to Oliver: 'Is it true that a clergyman down south objected because at some show in a village hall you made a country boy kiss a broomstick?'

'Too true. He did worse. I said to him that the parochial hall broom was the girl he fancied most in the parish. The pent-up forces I released.' Oliver was, clearly, the hypnotist.

'Don, here,' Emily said, 'is interested in whatever you call it.'

'Hypnotheraphy,' Catherine said.

'We'll get down to that later. Cognac first.'

'The Pyramid first,' Catherine said. 'Then cognac. We'll go up to our place from the Pyramid.'

Emily asked: 'Won't your landlady throw us out?'

'She's out herself. Nights she goes out prowling. For what, I don't know'

Catches little boys in back-lanes and eats them,' Oliver said.

'Mutilates them,' said Catherine, 'with her fangs.' Then she turned around to me and said: 'All this is mystery to you, Don. You've never heard of our landlady.'

'No, never.'

'She's mad,' Emily said.

'Not mad. Peculiar. She makes artificial flowers and keeps saying she's not one of the nouveaux riches.' And for the rest of the journey to the city, to the Pyramid, I heard with a half interest about the woman who owned the house in which Catherine and Angela shared a flat. Emily's body was so blessedly close to mine that I could have simulated interest in public readings from a treatise on traction engines. The landlady was such a card. She sat all day in a corner of her sitting-room, sheltered from draughts by a Japanese screen, and made away at her artificial flowers. She had boxes of dusty books, none of which she ever opened, preserved from the wreckage of some great house where she had once lived. She had the most beautiful tinted glassware and two toasting- forks with handles that had once been the proud, high, spiral horns of spring-bok. She never washed. At night she prowled the streets alone, standing in doorways, peeking out at people. She wrote letters to the papers about the immodesty of the modern woman. She had a Jewess and a mannequin living in her house who suspected that they provided her with inspiration for her letters. She was wonderfully, wonderfully funny.

Drunk with the warm feering of the girl close and willingly beside me, I laughed until my ribs ached. Oh, Emily, come closer, come closer; and Butler, be brutal and dig your own grave, destroy with harsh manners what place you ever had in my love's heart.

III

The girls lived in the basement flat of a high ramshackle house in a square in the south of the city. We went merrily, noisily from the crowded Pyramid, where all sorts of things in tweeds and flushed faces were conducting a post-mortem on the races. The two cars were parked at a safe distance from the house of the deft old dame. 'She's not in, for mercy sake,' Catherine said. 'We could drive up all the way and not go walking in the rain.'

'The cars'll have to move off again some time, I hope,' Angela said. 'If they were any nearer they'd rev the old creature out of her sleep.'

'Her scented sleep,' Butler sneered. Emily had to my agony sat by his side on the journey from the Pyramid. 'She'd write another letter to the evening papers,' Angela said. 'Bad women and motor-cars. She wrote a screamer after the Walsh and Morgan murder case.'

Oliver said: 'I wonder did that fellow do it.'

'Ask George or Donagh,' Emily said. 'They were there.'

'The jury found him guilty,' I said.

'And the judge he wrote it down,' Butler went on, and as Angela led the way down a narrow iron stairway to a basement door he sang in his best voice and braggadoccio manner:

> *For the breaking of the Union Bank*
> *You are sent to Charlestown.*

'Broke more than a bank, he did, that Walsh fellow, by all accounts,' Oliver said.

'Please don't be gruesome,' Catherine said.

'That's my occupation.'

Jacques stumbled in his big boots, clattered down two steps, cursed, steadied himself with an effort. Catherine whispered to me: 'Know why Jacques wears big boots?'

'The old joke,' Jacques said patiently. We stood while Angela fumbled for her key. Through the heavily barred basement window the street light above us illuminated a dim corner of a sitting-room. 'Somebody asked him when he came here first,' Catherine said. 'May I tell it, Jacques?'

'*Pourquoi pas.*' Jacques clearly liked Catherine, but the French are not an oppressed people and he hadn't a chance.

'And he said: I walk a lot. These boots they will be useful for trampling on the Irish collines.' Several laughs. The key clicked in the lock. 'We thought,' Catherine said, 'that he meant little girls when he really meant little hills.'

Jacques said earnestly to me: 'They thought I was a sort of perversion.' He went ahead of me through a small hallway into the sitting-room behind the barred window. 'She's out all right,' Angela said. 'She makes her flowers in here.'

Somebody switched on a light and I saw the things I had already heard about from Catherine, and several others she hadn't mentioned: the Japanese screen and behind it a table piled with the makings of paper flowers, tomato packing-cases filled with dusty books standing high in one corner, the cut glass shining clean, the springbok toasting-forks. The air was musty. 'She never lights a fire,' Catherine said. In the corner behind the door was, grey and sagging with age, the largest couch I'd ever seen. We escaped into a stone-flagged corridor. 'Our own door is at the back,' Angela said. 'But it's so far around we only use it when the witch is at home.'

'Brewing her spells,' Emily said. 'Making her magic flowers.'

Butler sniffed. He said: 'Her smells.' He was still in a nasty mood.

From the corridor we stepped into another world: a warm, well-furnished, lively sitting-room, a spotless kitchenette all enamel and chromium, two cosy bedrooms, a sideboard literally lined with bottles of the most wonderful cognac. 'Great God,' Butler shouted, and Oliver said: 'Thank you, darlings, even if you do get it for nothing;' and in half an hour, with the company stinking drunk, Oliver had Jacques in the middle of the floor, was gazing into his eyes, waving hands before his face, saying: 'Look deeply deeply deeply deep deep into the pupil of my right eye,' and: 'Let your body relax and fall forwards against me, falling falling, fall, gently, gentle,' and so on. We screamed and roared with laughter when

Jacques, big boots and all, stalked off like an automaton down the corridor to return with the two springbok toasting-forks.

'He looks dangerous.'

'He could do murder now.'

'Forget about murder,' I drunkenly wailed. 'I've seen enough of it to do me for the remainder of my days.'

'Oh, Harty, forget about it. It's all over bar the hanging.' 'I'm trying to forget about it, Butler, old pal.' Cognac had made us friends again. 'But they won't allow me. Somebody mentioned murder.'

Several voices chorused: 'Who the hell mentioned murder?' 'I did,' Emily said. 'Who has a better right? Wasn't it my next-door neighbour who was done in?'

'Can a cottager,' I said, slowly waving my arms which felt as if they belonged to somebody else, 'be next-door neighbour to a princess?' And I did, I shudder to remember, go on to quote: Sui-je, sui-je, sui-je, belle? They listened in profound wondering silence. 'It's the cognac, 'Jill said, 'straight from France.'

'Harty's a poet,' Butler explained.

Catherine said: 'He's switched the talk from murder to love and that's an improvement.' Love. Trust a Jewess to understand what I was about.

'Does Catherine want love?'

'Not from you, Oliver, darling.'

'Love. Love,' Angela screamed. 'Oliver, do please make Jacques kiss a toasting-fork.' 'What about the yokel and the broomstick,' Catherine warned, and somebody said: 'But the French are different.' Jacques, obedient to Oliver Magus, kissed the two toasting-forks and later on, when Oliver clapped his hands, came unharmed out of his hypnotic trance. 'Now it's your turn, Harty, Jill said. Under Oliver's guidance I allowed myself to be made as sniff as a board, then lay with my head on the rim of the seat of one chair and my heels on another chair, and Emily sat on my knees to show the world how rigid I was. When I recovered Angela was saying: 'Now for George Butler.'

'No bloody fears. I like my hypnotists neat without cognac. Oliver's due to pass out in about two minutes.' To show the excellence and wisdom of Butler's judgment, Oliver did pass out in about five minutes, was reverently laid on Catherine's bed, a basin beside him on the floor, and the party progressed to singing and to dancing to music from some continental radio station. Somebody slipped out for a while, returned with a monstrous steaming-hot parcel of fish and chips to save—said Angela and Catherine in one breath—the bother of cooking. Oh, the taste of potato chips fried in rancid fat, incongruously in the mouth with the flavour of cognac; and the odd way the browned skin peels off the fish to show phosphorescently white substance underneath. In a loud voice Butler boasted how the previous day in his office he had made a most successful effort to get the sound of a break of wind, with an imitation bugle preliminary, on to the office recording machine. From tightened lips and through cupped hands he showed us how it was done and we laughed and laughed and laughed; and the jest about the Irish collines went backwards and forwards all night long, like an aged faithful servant in a Russian play—axes chopping in the cherry orchard, until I saw a vision of Jacques the giant-walker, tramping miles, head bald as a blade, feet leaving bleeding marks of hobnails on prostrate screaming Irish virgins.

Said Jill: 'The fire's dying,' and: 'Burn my books,' screamed Catherine, and to please her we tore leaves from seven or eight books and piled them on until the flames roared up the chimney. The ninth book was a novel by Henry James and, a little sobered at the thought, I took it with me to a distant corner, tried to read. But the pages were blurred and the words danced stately gavottes and pavanes and lively minuets. Then Emily came beside me to lie down, to put her head on my lap and on Henry James. She said: 'Donagh the dope.' 'Donagh the drunk,' I said.

'We're all drunk.'

'Drunk or sober, you're beautiful.'

'Oh, Donagh, you say the sweetest things.'

'Come out with me,' I said, 'until I put back auntie's toasting-forks.' And I thought, naturally: that which hath made them drunk hath made me bold; and, St. Ruth in his stirrups stood up and cried: the day is ours, we will drive them back to the gates of Dublin.

In the dark musty sitting-room where by day a dirty old woman made dusty paper flowers in a sheltered corner behind a Japanese screen, I dropped and damned one springbok horn, put the other into my pocket, grabbed my Emily, and we sank like one body to the vast ancient couch, saying, I love you, I love you, and do you love me, and, yes, darling, I do, and mingling our winey breaths.

'It's George you love, not me.'

'It isn't George, Don, darling.'

'He's more worthy of you. He's a big he-man.'

'I hate he-men.'

'He's a hero.'

'I hate heroes.'

'He'd fight for you.'

'I don't want anyone to fight for me.'

'Do you really love me?'

'I do. I do. I do.'

Many kisses. The din from the other room came booming along the stone-paved corridor.

'Do you fear me as you fear George?' My hands hadn't ever touched so much of her. She had never been so close to me. She said: 'No. No. No. No.'

'You do. Tell the truth.'

'No. I've told you everything. I'd go anywhere with you.'

'Come away with me somewhere.'

'Where?'

'Agree to come. I'll find a place. Are you afraid?'

'No. No. No.'

'Come then.'

'When?'

'As soon as you can.'

'Yes. Yes. Yes.' And more and more kisses and life, warm and beautiful, in that dead, decayed room. Then Angela came in, switched on the light, said Oliver had woken up fighting drunk, and wanted to hit George Butler because Butler had refused to be hypnotized and said Oliver was a phoney, all hypnotists were phoneys. Would I please, please come and help Jacques to separate them before they hurt each other or smashed her bric-a-brac? She collected bric-a-brac and eighteenth-century mourning broaches. But by the time I had staggered as far as the field of battle Jacques had taken ill from overmuch cognac and Oliver and Butler, shocked and reunited before the catastrophic failure of a Frenchman to carry unflinchingly his skinful of French drink, were in the bathroom helping Jacques to bathe his face.

We had a very fine party indeed. Lots of fun at Finnegans wake.

The landlady later had a row with Angela for tossing one toasting-fork to the floor and mislaying the other. But by that time Butler, Emily, Jill, and myself had left for rural places. Dustbins, stray dogs, chill morning and milk-carts, between them possessed the streets. The toasting-fork I didn't steal was broken, and Angela had to pay the cost of repair and the cost of the missing one. The wind made the river (morning tide against hailstones melted from distant brown mountains and sapping fields and city gutters) look like frosted glass. Emily drove slowly. Butler sat beside her and sang songs.

IV

All the way on my second journey to the jungle the thought kept annoyingly recurring: How mad I was to imagine that she could possibly mean to hold herself to a promise given in the deeps of drink. Under the glass, in among the plants and trees, the Kentiopsis Macrocarpa, the Indian Otochilus Fusca, the spiny phallic Esposita Lanata she'd meet me now and say: Let's forget all about it, Donagh. It was all foolish talk. You know I could never face it.

And I'd accept her will, thinking bitterly that everything was for the best, that we were, perhaps, escaping an embarrassing agony.

Children on roller-skates again streaking along the footpath as I stepped down from the bus. Fresh clean red carrots in boxes outside the greengrocer's shop at the corner. Suburban gates idly half open. Nosing dogs. Suburban peace. Suburban suffocation. My mother and reality waiting for me half a mile away. A girl in a blue car waiting for me at the gates of the gardens. This time she wouldn't trust herself with me in the hot, moist air of the jungle.

She hooted the horn as I approached: a comic Laurel and Hardy rhythm suited to the movement of my feet. This would be the beginning of the push-off, but she'd do the dirty work as lightly, as gaily as possible. My memory was sour with joyous Elizabethan prothalamions, wine flowing red, virgin snoods unbound, and candles burning to bedward. What had I to hope for? The afternoon was grey and lifeless and cold. 'Hop in, Don. Let's go somewhere.'

'Is the car fixed?,'

'What do you think?' She made room for me, tucking around her

123

thighs the skirts of a warm coat of grey tweed. 'I called into the garage just in the hope. And there it was. just as good as new.' My throat was clogged with nervousness, with agonized waiting for the moment when she'd say: About that night in Angela's place. I was foolish, Don. I'm ashamed of myself. Can we agree to forget about it?

I said: 'She runs beautifully.' We drove northwards. The country came to us in green billows, swamping suburbia's poor cockle-shells. We swung westwards following a wide arc towards our own village. She didn't speak until we pulled up at a whitewashed roadside pub, ancient sign the shape of a riding boot hanging above the door, to one side of the threshold a worn mounting block that once had helped drunken gentlemen to hoist their broad beam-ends to the saddle. 'Have a drink, Don?'

'That's a good idea.' In the dark, quiet pub we sat in a corner at a distance from the barmaid, and three solid country-men contemplating black pints. 'You're very quiet, Don.'

'So are you.'

'You're not regretting anything?'

'Why should I regret anything? But I was afraid you were.'

'Well, I'm not.'

'You remember what you promised?'

'I do. I wasn't that tight.'

'And you don't regret it?'

'Buy me a gin and lime and don't be silly.' The pub brightened as I walked to the counter. The solid men at their pints were the noblest specimens of God's creation. The sour black drink sparkled and danced like rich wine. Ghosts of slim gallant swordsmen leaped lightly into caparisoned saddles, disdaining the aid of the mounting block, and went off with a lively clatter of hooves into a glad spring countryside. Over her gin and lime and my ale and lime—lime from the one green bottle linked us together—she asked, her lips opening above her drink, her eyes not looking at me: 'Do you know where?'

'There's a little town,' I said, 'away inside in the country. Off main roads and beaten tracks and all that. You'd never meet anybody you'd know there.'

'You cunning fellow, Don. Who'd ever suspect you'd know about such places.'

'I like quiet, that's all. I found this place by accident once when

I was cycling.' She locked her right hand in mine and moved closer to me and laughed a little and said: 'There's somewhere to sleep, I suppose?'

'A hotel. Very good, too. Good food and drink.' Daring the sky to fall and the roof above us to be flattened by crashing clouds, I said: 'The beds are beautifully sprung.' 'Tell me more and then we'll have another drink.'

'There's a hill above the town and an old fairy forth on the top of that hill. From the mound of that forth you can see the world.'

'That's just what I want to do.'

'There's a diamond-shaped market-place with men in big boots moving slowly and carts with shafts tilted up to the sky, and the smell of straw and horse dung.'

She was giggling. She said: 'How real. How earthy.' 'It's always windy in that town. A wild, warm sort of wind. You have to struggle to close the door of the hotel against it. But inside it's so snug and cosy. Good whisky. Food steaming hot. Huge steaks.'

'Greedygut.'

'In the room where you sit and drink there are old pattern plates balanced on the picture rail and two huge china urns on a mantel-piece as broad as a battlefield.' An old rascal of an Irish writer had, I remembered, used that phrase to describe the vast double bed that in a hotel in a French town spread itself before himself and his love; and I was momentarily embarrassed and tantalized by the memory. 'Below the town there's a river. It's wide and deep and smooth and slow-flowing. 'There's a river-walk under the loveliest beech trees in the world. They'll still have a few red leaves.'

'I love beech trees.'

'There are some beauties in the little wood between the bridge and Morgan's house.'

'Morgan's house. Morgan's house. Will we never get away from that name?' She was agitated, her voice trembling. 'I know you'll think I'm foolish,' she said, 'but from my bedroom window I can see right over the trees to the cottage. No matter how dark the night is, I can still see it just like a white spot in the fields. I can't help thinking that one night when I was comfortably asleep that creature was raped and murdered, or whatever happened to her.'

'Not your fault.'

'But it was so near and so horrible.' The pub was darkening again.

My idyllic picture of a heavenly town had pitifully dissolved. Was she linking up the hands that closed on Lily Morgan's throat with the hands that untied a child's hair-ribbon in a Brighton lane: virgin snood unbound, but no candles ever to burn to bedward? 'Don't think about it,' I said uneasily. 'It'll soon all be over.'

'That makes it even more horrible. That wretched man. What was he like the night he came into your place?'

'Seemed decent enough. But, then, you never know what anybody may do. I knew a man once who knew a man.'

'Go on. Tell me a story.'

'It's about another murder. I'd better not.'

'Please do. Another murder, for a change. Anything but the Morgan murder. It happened too close to us.'

'Another drink first.' And over the second drink we chatted cheerfully about distant murders, poison, husbands hatcheting wives, acid baths, pushes down deep wells, stranglings, and suffocations, until murder became for us another of the funny things that people unaccountably did, like dancing or drabbing or drinking, or diving from high resilient planks into deep pools. Over the third drink she said: 'When will I see your wonderful town?'

'You still do want to see it?'

'Don't be tiresome, Don. You know I do. I'd like to be somewhere away with you, even for a little while.'

'Where nobody else can bother us.'

'Where nobody else can bother us,' she repeated, and George Butler died then by our hands as fearfully as heavily insured old husbands with young wives who have lovers die in American crime stories. Oh, how lovely she was, her firm breasts high-seated, her cheeks smooth as petals, her lips a little apart, and her eyes brightly and honestly looking into mine. What could friendship or fame or gold or any damned thing matter against being alone with her in a paradise of a country town? There and then we settled on a day. I didn't tell her that I had already written to the hotel to book two rooms for the next Saturday night and had had that morning the acceptance of my booking. We drove home in the wintry dusk, together in a small cushioned space in a darkening world that didn't matter. At her father's gate I left her, kissed her gently many times before I stepped from the car to go walking as light-footed as a lamp-lighter towards the village and my hut, no longer horrible with loneliness. The feel of her hands, of her body under my hands, of her warm breath around my face and throat, went with me for glorious company. It didn't worry me that I had never, except that one time to use the telephone for the public good, gone with her along the sweep of the gravelled drive, by the narrow artificial lake and up the gentle slope and the three or four broad steps, to enter the house she lived in. There was more between us than a house built with hands could signify. There was the poem by Eustache Deschamps, the secret told only to me, the promise to spend a night in a lazy, quiet old town.

In the hotel bar I had two whiskies because I was so elated that I felt I needed strong spirits to shock me back to normality, to keep me from dancing, knees rising, fingers clicking, up the village street, up the steep fair-green. Butler hadn't returned from the city. He'd left a message for myself or for Miss Rayel, to say, if we called, that he'd be exceptionally late. He had considered us. He had linked our names together. The thought troubled me for a while. Then my worry melted to pity for big Butler, the betrayed friend. But out in the air again, as proud as a demon in the dark night, pity was swept away by joy in the thing that had happened to me, the most unlikely of men.

From the summit of the fair-green I looked down on the bundled, shadowy shape of the village, on the dark land beyond, where the cold river flowed invisible, and I felt as if I owned the houses and the land. When the three street lamps came to life it seemed as apt as if some god of light had paid direct tribute to myself and my triumph.

V

The Kavanagh woman must have heard my step as I walked past in the darkness, for the door of the hut opened suddenly. An oblong of released light caught me, went beyond me towards the bare trees. A rising wind was rattling the branches. She called: 'Who's there?' But I knew she knew it was myself.

'This is Hartigan.'

'Oh, hello, Mr. Hartigan. How are you?' Her silhouette was bulky in the doorway. She wore an overcoat with the collar turned up around her padded chin. She said: 'I haven't seen you this long time.'

'No. Not for a long time now.'

'Won't you come in out of the cold?' I hesitated. The thought of the hostile face of the sallow man wasn't too inviting. But she said: 'You won't mind my shouting after you as you passed. Himself's away and I get nervous every time I hear a passing footstep.' I walked towards her door. She was lonely and needed company. Out of my largesse I could afford to give to the world. 'It must be lonesome for you when you're on your own.'

'He's not often away this late. He goes now and again to his mother's and stays there until they say the rosary at a quarter past twelve. Then he cycles home. It's a half-hour's ride on a bike.'

'He's a regular man.'

'As regular as a chiming clock.'

'It's a good thing.'

'It is. Sometimes.' The light hurt my eyes, and I blinked my way past her into the hut, conscious of the clean straw mat under my feet, and then, as the blinking ceased and my eyes cleared, of the pictures of Christ in His agony and His saints contemplating skulls. But tonight they affected me only as any coloured thing affects a happy man. She closed the door behind me. She said: 'I have a wee drop salted away for the cold weather.'

'You should hold on to it for a while. The cold weather hasn't commenced yet.'

'God sees it's cold enough here tonight.' She pointed to the grate and its cheerless smutawn of a fire. 'Whatever way the wind's set tonight the smoke comes blowing down again. And he won't have electric fires in the place. He says they're dangerous.'

'Everything's dangerous. Especially fires.' But she was too cold to be coy about references to danger and fires and heat. She said: 'He's terrified out of his life of electric shock. An uncle of his that worked in Chicago met his end that way.' To every man his own hobgoblin. Her figure strained at the dark nap coat she wore to keep herself warm and her fair round face above it looked incongruously pale and young. From the cupboard that made up the lower half of the dresser she took, after much rattling and clinking behind cups and crockery, a naggin bottle. Whisky had to be hidden carefully from the disapproving eyes of himself. 'Come over to my place,' I

said, 'and we'll drink it hot. I've some lemons and cloves.'
'I'd love to. You wouldn't think me cheap if I did?'
'Good God. Not at all.' The pine stick lay on the scrubbed table.
As I turned again towards the door I picked it up, balanced it, said:
'You're well armed, anyway.'
'A woman'd never know what would come to the door and she
alone.' She slipped the naggin bottle into a brown leather handbag.
'Like myself, for instance,' I said.
'Oh, Mr. Hartigan.' She laughed until her face reddened and
mercury-bright tears sailed slowly down the globes of her cheeks.
I laughed with her, although I wasn't quite sure whether one should
be complimented or insulted by her laughter and its implication of
my harmlessness to lone women. 'Now, if it was a rampager like
Mr. Butler,' she said, 'a woman'd need to keep her eyes skinned.
But there's the signs of decency about yourself, Mr. Hartigan.'
'Butler's not as bad as all that.' I felt guilty at hearing him abused.
I'd done him enough harm.
'Not so bad,' she said. 'He's the world's best. But the same world
knows he's the divil for women.' In the outer darkness she took my
arm. Years ago, it seemed, I had dreamt of clutching her and
supporting her in a wobbling, dissolving world. The length of sticky
pine was still in my free hand. 'I remember for the first two months
after I was married,' she said, 'we had rooms in a wee house across
the street from the hotel. Lo and behold you, the things Mr. Butler
used to bring home with him. Like something you'd see in the
American magazines. All with the best nylons and heels as high as
stilts.,
'What did the hotel people say?'
'Say? Sure, they do what Mr. Butler tells them. He has a way
with him.' A remark of that sort had no longer the power to depress
me with a sense of my own inferiority, for in one notable instance
Butler's way had betrayed him and a shaky, unstable man now
possessed the hero's kingdom. The thought of Butler and his
long-legged mannequins washed away my remorse, my feeling that
I had nastily betrayed him. He had had so much and I so little. 'The
first night I met him,' she said, 'was a night just like this when the
husband was away in his mother's. Mr. Butler came home on his
own and he so royal drunk he fell on the pavement between his car
and the door. It was midnight and not a sinner on the street, so I ran

129

across and helped him in and up to his room.'

Did you, I thought, did you, and was he grateful, and did he sober up in five minutes, as he can do, and find you within arm's length, and was that why you called him a rampager or a rummager or whatever it was?

'Drunk as he was,' she said, 'he was a perfect gentleman and the best of fun.'

'What's your idea of the best of fun?' At the door of my hut she giggled her reply: 'Oh, Mr. Hartigan, don't embarrass me. I'm afraid there's a bit of the divil in you after all.' A bit? Once upon a time, woman, I was possessed by seven grey demons, each one as high as a church tower or a pillar supporting the roof of hell.

She sat on the edge of my bunk, her legs dangling, wearing her coat until the room would warm up or the whisky warm her; and although I half wanted to sit beside her I found I could get no closer than the rocking-chair where Jim Walsh had slept. For all practical purposes this night had happened on the wrong side of my meeting with Emily Rayel.

She wasn't a good drinker. Half a naggin hot and she was ready for the world of gossip. 'Yourself and Miss Rayel are great friends.'

'She's a lovely girl,' I said recklessly.

'Does Mr. Butler think so?'

'How should I know?'

'Aren't the two of you as thick as thieves?'

'He's a good friend. We found a dead body together.'

'I always jeer him about wanting to marry Miss Rayel for her money.'

Always? How often did she meet and speak to Butler? How well did she know him? I said: 'Miss Rayel has more than money.'

'I don't know her well at all. She wouldn't speak to the likes of myself.' The jealousy in her voice angered me; it never occurred to me to think she was telling the truth, that Emily in her own village could be all that of a snob. Our glasses were empty. 'Here, I have some more,' I said, unlocking the cupboard. Sooner or later, before the man was hanged, the whisky he had taken without the publican's leave would have to be drunk. She said: 'That's a good drop.'

'The very best.' Our glasses refilled, I sat down again on the rocking-chair, even though she moved a little to make room for me to sit beside her on the bunk. Then after the sort of uneasy silence that had once before perturbed me in her company, I said, looking at the whisky and trying to remember what the man who had provided it had looked like: 'He'll soon be for the high jump.'

'Who?' She knew well who.

'Jim Walsh.'

Another uneasy silence. Then she said: 'Wasn't it wonderful how he was in here with you the very night after the murder?'

'What's so wonderful about that? Seeing he was with you the night before. And brought you a bottle of whisky, too!' The last touch was the result of sudden aid from my imagination, was based on probability and added with irrational malice. But her sudden little gasp and the way she sat up straight as if a pain in her spine had stung her made me feel as a soldier must feel when he bayonets his first enemy—his power, his fatal power. She shivered and her cheeks went as white as flour. 'Who in the name of God told you that?'

'Jim Walsh. Who else?' I was sorry for her until she said: 'I hope you never breathed a word of it to any living being.'

'I don't gossip. What you do is your own business.' She didn't even attempt to pretend, as you'd think a woman would, that she had been doing what they call nothing wrong with Jim Walsh, that he'd come to her just for old time's sake, or to look at the gas meter, or with a message from her sister in Liverpool or anywhere, or to mend a leaky pipe. 'Don't take me up wrong,' she said piteously. 'I don't mean to insult you. I know you don't gossip. But he'd kill me if he ever suspected. He'd throw me out.' I looked at my watch. 'He'll soon be on his knees for the rosary.' She shivered again and pulled her coat more tightly around her and hid her face for a second in her hands as if she was about to cry or to pray. But she didn't cry and she didn't pray out aloud, except by implication to me, the great god Don, down in the chair by his creaking bunk. 'You see, to tell you the honest truth,' she said, 'Jim Walsh was my old beau.' Such an ineffectual, unsuitable word to describe the desolate unshaven wreck I had spoken to, or the damned white-faced man between two policemen in the dock. 'That was before Lily Morgan got her hands on him. I ask you, Mr. Hartigan, what could men ever see in a woman like that?'

I thought: Quietude, mystery, something different and unexplained. But I said: 'God only knows.'

'When Jim let me down after all I'd done and endured for him, I was so mad I'd have married a black. So I married him.' The stinging emphasized pronoun could mean only one thing. You didn't, you couldn't love that sort of a him. 'I didn't marry a black. I married a monk. A walking saint. You saw those pictures on the wall.'

I had. I said: 'I did.'

'It broke out in him a week after the wedding. The praying. He never knew beforehand what it meant to be married. And he found out things. Somebody must have told him, because he'd never have known himself. That wicked old mother of his. Somebody told him about myself and Jim. So you can see what'd happen if he knew about that night.' Her face again went down to meet her rising, bewildered hands. This time she did cry, her round heavy shoulders shaking, the bunk shaking; and I sat for a time sipping whisky, not knowing what to do, then venturing to lay a hand on her hands and say: 'Cheer up now, Mrs. Kavanagh. Things could be worse.'

'They could be better too. I hate them all. Himself and his ma and his prayers. And Jim Walsh and that girl he killed. He swore to me that night that she was no more to him than chaff in the wind.'

'Maybe she wasn't.' 'And she dead in her bed by his hands at the moment he came to me. Isn't it enough to drive a woman mad? What did I ever do to deserve it?'

That I couldn't say, I thought, being neither Jim Walsh nor the yellow monk; and I forced her to dry her eyes, to sit closer to the electric fire, to sip hot whisky until the sobbing and shivering had ceased, and she smiled up at me and said: 'Mr. Hartigan, you're very kind. And you a complete stranger.'

'Not a complete stranger. I'm a neighbour.'

'No wonder Mr. Butler likes you.' She might as well have spat in my face. I hated her again. 'Did he tell you that?'

'He says you're a grand fellow and a most intelligent man.'

'That was nice of him.' I sat down on the bunk on the place she had warmed, hoping she wouldn't move from where I had placed her on the chair close to the fire. She said: 'Will he marry Miss Rayel, do you think?' For an instant I thought she was talking about myself.

'Will she marry him?'

'I'd hate to see him tied up. Matrimony'd kill him.' But I knew by the way she turned to her drink and tightened her lips over it that what she didn't like was the idea of any woman having a legal claim on big Butler; and, looking at my watch, I wished she'd go home to hell or to that heaven of holy pictures and leave me more whisky to kill on my own. She didn't move from her chair or cease from her senseless gossip until fifteen minutes before the monk was due on his velocipede. What would she do if choirs of angels caught him in their arms in the last ecstasy of family prayers at his mother's hearth, and bore him aloft and along and got him home half an hour too soon? For she really did fear that sallow, pious wisp of a man. She drank the last of her whisky. The bottle stood uncorked and drained empty. That whisky might, but for accident, have passed through the guts of Jim Walsh, warming and lubricating the way for the condemned man's splendid breakfast, but instead it had been shared between myself and the woman he had charitably pleasured on the night he choked his love. The sodden slices of lemon she tumbled into the palm of her hand, sucked out of them the last drop of bitter juice tinctured with whisky, then dropped them back into the tumbler. Her lips made an obscene sucking sound. For the first time I noticed that she wore false teeth. She placed the tumbler on the table, then paused, finger and thumb still resting on the glass rim, and said: 'Excuse me, Mr. Hartigan, but are you going on a holiday to that town?'

The letter lying open on the table before her said simply: 'Dear Sir, In reply to yours of the something or other inst., we are pleased to be able to inform you that two single rooms will be available for the night of the something else inst. Yours etcetera.'

Stiff paper crackled as impudently she took the letter up in her hand and read it again; and my eyes went crimson and my head rattled at the thought of her fingers—the fingers of Jim Walsh's discarded woman, of the thwarted wife of a monk of a man, of a fat woman with false teeth, of the confidential friend of the great Mr. Butler of the hotel—touching anything that Emily and myself had in common. God, I'd gone a long distance since the still nights I'd lain awake listening for the creaking of the neighbours' bunk— apparently it never had had occasion to creak—and a long distance from the windy days when my eyes would wander to watch her at her husband's door, her plaid skirt blown back against her strong wide legs. 'Not a holiday,' I said, and my voice, I'm afraid, was quivering with anger. 'I'm going down there for a night with a friend to see some people.'

'Who are they? Would I know them, I wonder? I know the town well. It's a dull hole of a place.'

'They're English people. They're new to the town. As a matter of fact, they live out a few miles in the country.'

'I know well a man who owns a shop and a pub there.' Would that be Jim Walsh's predecessor? 'If you've a minute to spare you should step into his place and tell him I was asking for him.' I wouldn't, I hoped silently, have a minute to spare for anything of the sort. 'I'd like to see his face,' she said, 'when you walk in and tell him you know me. He'll be surprised.' Then she mentioned some name that I didn't bother to remember and I left her halfway home and came back and securely bolted my own door.

The pine bludgeon still lay along the coverlet of my bunk where I had dropped it when we came in. With a vague intention of returning it, I picked it up, but heard just then the whirr of wheels as the saint came cycling home again. In a mild way it was amusing to think that, if Butler at any time came rampaging, she'd have no stick to protect herself against him, that was if she wanted any protection against Butler, the world's best something or other.

VI

I could have gone, but didn't, to the jail gate in the early morning to see somebody pin to the barrier the jail governor's note saying that Jim Walsh had been safely and efficiently hanged.

> *The night before Larry was stretched*
> *The boys they all paid him a visit. . . .*

Pinning up a piece of paper is the miserable niggling modern way in place of the ceremony of tumbrils , hurdles, horses, and crowds shouting execration, making a man feel that in his last moments he's the centre of things. . . .

> *When he came to the nubbling chit,*
> *He was tucked up so neat and so pretty;*
> *The rumbler jugged off from his feet,*

And he died with his face to the city.

... that he's providing entertainment, brightening the lives of his fellows, discouraging evil-doers, encouraging the good towards betterment, being the life and soul of the party, being a great, great boy.

> *He kicked too, but that was all pride,*
> *For soon you might see 'twas all over;*
> *And as soon as the noose was untied,*
> *Then at darkey we waked him in clover,*
> *And sent him to take a ground sweat.*

It was all in the newspaper in a five-line paragraph. Reading that was handier than rising at dawn, rushing to town, waiting, perhaps in mizzling rain with a group of people who, some of them, whether the ground was wet or dry, would kneel down at eight o'clock striking, to pray for the safe journeying of whatever it was went out over their heads like a bird, over the city and the sleeping theatres, the still unopened Pyramid with its circle empty of eating beasts and no Circe in the glass box, the back-lane brothel where Jim Walsh had slept his last free night, over my sisters having breakfast and my mother still in bed, over villages and huts and holy yellow men and disappointed women, and Lily Morgan's grave, and Emily Rayel slowly opening her eyes and raising her petal cheek from the warm pillow.

But I did rise early the following morning. I took the bus to the city. Gripped in my fist was the pine bludgeon, more for singularity than support, and to signify to urban clerks that I was bound for adventure in country places. I took another bus south-westwards away from the city until I came to a village and a roadside pub. There I waited until Emily, driving her blue car, overtook me. That was how we dodged George Butler and drove off in the general direction of heaven.

VII

Apart from sides of beef in butchers' windows and red steaks on marble slabs, tins of fruit piled in pyramids in grocers' windows, a new cinema painted a sickly cream, the town had no bright colours. Browns and greys and blacks, and green grass all around. Behind churchyard railings at the bottom of a hilly street there was one splash of green, clipped lawn and yew trees, visible from where we sat and ate at the window of the upstairs dining-room. The walls of that room were solemn with a series of dark pictures of episodes in the life of George Washington. Our plates were overloaded with the biggest, richest steaks imaginable. This was cattle country. Heavy bullock bellies brushed against deep grass. Bullock jaws champed around and around the sleepy little overfed town. Sounds and smells of cattle came down entry-ways from lairs already filling for tomorrow's fair.

'Most unladylike,' Emily said, cutting deeply into steak. 'I don't normally eat like this, Don, but I'm so, so hungry. I never imagined I could be as ravenous as I am.' We drank good burgundy and had brandy in our coffee. Two yellow wisps of straw, escaped from a cattle lair and, blown gently around in circles on the Diamond, were finally entangled with the feet of seven people standing in a passive cattle-like queue close to a telephone kiosk and waiting for a bus to carry them to even quieter places deeper in the country. The dancing straw had brightened the street and sunshine followed, early afternoon sunshine defying winter and bare branches, softening the air out of all regard to the season, touching with colour even the dull useful clothes in the squinty windows of small drapery shops. 'The sun makes a difference,' I said. 'I feel warmer.'

She laughed at me. Her lips were wet with wine. 'Could it be the brandy, Don?' And to make certain, we sat for an hour in the room downstairs and drank more brandy, until the plates on the picture rail shone like gems and all words were like clear eloquent music. She stood up, still laughing at some secret joke the wine had told her, and gently with the tips of her fingers touched one of the large urns on the mantelpiece as if it were alive and might move sensuously at contact with her warm hand. Fingertips resting on the urn, body leaning a little forward, tweed skirt buttoned down the front and tightening around her hips as she reached upwards, she was more than ever a girl from another time, figure from a Greek wall, image from a *trouvère*'s dream, meant for the pleasures of prince or emperor, or to stir up a poet's ravings. Could I help feeling elated until my head whirled at the thought that she was here because of me, alone with me, ready to go with me to undiscovered places?

'We must see the town, Don.' The air around us was warm with sweet conspiracy and warm also with brandy. Slow voices talked somewhere in an echoing kitchen. There clearly couldn't be many guests in the hotel. The commercials were off home to their wives, and it was too late in the year for tourists. 'We must see the town and the river and the hill.'

'And the world, of course, from the top of the hill.'

'Let's go now while the sun's shining.' We went, almost running, hand in hand. With my free hand I grabbed from the hallstand Mrs. Kavanagh's bludgeon. 'To keep the cows away,' Emily said, 'and, Don, do look at that picture. Doesn't it remind you of the races?' It did, except that the costumes of the race-goers in that picture above the hallstand were eighty or ninety years old, and judging by the bright colours the weather had been warm and sunny, no hooves in slush, no hailstones. 'Where would George be?' she joked, peering at the picture, stretching up to touch it as she had touched the urn. The cold, slightly damp glass kept for an instant the print of her fingers. The glass would remember, and the urn, that she had visited this place, and chairs she had sat on, and tumblers, cups, and cutlery she had fingered; and upstairs a bed as yet unslept in. Thinking that way made—no wonder—the blood go to my head with a bang. Struggling for words, I said: 'Fighting somewhere. Off-stage. I suppose.'

'Being a hero.'

'Being a he-man.' And to show how infinitely our mood differed from the strained, uneasy, watchful moods of days and nights in the village and the city, we went laughing and happy out to the Diamond, my left arm around her waist. We had escaped from Butler. Every step left him farther behind.

Which pub and grocery is owned and inhabited by the man who'd be surprised to hear that I know Mrs. Kavanagh? Would he be that man proudly at his prosperous door, tails of yellow shop-coat hoisted so that he can dig hands into trousers pockets to jingle coins and keys? Why would he be surprised if the pale, thin-faced, dark-headed stranger now strutting the pavement, proud as a peacock because of the pretty girl by his side, were to halt and say: Look, I know a woman who married a saint called Kavanagh when a murderer jilted her, and who says she knows you.

Halfway across the Diamond we waited, Emily still in the crook of my arm and leaning against me, while a green bus came, windows loose in the frames and quivering noisily, devoured the queue of seven people, went off searching for sleepy roads where the only sounds at this season would be the rattling of its own decrepit body or the barking of dogs startled by that rattling out of the country's winter sleep.

We looked into seventeen shop windows. We had another brandy in a cubicle curtained off like a confessional in the corner of a grocery shop.

A lank wild-haired youth rode slowly by, toes trailing, on the back of a small patient donkey. Two corner-boys stirred themselves to shout: 'Go on, Steve. Ride him, cowboy,' then stirred themselves again and more sharply to look at Emily, to contort their claws in their trousers pockets, then relaxed, the exertion ended, shoulder-blades against greasy wall, and hoped against hope for free porter.

Little lanes of whitewashed cottages, vennels slimy with slung dishwater, led steeply down to a bridge and the deep river. A child cried. A woman sang. A gramophone played a schottische tune. A dog snuffled at our heels. An old man raised his hat to the strangers.

We looked at the weir slung slantwise from bank to bank, dividing with knife-edge exactness the deep delayed ebony water and the white feathery spray.

Machinery chug-chugged in a high grey mill. I remembered the ruined mill near Morgan's cottage, sunlight yellow like spilling wine through sightless window cavities, the blackbird rustling and fistling in the littered shrubbery, Butler and myself on the road towards Lily dead and Emily alive.

A steeply slanting roof, crusted with years of rejected chaff and husks, ran up to a point as sharp as an oast-house. Worn jagged steps descended from the road to the river path. Clusters of reddened beech leaves, like swallows on telegraph wires, still clung to the high trees. Beech-nuts gravelled the ground. A second old man sat on a bench, didn't raise his hat or even his head. Ten yards beyond him, and secure in the knowledge that he wasn't noticing a thing and seeing no other person on the path, we kissed until our lips hurt. I held her so tightly her feet left the ground and, her thighs pressing against me, she locked her legs around mine so that we staggered and almost fell. Here under the high beeches we were the world and more away from Brighton.

A second weir swung the river sideways. The lively water sang all around us. A tarred flat-bottomed boat lay upside down beside a brightly painted boat-house. The river escaped from the town and the trees, looped leftwards, a wide meadow to one side and green grassy slopes to the other. The path, high on a causeway like a Dutch dyke, bisected the meadow. To show the world, if the world was watching and interested, we kissed a million times on our way along the causeway to a wooden foot-bridge. Once across that bridge we turned away from the river, followed another and narrower path cutting between deep clay banks kept from crumbling and falling only by the hold of a few scraggy bushes, found ourselves on the road that led to the hill and the forth.

Sparrows chirped and quarrelled on the roof of a grey building that had once been a workhouse and was now a factory.

Two fat girls, capacious bums sagging over bicycle saddles, laden baskets unbalancing handlebars, went cycling slowly up the slope from the town. They laughed loudly as they passed, probably because Emily and myself had our arms fiercely locked, were walking shoulder to shoulder and hand in hand as if, as was the case, we'd been pulled together by something stronger than our own muscles. But for us their silly laughter only emphasized our joy in isolation from the rest of the world. 'Poor fat things,' I said. 'I doubt if a man ever had an arm around those waists.' They wore thick raincoats of brown leather. 'It would have to be such a long, long arm,' she said, and squeezed closer to me, if that were possible, and sighed and then we both laughed and excitedly stepped faster. Ahead of us the hill rose to the right of the road, summit crowned by the bushy grass-grown forth, sides green and smooth as a naked body, a hill that needed a haircut or even a scalping, but wouldn't get one or the other because traditions of dancing wild spirits were strong enough to preserve intact and unlevelled the clay ring and mound made for a dwelling-place by pre-historic people.

'To the forth,' I said.

'To the forth,' she said. Then we chorused: 'To the woods. To the woods,' and Emily falsettoed: 'No, no. No, no. My mother won't like it.' Butler would have had the gall and the crudity to complete the chant about what the mother of the hypothetical abducted maiden wouldn't like and wouldn't get. But I couldn't, because the thoughts in my head, and I suspected in her head also, embarrassed me almost to the point of blushing; and I took refuge in asking a man, labouring with a chopping spade at the road's grass margin, the shortest way to the summit.

Through the farmyard there, he told us, and let the lady mind her shoes. Then out by a gate with white pillars to the place by the stream where county council men are screening gravel.

Picking our steps through somebody's farmyard, we were guided and led on by the swish of sluicing water, the slap of gravel shovelled against riddling wires.

Up the zigzaggy path, said one of the county council men, and through the dry, withered whins. Don't trust your weight to the sagging wire fence and let the lady mind her stockings.

Halfway up, I felt, a satyr or a goat itself or an ancient crooked shepherd would carry on the wonder-tale rhythm, would show us a clear spring where every drinker of the pure cold water could find power to love and live for ever. But halfway up there was only the wind swaying thorn bushes and sunshine still yellow on old grass.

From this out we're on our own, men and the world and county councils all below and behind us.

Now we're over the rampart, down through hazels and up again and into the fairy ring. There's a robin singing somewhere and in the circle sheltered by the dry bushes there's no wind worth speaking of. If it wasn't for leaflessness and the poor state of the grass the month might be May or early June.

Behind some high whins we found a corner of secure and absolute shelter. Lining carefully down—a tip once learned from a school friend addicted to love-making in hedgerows—I spread my coat underneath us. Then we lay for a long time content with no talking. There was no smoothness in the world like the smoothness of her body under my hand and no singular thing so distinctively beautiful as the brown mole above her right breast. She whispered: 'I never thought I'd have gone so far with anyone.' Why with me, I still dazedly wondered, and not with Butler or any of the world's great men who'd be glad in their guts to be here in this windless, sunny, whin-sheltered corner? But I said, mumbling like an idiot: 'A little farther and we'll be at the beginning of the world,' and had no fear that the beginning might also be the end. Then for minutes

I lost sight of whins and sun and falsely blue sky. There was a tear on her right cheek that seemed to have come not from her eye but, like a welling spring, from the pores of her smooth skin. The sky, the sun, the whins returned shaking and blurred from a deep purple mist. The sun, though, was slipping away from us: the false blue revealing its true nature by fading to grey; the whins were as brown and crippled as they should be in the beginning of an island winter. 'Did I hurt you terribly?'

Pitifully she whispered to my ear: 'I was such a coward, wasn't I?' and shivered and sobbed where she lay by my side. But after a while she said, fiercely: 'I'm glad though, I'm glad, for now I know,' and I felt myself as discarded as galoshes when their user has dumped them behind the door of a warm, dry house.

We lay on the grass until the cold touched us. She fondled my face and ran her fingers through my hair and said sweet things until I was consoled, then drenched me with icy water by saying: 'You'll let me sleep in peace tonight, won't you?' 'I'm not a brute.' That was the correct thing to say. Moreover, I wasn't a brute.

'It's not that I don't want. But. You know.'

'We must go slow.' What were we talking about: driving a car, breaking in a young horse, strikes on British railways, hoovering a carpet, building a house, washing dishes? We did go slow: slowly back to the hotel, dawdled over dinner and drink, dawdled up the stairs to our separate rooms. I tried to sleep, but the room tried to keep me awake and suffocate me. So I went, this time rapidly, feverishly, down long corridors to the kitchen and, seated in a chair close to the heat of the range, drank bottle after bottle of stout, heard town gossip from the boots and a thin hunchbacked chambermaid. Then, to wear away the heaviness of the stout, I walked the dark path by the river, on an impulse climbed like a lunatic to the bushy forth, found and felt with my fingers the cold crushed corner where we had lain. The impulse continuing and strenghening, I strode back to the hotel, like a conquering hero to the door of Emily's room, found it unlocked and the girl awake and waiting. She said: 'Oh, Don, I was hoping you'd come. Your clothes are wet. Where were you?'

'Walking. Revisiting past scenes of delight, as the poet says.'

'You're such an odd darling.' She was laughing and happy, no fears, no tears. When the daylight woke me, we were still happy.

Her hair was loose all over the pillow. I gathered it in ropes and tugged gently until she too awoke. We lay until we heard the sounds of work beginning in corridors and kitchen, until the odours of food came filtering pleasantly upwards to tempt two tired, satisfied people.

VIII

We were at breakfast when the waitress said: 'A phone call for Miss Emily Rayel.'

'For me?'

'Yes, miss. A gentleman, and he says it's urgent.' She didn't speak until the waitress had moved away. Then she asked: 'Don, did you hear that?'

'Couldn't help hearing it, me dear.' Domesticated already.

'Who could it be?'

'Heaven only knows.' I wasn't without an uneasy feeling.

She said: 'But nobody knows we're here.'

'I told nobody.'

'Nor did I. Not even Jill.'

'It would hurt Jill.'

'Oh, Don, poor Jill. I know she has a crush on me.' She pursed her lips and thought and said: 'But who could this man be?'

'Only one way to find out.'

'Suppose it's my father. What on earth will I say?'

'Say you're here with a party.'

'So I am. A lovely party it was too.'

'It's still going on. Progress reported.' We laughed and she went away laughing, but when she returned her mouth was tightly set and her eyes serious. 'Don, it's George. And it isn't a trunk call. He's here in this town. He's followed us.'

'So what? It's a free country.' But I didn't feel all that happy about it.

'He's mad drunk. He says he's known about us for ever so long, but that he was giving us rope to hang ourselves.' She was angry, but she was also a little bit frightened. 'He has a neck to talk that way,' I said. 'He doesn't bloodywell own you.'

142

'He thinks he does. There'll be trouble, Don. You know there'll be trouble.' Her fears were getting the upper hand of her anger. 'We'll get away out of this quickly.'

'Because why?'

'We must, Don. You know he'll make trouble.'

'Let him try. This had to happen some time.' But I knew, and I think she knew, how hollow my words were. 'No, we must go, Don. We must go.'

'Run away. Not on your life.'

'It's not running away. It's just sense.'

'Is he coming here soon?'

'He says he'll be here as soon as he's drunk enough to kill the two of us.'

'What right has he to talk like that to you?'

'We'd better go, Don.'

'Why had we? You go, Emily. I'll wait and see how much killing he does.' Vividly I could hear again the crunch of his fist on the fool's face on the day of the races. I wasn't a fighting man. Even as a schoolboy a fight for me had always meant standing in one place as if my feet were screwed to the ground, closing my eyes, flailing emptiness with my fists, hoping that I'd hit something and yet afraid to augment my opponent's anger, feeling stinging directed blows on my face and hearing laughter from a surrounding circle as if I was being baited and mocked by invisible demons or demigods. How would I, could I, face big Butler? Emily mustn't see my fear, mustn't know that I expect slaughter, that honestly in my heart I know slaughter wouldn't be undeserved. 'You go now, Emily. I'll wait.'

'Don't be absurd, Don. I can't leave you.'

'You must.' For fifteen minutes I kept repeating at intervals those two words, and in the end she agreed dubiously and to my disappointment. We walked to the hallway, stood for a while dumbly and miserably looking at the picture of races run a century since. It didn't amuse us any more. Butler was now too close to that tightly corseted, long-skirted, sun-blessed crowd. She said: 'Must I go, Don?'

'You must.'

'But it seems so mean.'

'I'd prefer you to go.' In a room off the hallway, the room of plates and urns and pleasant drinking of brandy, the telephone rang. It occurred to me then that I genuinely would prefer her to leave: her presence couldn't halt the slaughter and would add to the pain, eternal humiliation, for herself and myself. Butler wouldn't, if she fled instantly, have the triumph of meeting her, taking her from me, driving her back to the city and the village.

'It is mean to go.'

'No, you must go. You must. I want you to go. Don't let's argue about it all morning.' Behind us the hall porter said: 'A telephone call for Miss Emily Rayel.' We went together to the telephone. We knew it was Butler playing at cat and mouse. This time I picked up the receiver. Butler's voice, shrill and unsteady, said: 'That you, Emily? Tell that Hartigan bastard I'm coming now for his blood.'

I said: 'Hold on a minute, Butler.'

I want to speak to Emily, not to you. I'll talk to you later.'

'Emily doesn't want to speak to you. If you're coming here, come on ahead. I'll wait for you.'

'You bloody well better, you lousy traitor. If you're gone when I get there, I'll follow you to the ends of the earth, I'll follow you to hell and back, you. . . .' I cut down the receiver on the names he chose to call me. What was it, if anything, that Valentine, when he found out the truth, called Proteus? At least, in Emily's presence I had spoken to him without any sign of fear. We went out by a side door and around to the garage at the back of the hotel. When she was seated at the wheel and the road to safety open before her, I kissed her a few times and came back alone, collecting my bludgeon in the hallway, sitting in the room of plates and urns to wait for the avenger to come, drinking rum to build up my courage or, more honestly, to burn away my fears. He didn't come in five or in ten or in fifteen minutes. I drank more rum. An antique wag-by-the-wall slowly ticked away the seconds. Could he have met Emily on the way, stopped her, taken her with him, leaving me to wait like a fool, content to know that some night he could come quietly to my hut and beat my face in? What would he do to her if he did meet her and take her with him? He couldn't, I gloried, even in my cowardice, do to her what I had done, couldn't help her towards first knowledge. The clock chimed. A waitress brought me another rum, told me the next bus left for the city in half an hour. I'll give him that half-hour and no more. Courage came at last from the burning liquor and I was even beginning to hope he would come quickly so that I could talk to him plain and straight. Fifteen minutes. Two more rums. Twenty minutes. On the twenty-seventh he came, lurching into the room, face red, hair tousled, swaying from heels to toes as he stood and looked at me across three tables and the intervening spaces. Gripping my bludgeon, I expected cavalry, a rush and a blow. Pine was, as the sallow saint had said, a poor light wood when compared with ash or blackthorn. But no rush came and for the moment no blow. He came across slowly, unsteadily, and sat at my table, pushing away from him with a sweep of his left arm the water-bottle and two empty glasses. His eyes were bloodshot. By comparison I felt cool, almost master of the situation: but that feeling was the work of the valorous rum.

'Who told you we were here?'

'Would you like to know?'

'Not particularly.'

'Your next-door neighbour. She's a friend of mine.'

'So I gather. She was a friend of Jim Walsh too.'

He leaned towards me, his fingers gripping the edge of the table. 'What do you mean by that?'

'Nothing.'

'You'd better mean nothing.' His abrupt quickening of hostility shook my spurious confidence and I needed another drink. So I said: 'Have a drink, Butler?'

'Sure I'll drink your drink. We'll talk then. Outside this place.' And while we waited on the drinks he laughed quietly and wickedly as if I wasn't there. He said: 'I drank in every pub coming up the street just to keep you waiting. To keep you hopping.'

'You're a cruel fellow, Butler.' Out in Africa he should be, said the Jewess, maltreating blacks. 'And you've a fine notion about your power to keep anybody hopping.'

'I'm honest about it, Harty. I don't cheat.' The truth of that and the way he used my name as if we were still friends stung me. 'Tell the truth, Harty. The guts are scared out of you.'

'I'm ashamed. Not afraid. I should have told you long ago.'

'Told me what?'

'That Emily and myself were in love.'

'Emily in love with you. You're not a liar, you're an imbecile.' His laughter went on for a long time, but knowing what I knew, it had no power to hurt me. 'Laugh away,' I said. 'It's the truth all the same. There are things about Emily you don't understand.'

Louder laughter. 'How nice of you to tell me. I don't read the books you read, Harty.'

'You certainly don't.' Then I said: 'I slept with her last night,' and thought: He'll hit me now and put an end to this agony. For a while it looked as if he was going to strike me. His body, rigid, rose a few inches from his chair, but he didn't move his hands; and his eyes were glazed and turned upwards like the eyes of a lunatic or a dead man. 'God Jesus,' he said. 'You bastardin' liar. I'll kill you for that.'

'Kill away. It's still the truth.' I wasn't afraid any more.

I'd struck the hardest blow I could strike. 'Come out of this,' he whispered. 'Come out if you're a man at all. Come out and give me a chance to choke you.'

Bludgeon in hand, I went with him for a mixture of motives and with a mingling of feelings, none of them having anything to do with common sense; remorse, the feeling that I deserved what was in store for me, that I'd ruined a girl and betrayed and maddened a friend, also a pride that I had the power to do such things and that having known greater agonies in my time I now cared little for what Butler's blows could do to my body.

IX

At the bridge where the worn steps descended to the river path he brought the sky crashing down, not with blows but with words, ridiculously few words. He said: 'Harty, you were my friend and you did that to me. I've done murder for what you stole from me.'

'You've done what?'

'Murder. Murder. Murder. With these hands.' I think he held his hands up above his head, but if I did look at them I mustn't have been able to see them. 'For Christ's sake, who do you think killed Lily Morgan? Not the poor oaf who got himself hanged?'

'Butler, you're demented. You don't know what you're saying.' I couldn't stop shivering. It wasn't fear or cold.

'I know what I'm saying. Who should know if I don't? I killed her. And then I raised you from the gutter. From your own neurotic excrement. Made a man of you. And this is my thanks.' His face seemed to be miles away. But I could see it distinctly. The awful rigidity of jaw-bones and throat sinews. The eyes staring, but not staring at me. There were no beech trees or old men on benches, no talking water, no river path, no morning or evening or danger or anything, only the words I was listening to—and believing, because it wasn't possible to disbelieve their sound, the accents of excruciating pain.

'Why? Butler, why? In God's name, why should you have killed her?'

'She was a bitch. A low bitch. The lowest ever walked.'

'The world's full of them. You don't kill them just for being bitchy. What did she do to you?'

'What did *she* do to *me*.' He was hideously amused. 'You mean what I did to her. She wanted to talk about it across the road to Emily's father. I tell you she was a low bitch.' His eyes were bright, and protruded until I thought they'd burst like shot out of their sockets. 'Do you see now what happened to me, Hartigan? Do you see what you've done?'

'You must have given her good reason to make her want to talk.' Calmness, cold with anger and hate, had returned to me. The face of Lily Morgan came before my eyes, quivering up from the water, gradually growing more distinct and taking a shape. She was dead, could talk no longer on her own behalf, and I must defend her memory against this monster. 'Maybe she wanted to save Emily from what she herself had suffered from you.' The rattle of the bare branches above us was like the uncovering of swords for a murderous battle. He was so drunk with hot spirits and insane egotism that he didn't notice my studied insult, or perhaps it never could have occurred to him that under any circumstances I'd dare to insult him. 'I did her no harm. She put herself in my way and I took her. I gave her a good time.'

'I can imagine.' I could; and the imagination, even if I had snatched Emily from him, was hot hell.

'It wasn't easy taking her. She wanted a husband. They all do.'

'They all do.'

'She was a virgin too.'

'They all begin that way.'

'But she wanted something better than the Walsh fellow, and at last she made up her mind and took her chance.'

'It's your word against the world.'

'What do you mean?'

'She's dead. Walsh's dead. They can't contradict you.'

'Think I'm lying, do you?'

'She loved Walsh.'

'She did in a way. But I was a big man like him and that worked wonders. I had the car too. And money. There's nothing like the car.' My hand gripped tighter and tighter until the pinewood hurt my palm. 'Then,' he said, 'she wanted to hold on to me. They all do.'

'They all do.'

'She showed her claws when she heard a rumour I was engaged to Emily.'

'You could have told her there was nothing in the rumour.' 'Why should I? I was tired looking at her. But I never thought she'd turn out so nasty. You know the feeling when a woman gets her claws into you and means to hold on.'

'I don't.'

'You wouldn't.' The contempt in his voice couldn't touch me. I was away beyond such things. If it did anything to me, it made me ferociously glad, certain that he was no longer my friend, that he never could have been my friend.

'What did you ever want her for?'

'She put herself in my way.' Her face was before my eyes, so vivid as bright enamel. I asked: 'Hadn't you mannequins and brassiered beauty queens?' The Kavanagh woman had talked of his visitors, like something out of the American magazines, nylons and heels as high as stilts, every small man's dream of impossible conquests, models and cover girls flat on their backs and liking it. 'You don't understand, Hartigan. There's a fascination in doing things like that.'

'Like a man doing ninety in a big car on a highway. Then he leaves the car and the highway and foots it along a twisty country lane.' Words and words, said slowly and preciously, so that he'd think me an utter fool, so that I'd have time to watch him, so that without sign of cowardice I could walk with him from the seclusion of the trees where anything could happen. Since he told me all this he must feel as secure as Lucifer. He wasn't afraid of me, or of

148

judgment. Jim Walsh was hanged and the law satisfied. Who'd credit my story? I could hardly credit it myself. I only knew that I hated him so much that this revelation, made without its appropriate thunder and lightning and witches screaming through sulphury air, must nevertheless be true. Or did he intend that I'd never go from that place even to tell the story that nobody would believe? Or did he think that I'd stay silent to keep Emily's name out of it, that I'd accept the horror of injustice unalterably done? 'So you went along and killed her,' I said. Fifty yards away the trees ended. Once out on the causeway, and the world would be able to see us. What did he mean to do? I knew what I meant to do. 'Why tell me all this?'

'It won't do you any good.'

'Why not?'

'You'll find out. Anyway, it does me good to talk to somebody. I'm not a brute. She drove me to it. I didn't kill her in cold blood.'

'The night Walsh went to her cottage she had the door open. She was waiting for you.'

'I'm not a brute. I only intended to shake her hard, frighten her, put the fear of God into her.'

'You did that.'

'I didn't mean to kill her.'

'But you did, Butler.' He was absorbed in his story, in himself, in his memories. He seemed for the moment to have forgotten his purpose in pursuing Emily and myself to this town. After months of silence he was talking, talking, talking, as even the prince of devils must surely talk confidingly to some other black angel. 'Then you came along with your nerves. Jesus. Nerves. How little you knew about it. What do you think my nerves were like all the time? Jitters. Jitters. I could hardly keep myself from driving the car under a bus or something, or into the river off the city quays.' He had stopped walking. The beginning of the causeway and the open, exposed places were thirty yards away. No old men or young men or any men to be seen. He looked straight at me. He said: 'It's all over now.'

'How do you know?'

'Walsh's dead. You'll never talk.'

'How do you know?'

'I'll make sure you won't.'

'You can't kill me as well.' I knew then he was deranged. Nerves.

Worry. Anything you like. I was there in that lonely place facing a lunatic who had good reason to hate me. 'You won't talk,' he said. 'I'm for England tonight. I'm getting out of this bloody country. You won't talk. I'll see Emily before I go. She'll come with me.'

'How do you know?'

'I know. That's all. I know.' He led me, his hand on my arm, around two tall trees towards the clay bank crumbling above deep water. He wasn't steady on his feet. His hand trembled. I walked a pace behind him. I wasn't afraid. I knew I wasn't going to die. 'Butler, be reasonable,' I said. He laughed at me, threw back his head and laughed. Unhurriedly I thought: All the time I spent reproaching myself because I thought I had betrayed you, you murdering bastard, devil in the daylight, blot on God's earth. 'Butler, be reasonable,' I said again, and struck him in the eyes with the heavy end of the pine bludgeon. Light as it was, it was accurate as a knife. A rajah suddenly spat on by the lowliest, most neglected creature in his harem, or cuckolded and assaulted by a flabby, amorphous eunuch, couldn't have been more astounded. I swung the bludgeon and struck again. Then my coolness snapped like overstrained elastic and I was striking, screaming, crying in the centre of a blood-red mist, and hearing another voice roaring with pain, and hearing a splash as of feet in water, and a scrabbling as of hands or claws grasping at clay; and then I was running and running and running, perhaps along the causeway or perhaps over fields or among clouds or mountain peaks, but finally, when the mist cleared and the world turned green again, I was on the road that led back from the forth to the town, that pleasant peaceful town with cart shafts tilted heavenwards and aproned men idle in shop doors, with polished plates on picture rails, blue urns on mantelpieces, with Butler's car parked beside the telephone kiosk in the Diamond.

The sight of the white naked digits of his registration number recalled me completely to life. People were staring at me. The left sleeve of my jacket was ripped at the shoulder. My shirt and collar were torn. One trouser leg was streaked with mud, one hand dripping blood; and when I raised the clean hand to my face I felt a fresh gash under my right eye. So looking neither right nor left, afraid of comment, afraid of sympathy, I crossed the Diamond to the hotel, raced upstairs to the bathroom, did what I could to cover the signs of the struggle. In my bedroom I found my rainproof; and, the rents in my clothes blessedly hidden, I sat in the dining-room at the table near the window where last night I had sat with Emily. His car was still there in the Diamond. I watched for a century. My lunch went cold before me. My lips tasted of ashes. The waitress came with coffee. My hand trembled so much that the brown liquid spilled. She mopped it up, said reproachfully and pityingly: 'Is there anything the matter, sir?'

'No. Nothing the matter,' and just then Butler entered the Diamond, walking with difficulty towards his car. 'No, thank you. There's nothing the matter.' Even from a distance I could see what my first lucky blow had done to his eyes. Occasionally as he walked he shaded them with both hands. People stopped to look after him. Below the knees his trousers clung damply to his legs. For minutes as long as years he fumbled with his keys. The revelation and experience of the last while were still so recent and incredible that I almost rose from my chair to go to his aid. Under the table-cloth the waitress slipped a saucer to give the damp brown stain a chance to dry. Butler drove slowly out of the Diamond along the city road. His plight caused me no elation, no remorse, no emotion of any kind. The mesmeric skian was wrenched out from under the eaves. The sense of finality was as dead as lead. I had a job to do and then everything would be over. The next bus brought me back through green soft bullock country to the city.

X

Never before had I entered a police station, and this one was a dreadful disappointment. There wasn't a thing to indicate that the large blue-uniformed men who lived in the place were engaged in the detection of crime. There wasn't even a reward notice, with sullen bearded photograph, for a wanted man. But there were three blotchily printed notices, one about grass-seed, one about bulls, one about the licensing of dogs. They stood out hideously against the whitewashed walls of the passage that led in from the street. Two or three of the flags in the floor were loose and moved and rattled disconcertingly under my feet. The hallway was empty and unconcerned. The air stank of disinfectant to keep it, you couldn't help thinking, from stinking of chamber-lye.

I walked back again to the door, looked out at the dark village street, and again rang the bell. Nobody answered. Then bold because of impatience, I opened the first door to the left of the hallway, walked into the room, saw the scholarly-looking sergeant sitting at a table, small gold-rimmed spectacles perched on his nose. He was reading a magazine and didn't look up until I had shuffled and coughed. How in hell, with their dullness and nonchalance and their concentration on magazines, did they ever manage to catch Jim Walsh? But then they—these village police—they didn't. It was the shabby fellows in the city who found him in a back-lane brothel, and seeing that he happened to be the wrong man, catching him and hanging him hadn't been such a hell of an achievement. Perhaps there was some reason in the number of knowing books that brought along glick amateurs to give points to the police.

With a delicate right hand the sergeant smoothed his silvery handsome hair, outlined distinctly against a brown press bulging with documents-or, perhaps, back numbers of magazines.

'Were you looking for someone?'

'Yes. I was ringing the bell.'

'It rings in another room. Is there nobody there?' His voice was the voice of a dress designer and his person was part professor and part actor with only blue cloth and buttons to remind one of the police. 'I didn't look,' I said.

'Who was it you wanted? Could I do anything for you?'

'Nobody in particular. I wanted to make a statement.'

'You might as well make it to me, so. What have you done?'

'Nothing. I've found out something about somebody else.' Did this make me a police informer? Nerves were getting the better of me. This was a dreadful thing to feel compelled to do. My palms sweated. My fingers twitched. To reassure myself, to prevent the world from shaking, I said hurriedly: 'Something serious. Something very serious.'

With startling loudness and roughness he roared: 'Sullivan, Sullivan, I want you.' Quietly to me he said: 'Take a seat,' and I sat uneasily on a hard cane chair and he read his magazine until the door opened and another man in uniform came into the room. It was the man I had once talked to in the porch of Morgan's cottage. He nodded, but there was no real recognition in his prominent blue eyes. The sergeant said: 'This gentleman wants to make a statement.' They both looked at me, not curiously, almost bovinely and yet analytically, if you could imagine a cow giving an analytical glance. My knees quivered. Christ, I thought, it must be a sweet business to have a crime on your chest, a murder, a theft, a rape, and to come to confess to these half-interested men. Rapidly, my voice very near a squeak, I said: 'I want to make a statement about the Morgan murder case.'

'About the what?' the sergeant, I think, said.

'About the Morgan murder case.'

'We don't need another statement about that. It's all over.'

Behind me Sullivan said: 'A closed book.'

'It's not all over.'

The sergeant looked at me steadily. He said: 'The man's hanged. It was a clear case. What more could you expect the police to do?'

'To hang the right man.' That was the wrong way to speak to them. The sterilized air was noticeably immediately hostile. With excessively smooth politeness the sergeant said: 'A judge and jury thought the right man was hanged.'

'They were wrong.'

'Can you prove that?'

'I can.' Then I hesitated, fatally. What proof had I except Butler's lunatic statement made when he was demented by the thought that Emily and myself had shared a bed? Suppose he should now choose to deny that he had ever said anything of the sort? And it was practically certain that he would deny it, that he wouldn't have told me if he hadn't known that my knowledge and my enmity would be harmless. The police were against me, and the weighing words of a judge and the findings of a jury in a case as clear as spring water. They eyed my hesitation. Oh, those seemingly bovine glances were really as sharp as the glinting eyes of ferrets. The sergeant laughed. The room shook. 'Look, mister,' he said, and then: 'What's your name?' My part in the Morgan case had made so little impression on him that he didn't even know my name.

'Hartigan.'

'Hartigan. I see now. You were there when the body was found.'

'I found the body.'

'Along with Mr. Butler of the hotel.'

'Yes,' and I thought with evil joy: no longer of the hotel nor of this village.

'You suffered from nervous shock afterwards.'

'I . . .' But Sullivan said: 'He was excused attendance at the inquest on that account.'

The sergeant sucked his lips. I didn't like his lips or the calm way he sucked them, drawing in his underlip, releasing it again momentarily whitened by the scraping of his teeth. Again he said: 'I see.' Then: 'You know, Mr. Hartigan, that statements of the sort you wish to make must not be made lightly, that it would be possible to find yourself in trouble if you went about making such statements just for the fun of it.'

'I know that.' Why in Christ's name had I come here at all? Jim Walsh could never come out of the grave, return to life and liberty by way of the gallows, the condemned cell, the dock, the back-lane brothel, my hut, Kavanagh's hut, Morgan's cottage. Why had I come? Was it for no better reason than that I hated George Butler?

'If you insist on making this statement we can't stop you. But it's only right you should be warned.' My sweating hands gripped the seat of the cane chair. To cut short this trying palaver, I said: 'I know the man who killed Lily Morgan. The real murderer.'

'You do? How?'

'From his own lips. He told me.'

'He confessed to you?'

'Yes.' The sergeant's eyes looked beyond me to find Sullivan's eyes. The cunning, amused, swivelling movement maddened me.

'Why did he tell you?'

'It doesn't matter why. He told me.'

'Everything matters in a case like this.'

'I don't know why. He did tell me.'

'Who is he? Do we know him?'

I knew they wouldn't, couldn't credit it. With apparent despair in my voice, with no feeling of conviction inside me, I said: 'George Butler.'

'Who?'

'George Butler.'

The sergeant asked: 'Do my ears deceive me?' Sullivan said simply: 'Jasus.'

'You mean George Butler that I've played pontoon with in the hotel nights and nights.' The sergeant was one of the select circle that met, drank, and gambled in the hotel. I said: 'He won't be there tonight.'

'We know that. He's going to England for a month on business.'
They knew a lot. The room shuddered. Butler, the bastard, had his
plans made with mad evil cunning.

'You say he killed the Morgan girl. Why?' Another fatal hesitation. The name of Emily Rayel couldn't be mentioned. It was all
too impossible. How mad, mad, mad I had been to think that things
gone irreparably wrong could ever be set right. I said: 'Because he
was her . . . lover.' The sergeant laughed coarsely, probably at my
stuttering, faltering before the word lover, and Sullivan slowly blew
out his breath as if he was about to say: Well, wonders will never
cease, or, Now, bejasus, I've seen and heard everything. 'I wouldn't
be surprised at that,' the sergeant jested. 'The same George laid a
good few low in his day.'

I almost screamed: But one he failed to lay low.

'But that's not the same thing as murder,' the sergeant said, and
Sullivan, like the bass voice assisting a sports commentator,
intoned: 'Not even a motive.'

'If you love a girl,' the sergeant said, 'she's better fun alive than
dead,' and the two of them laughed fit to rock the room.

Shaking with fury I stood up. I said: 'This is serious. It's no
laughing matter.' Their laughter stopped with a crack and they
looked at me thoughtfully, the sergeant tapping his left ear with a
blue pencil. 'Sit down, Mr. Hartigan. Take it easy.' I sat down, but
I said: 'If you think this is a joke I'll take it higher up.'

'Look now, Mr. Hartigan. We're not fooling. This is a serious
matter. It's your accusation without, I doubt, a proof in the world
against the verdict of the court. It's a dangerous thing to go making
charges like that with nothing to base them on. We all here know
George Butler.'

'You don't know him as well as I do.'

'We've known him longer. He's hardly the man to do what you
say he's done. The law's already satisfied that another man did it.'

'How are you so certain George Butler wouldn't do it?'

'You don't like George, Mr. Hartigan. Isn't that the truth?' I
didn't answer. 'Yet the whole village here knows how good he was
to you.'

'What good did he ever do me?' That wasn't what I had come to
say. I amended it to: 'What's that got to do with the case?'

'Look at you now, man. We all know you came here a nervous wreck and George Butler took you under his wing and made a new man of you.'

'I didn't come in here to be insulted. Will you take my statement or must I go elsewhere? A few hours ago Butler told me that he killed Lily Morgan.'

'If he ever told you anything of the sort. . . .'

'I say he did.'

Sullivan again sighingly blew out his despairing breath. The sergeant this time bit, not sucked, his lips. He said:

'Give me time to talk now. If George Butler told you that, then he was pulling your leg as long as from here to Cork. You can't just walk in here and say a man told me he killed somebody.'

'Why can't I if it's true?'

'It couldn't be true. The police and the law took a long time to find out the truth. Your bare word isn't enough to overturn all that.'

'I tell you Butler told me he killed Lily Morgan.'

'Had you a row with Butler?'

'What's that got to do with it?'

'You had a row with him. That's how you got your face cut. Wasn't it?'

'That's nothing to do with my statement.'

'All right so, Mr. Hartigan. But here's my advice to you. What you have to make isn't a statement. Go home and think it over for forty-eight hours. See your doctor and your confessor.' They knew I had been a nervous wreck. They thought now that through spite against Butler I'd gone clean mad, mad enough to accuse him of murder. What had he said about me to them? What sort of picture had he cunningly painted? 'Get things in order in your head,' the sergeant said. 'Then come back here if you still feel like it and say your say. You see, you can't just rush in and make a claim like that to the police and expect them to act on it. You'd be up for public mischief. I'm advising you for your own good.'

'Tis the truth,' Sullivan said. 'Take the sergeant's advice, Mr. Hartigan.'

'I'll follow this further.' But I wasn't at all sure that I would or could. I was shivering with impotent fury, made all the worse by the realization that they were doing the right thing, treating me gently, refusing to take seriously a statement more incredible than anything they had ever before heard. Again I said: 'I'll follow this further.' But Sullivan was saying soothingly: 'Now, Mr. Hartigan, be patient. It'll all work out grand. Sure, if there's truth in what you say we're the boys to ferret it out. Don't fret now. Don't fuss. Isn't it down here for a rest you are?' All the time, as he soothered, he was inching me towards the door. The sergeant had returned to the reading of his magazine-probably *The True Detective*.

XI

But fifty yards up the dark unevenly surfaced street I knew Sullivan was following me, not by the sound of his steps coming after my own stumbling steps, for he came rubbery- footed, but because to my agitated sense the air smelled of Sullivan. I'll be trailed by no damned policeman, and I turned and ran back towards him. He neither moved away nor attempted to hide. He didn't, as far as I could see by the popping brown light of one dim street-lamp, even show surprise at my race back towards him. It probably made him more certain that I was queer in the head. He said: 'Did you forget something, Mr. Hartigan?'

I said: 'Are you following me?'

'Heavens save us, I weren't,' he lied. 'What would I follow you for? It's only in the city they do things like that. Sure, if we want you we know where to find you.' I turned from him. He said: 'I'll walk a ways with you. I go that direction.'

'I don't want you. I prefer to be alone.'

'Ah, now don't be uncivil, Mr. Hartigan. Sure, we're old friends. You remember the day we were chatting in the cottage that the poor girl was choked in?'

'I do.'

'This murder case has been a great strain to you.'

'That's my own business.'

'We're trying to help.'

'In a damned odd way.'

'Ah, now we've our own ways and means too. Between ourselves you mightn't be as far out as the sergeant lets on to think.'

'Some day soon the sergeant will know that to his cost.' That was the way a nervy spoiled child, not a rational well-read man, would talk. Stand by me in my hour of need, old romancer Malory, Pascal the pure, Marcus the hell-hearted emperor. 'Wouldn't it be better,' Sullivan asked, 'if we worked together?' Had I alarmed them?

'I did my share in offering a statement. You wouldn't listen.'

'We listened right enough. But it's a hard one to credit.' 'I didn't invent it. I told you what Butler told me.' The fair-green rose into the darkness above us. If I climbed up the short cut Sullivan would certainly leave me. He had no excuse for climbing with me up that muddy way, for the house where he lived with his school-teacher wife was beyond the big bridge on the main road to the city. Yet when I stepped from the street and began the ascent be came with me. I didn't protest. I knew it was useless. But I bitterly remembered the happy times I'd walked that way, with Emily perhaps, or at the least thinking of her with a full amber mind, untrammelled by Butler's hideous revelation and the responsibility it had burdened me with.

'He weren't drinking, were he, at the time?'

'At what time?' There was no ruffling his patience. I tried to remember what he had looked like in the porch of Morgan's cottage or in the disinfected police station, for in the night, on the muddy steep slope, I could see only a dark figure by my side.

'When he told you.'

'He was stinking drunk.' Sullivan clicked his tongue. The wind strengthened as we neared the top of the fair-green. Raindrops spattered our faces. Across the fields was the light of Kavanagh's hut. 'Were you drunk yourself, Mr. Hartigan, if I may ask?'

'I wasn't.'

'Had you drink taken?'

'I had.'

'You had a row?'

'We had.'

'What about?'

'Look. I said, 'why cross-examine me? I didn't kill Lily Morgan.'

'We know well you didn't.' He laughed.

'I'm sober. I'm sane.'

'Sure, we know that.'

'George Butler told me a certain thing and I thought it my duty to tell the police. I've done that. Now shag off to hell and let me go home alone. At the moment I don't give a damn if you arrest and hang half the village, provided you leave me alone.'

'That's a bad attitude to take.'

'No worse than the sergeant's. As he'll find out if I live long enough.' Irresolutely he stopped walking. His patience at last was tried and shaken. But I was weak and empty of substance at the thought of the little conviction there was behind my bluster. I'd never go with my mad story to higher authority. Butler could go where he liked, do what he liked; and if Emily Rayel went with him the reason was that by nature some men were monarchs and some men worms. I'd had my bellyful of interfering with the shape of things, the way water flowed, winds blew, wheels turned, tide-ruling moons waxed and waned. Suppose, too, that Butler was out there hiding in the darkness, or waiting in my hut, his eyes bleeding, his heart murderous, where Jim Walsh had once waited. When I walked on I wasn't sorry that Sullivan walked with me. 'Would there be anybody who could back you up in the story?' he asked, just as the light of Kavanagh's hut flashed through somehow as far as my brain, and across the dark fields I seemed to see Jim Walsh, leaving his love alive behind him to be strangled by George Butler, go broken and pitiful to be charitable to the saint's buxom woman. 'By God,' I cried. 'I'm thick in the head. I never saw it until now.'

'Saw what?'

'The truth. It's down there where that light is.' Even in the darkness I could feel that he looked at me as if finally convinced of my lunacy. But he said quietly: 'How do you make that out?'

'You and the sergeant may not believe it, but Jim Walsh was probably in Kavanagh's hut at the time he was supposed to be choking Lily Morgan.'

'If you could prove that you'd have something.' He sounded as if he was humouring me, as if he hadn't a hope in the world that I'd prove anything except the necessity for my own certification for lunacy. So, for hellery, I said: 'Will you come with me now to that house?' He didn't speak for a while. Then at last he said: 'I'm not against you, Mr. Hartigan.'

'Will you come?' He was worried. He had followed me, probably on the sergeant's instructions, to make sure that I did no damage to myself or to anybody else. 'It would be irregular.'

'A hell of a lot you boys worry about irregularity.'

'Now Mr. Hartigan. . . .'

'Will you come to test my story?' He followed me, but hesitatingly, either because of the darkness on the narrow bumpy field path or because of the doubt in his mind. 'Look now,' he said, 'why didn't Jim Walsh himself say where he were at that time?'

'Maybe he didn't want to expose the woman.'

'Not even to save his own life?'

'I'm certain he didn't care much about his life. People get that way even when they have money and health and everything. He was ill. He was a wreck. He had nothing.' . . . And one has nothing and nobody . . . what sort of a life is it really: without a house, without inherited possessions, without dogs . . . ?

'It could be,' Sullivan said. 'Anything can be. I learned that much and me a policeman.' Under our feet the ground turned to champing gravel. We were approaching the holy of holies, the temple of the inner shrine. The gramophone was playing. I can't remember what the tune was. 'I'll go with you,' Sullivan sighed, 'though jasus knows, I think I'm as mad as you are.' Then I knocked on the door. The saint opened to us. He was in his stocking soles. He wore dungarees, but the top of them was relaxed and dangled down in front of him like a mason's apron. He wore no collar and a huge naked collar-stud shone like a brass knob just below his Adam's apple. He looked at us out of dull colourless eyes. For the first time I noticed that his face was a brown triangle, base up, the apex pointing to the shining stud. He said: 'What do you want at this hour?'

'It's not so late yet, Mr. Kavanagh,' Sullivan said, his voice soothering yet firm with authority now that he was dealing with real village people and not with puzzling imported madmen. 'We want to speak a word to your wife.'

'What could either of you have to say to my wife?' Behind him the needle was smartly lifted from the record, the turntable clicked to a stop. Now I seem to remember that the music, whatever it was, had not been a hymn tune. Were things, then, beginning to happen in the Kavanagh hut? There she was behind him without any sound of feet approaching: she was leaning over his shoulder. I couldn't see her face, for the light was behind her, blinding me. She was only a black silhouette. Her hair was tossed and tousled. Had she been out walking in the stormy woods searching for another pine bludgeon to replace the one I had wielded on Butler's eyes? 'What

160

is it, dear?' she whispered to him. At that instant I knew it wasn't worth while asking my question. He said: 'This Hartigan man and guard Sullivan wish to speak to you.'

'To me?'

Sullivan said: 'Yes, missus.'

'What about?'

'Just a question, missus. We're looking for some information.'

The saint growled: 'Never saw you better.'

'What information could I give you?' Oh, her voice was as innocent as sixteen. Or in these days should it be thirteen or eleven or seven itself? Neither of them asked us to step in out of the night. Sullivan prodded me in the back as much as to say: Go on, your turn now, do your stuff. Daftly I said: 'It might be better if Mr. Kavanagh wasn't present.'

'Why? Why? What is this all about?' I couldn't blame the man for his yellow wrath. It was a daft thing to ask. 'I've a right to hear anything said to my wife by the police or anybody else.'

'Understand,' said Sullivan, washing his hands of me, 'this isn't a police question.'

'Then what are you doing here?'

'Mr. Hartigan heard some rumours about a recent happening which he thinks Mrs. Kavanagh may be able to verify.'

'Why should he think that?'

'I don't know in the world. But he do think so. I'm here just in a friendly capacity to all concerned. Mr. Hartigan, you see, came to us with certain information.'

'So he's an informer. I always knew there was something nasty about the look of him.'

Weary of it all, I snapped: 'The same to you and more so. Did we interrupt you at the thirty days' prayer?' I'd tell my grandchildren. I thought: When a man tells you he murdered somebody, don't listen to him; if you can't help hearing him, don't believe him; if you see somebody murdering somebody, quickly close your eyes and run away and leave them to their sport. That would be if I ever had grandchildren, and I saw Emily prostrate on my rainproof on fairy earth and sobbingly calling herself a coward. 'Enough of that,' Sullivan said. 'At the least it's my duty to prevent breaches of the peace.' But peculiarly my outburst had squashed Kavanagh. Deflatedly he said: 'Ask your question and take yourself away from here.' Had remorse, coloured a dirty white, already overtaken him for letting down his dungarees to the rhythm of gramophone music? 'Mrs. Kavanagh,' I said, 'you once told me that on the night of the Morgan murder Jim Walsh visited this hut.'

Remember, I couldn't clearly see her face. Her voice was as flat as a pancake and, oh, as cool as cool could be. She said: 'I never told you anything of the sort. I don't know what on earth you're talking about.'

Honestly I wasn't even surprised. How could she admit the truth and his holiness standing by? How could I ever have imagined that she was one who would tell the truth except in a moment of loneliness and weakness and the melting influence of whisky? But I said, just for the sake of saying it: 'Now try hard to remember, Mrs. Kavanagh. You must remember the night you told me. Over there in my hut.'

She repeated: 'I never told you anything of the sort.' Then, quickly and shrilly: 'You're mad. The whole place knows you're mad. I was never in your hut in my life.' She went away from the door. The saint said smugly: 'Are ye satisfied now?'

'Sorry for bothering you,' Sullivan said. 'It's only the way that everything has to be checked up. That'll be all for tonight.'

'No bother at all, Guard. You're welcome. But will you ask that fool who the hell he thinks he is, trying to mix decent people up in a mess like that.'

'I'll look after him,' Sullivan was saying when the door was slammed forcibly enough to rattle the hut, and there were Sullivan and myself in the darkness and the rain beginning to fall in earnest. The very wind in the bare branches of the wood was having a laugh at my expense. He said: 'That's that. And here we are. High but not dry.'

'You might as well arrest me now for public mischief or whatever you call it.' To my surprise Sullivan was laughing as we walked away together through the rain. 'Mr. Hartigan, I never were inclined to believe you until this blessed minute. I know that pair of old. I know a lie when I hear it, too. I know bloody well that that one and Jim Walsh carried on like heroes once upon a time.'

'That proves nothing.' At the door of my hut I said: 'Come in and shelter and have some tea.'

'She's a renowned lassie, that one.'

162

'Her renown doesn't prove I'm not mad.'

'You have something in your story, somewhere. I'm convinced of that. But you'll never be able to do a thing about it. You haven't a proof. The whole power of the law is against you.'

'So I see. Step in out of the rain.' But for a while he stood where he was, very merrily laughing. 'That was a good one you gave to that holy Joe. 'Twasn't at his prayers he was when we came beating at the door. No wonder he was annoyed.' It seemed I had appealed to the Rabelaisian in Sullivan. 'Come inside. You'll be soaked.' The rising wind caught the rain and bent it, slapping the drops coldly against the panes of my front windows. 'I will and thanks,' he said. 'Then we'll trot like hares, get out the wife's car, and take a run as far as the airport.'

'Whatever for?'

'We could still have a word with Butler before he flies away.'

'How do you know he's flying?'

'Ah, now, we have our ways of knowing things.' You wouldn't, I supposed, have to be a Sherlock Holmes to find out how a man was leaving our island. There were only three ways: wind, water, a hole in the earth. Cremation wasn't Catholic and burning at the stake had never caught on. 'Talking to Butler will do no good. He only shot off his mouth to me because he knew nobody would believe me.'

'Sure, I know it'll do no good. It'll change nothing. But we'll go, anyway.' As I poured out the tea he said: 'No sugar and little milk. I'm all curiosity.'

XII

Sullivan's wife's car was an ancient two-seater Morris Cowley with a crack, carefully puttied, all the way along the wind-screen. We drove across country to the airport, threading our way through a maze of dark twisty by-roads, steering cautiously across two bright wide main roads where traffic ripped northwards in the rain. The hood on the ancient wreck flapped in the wind and leaked in two places, one of them so close to the nape of my neck that I had to pull up the collar of my overcoat to my ears. 'It's seen better days,' he said apologetically. 'The wife just do use it going to and coming from the school.' We increased speed to twenty-five miles an hour and rattled like be damned. Justice had seldom gone pursuing in a more absurd chariot. We talked about circumstantial evidence. Above the uproar of the engine, the rattle of the body, he shouted in a voice that would have made Blackstone sound like an election address: 'You know the law's a queer bloody thing.'

'Who're you telling?'

'I've seen a lot if I were at liberty to talk. Begod, the good woman should invest in a new car.'

'It moves, doesn't it?'

'You're right, it do move. In every direction at once. Did you see the queer case in the English papers the other day?'

'No.'

'Well, there was this poor fellow, you see, walking the street in London, and he stops a seventeen-year-old boy and asks him the time of the day.'

'No harm in that.' I was at ease with Sullivan. He didn't think I was mad or a liar. He, with me, was hunting the brute Butler, as he, with all the other police, had once hunted Jim Walsh; and I saw lean savage hounds straining and stretching after the hare's bobbing white scut. He said: 'Listen a while now. That's not the half of it.' He was at ease with me. 'Off walks the boy, puts his hand to his inside pocket. No wallet. So what does he do?'

He waited for question or comment. So I said: 'What?'

'Tells the police. What else?'

'And what did they do?'

'Lift the man. Charge him. Try him. And in a few hours he's on his ass in Pentonville Prison with a three months' sentence on his plate.'

'And that was that. That was fast work.'

'Too fast by far, if you ask me.'

I did ask him. I said: 'Why?'

'Because the bright boy stamps off home and finds his wallet safe and sound on the mantelpiece.

'Good God.'

'He has the guts to go back to the police and the man is set at liberty. But I ask you, Mr. Hartigan, what would have happened if the boy had really and truly lost his wallet and never found it, or if he hadn't been honest enough to own up to his mistake. That's circumstantial evidence for you.'

'That certainly is.'

'Anything can happen.'

'Anything can.' Then, there above us in the sky, were the crimson guiding lights of the airport, below those lights the white unearthly glitter surrounding buildings, bars, offices, and the nylons of high-stepping, desirable, but very cagey, hostesses. Up to that night an airport had always been for me a thing of bright morning and flashing white wings. I had never flown. The airport was a place I had visited two or three times with departing friends, a springboard shooting them up into blue places that were not part of my experience. The few friends I had, always seemed to go flying on sunny mornings, and on sunny mornings the airport from a distance was a block of white concrete and shining glass perched on a green horizon. A plane would shoot out and up, banking and glittering for a moment like a fish twisting in a pool. Uniformed, clean-shaven men stood attentively at high-pillared gateways. Bright flower-beds dotted the lawns that sloped up to the buildings. Cars came and went continuously. Officials walked smartly along concrete paths or darted like rabbits in and out of swinging glass doors. From somewhere unseen would come the reverberation of an engine like the beating of a Cyclopean heart. Then another plane, four engines roaring, would rise over the roofs, over the tall flagstaff with its flapping tricolour. Within the buildings pretty girls in green uniforms smiled from glass boxes or went, flashing nylon calves and certain-footed as chamois, on high heels across slippery floors. But on a wild rainy night the airport was unwelcoming and unreal, an artificial place menaced by powers that kept the aeroplanes on the ground and in shelter. 'He won't fly far tonight,' Sullivan said.

'He may have gone up while the weather was better.'

'We'll find out soon.' The uniformed man at the gate stayed snugly in his neat shelter, looked at us through protecting glass, then boredly waved us on. When we ran through rain from the car into the main hall the girl at the inquiry desk looked at us as if she disliked us intensely. We crossed the floor towards her. My crêpe soles left wet blobs on the polished surface. Sullivan's shoes squeaked embarrassingly. She was a red-haired, full-lipped young woman. She brightened up when we mentioned the name of the great brute, Butler. 'He had a booking for two. But he rang to cancel it.' Why hadn't I telephoned Emily? 'Yet what exactly could I have told her? Not certainly what Butler had told me before I fought him and marked his face. Had he run to her, his eyes dropping blood, looking at last for sympathy, the strong man, the he-man, the hero mightily fallen, and had she, now that with my aid she had conquered fear and leaped the dark initiatory threshold, gone away happily with him? Sullivan said: 'He didn't just postpone the trip?'

'No. He cancelled it altogether. He said he was sailing tonight instead.'

'Why was that, I wonder now.'

'Well, honestly, I haven't a clue.' Then she looked up from her record and said to me: 'I think I saw you one night at a theatre with Mr. Butler.'

'So you know him?'

'Of course. We all do. He's popular around here.'

'He's popular everywhere,' Sullivan said. 'He's a great man,' and we smiled at the girl, who smiled back at us, and we went out to the car. 'How'm I fixed for petrol?' he asked his dashboard, then, answering himself: 'Not so bad now. We'll make it at our ease.' He drove at what speed the car could make down sloping roads into the drenched city. The pavements were practically deserted. One brave crocodile of cinema-goers queued half in and half out of a gaudy foyer. Sullivan smoked and didn't talk much. I thought, if I said stop while I made a phone call, he'd say who, and Emily's name would be in the muck. He bent down his head to look at a clock on a public building. He had no watch and the dashboard clock had no hands. 'It'll be a tight thing,' he said. 'The boat sails in twenty minutes.' We went southwards through an older sort of suburbia. Great high red houses stood well back from the road. One wide door was open to show, as we whipped past, a bright hallway and people in evening dress. We passed crossings that had once been villages, and a grey square factory set incongruously in a non-industrial area; then swung left, avoiding bus routes, until the dark sea was on one side and on the other the still higher houses of an earlier period; then around a corner and we saw the arms of a harbour, pimpled with lamps, reaching out to hold, like candles guttering in a draughty place, two winking lighthouses. Between the lighthouses and gallantly tossing towards the open sea was the ship, as eerily illuminated as the airport. 'The luck we have,' said Sullivan, 'would make a man kick his own arse. There he goes.'

There he went. There with him, ten to one, went Emily Rayel. I felt no hope and no regret. The rain soaked in at the nape of my neck. This was the way things happened to people like me. 'Best go home to bed,' Sullivan said, 'and forget all about it. I doubt if any of the higher ups would chase him to England on the strength of your statement.' He intended no insult. He liked me, I think, and almost credited my story. He left me nothing to resent. I said: 'Let him go to England.'

'That's sensible, now.'

'Let him go to hell.'

'If he told you the truth he's well on the way there already.' Taking Emily with him, I thought, and I said: 'There's nothing can be done.'

'Not a lot, I'd be afraid. But give us a while to think it over.'

'By then he'll be in the Argentine or Africa or somewhere.'

'He won't run far. To tell the honest truth, he's little cause to run. Come and have a drink.' He meant: Only for you I wouldn't be here on such a hoor of a night, so come along like a decent man and buy me a large whisky. We drove a hundred yards ahead and then were halted by the crowd.

It was a restless, curious crowd, but it wasn't gay. Obstructing our path, it had gathered at what looked like the junction of four roads. We were approaching that junction at a sharp angle with a road that came steeply downhill from the town above the harbour, and to get to that harbour we would have to swing around an obtuse angle and follow a third road. The fourth road wasn't really a road at all. Twenty yards away from the junction it ended abruptly with a fifteen-foot drop into the water, an unprotected, dangerous, dimly lighted place. That was why the crowd had gathered there, why a policeman in glistening oil-cape held up his hand before us, bent to say: 'You'll have to turn back and detour to the left past the hotel.'

Sullivan said: 'Howarye, Mac? What's all the hullaballoo?'

'Is it Tim Sullivan I have?'

''Tis indeed. And no other.'

'What the hell are you doing out here?'

'On a joy ride in the wife's Rolls Royce. What are ye all at?'

'Some poor fellow went into the harbour, car and all. That corner's a regular death-trap. There'll be ructions at the inquest about the state of the lighting and no protection for man or beast.'

'Inquest? Is he drowned?'

'Well, they haven't got him yet. They have the car hooked on, but he's not in it. They think he might be under it in the mud.'

'Any harm if we have a look?'

'Not a pick. Sure, why would there be? We're only holding all these cods back in case a few more fall in. We've woes enough on our hands.' He led us through the crowd and the cordon to the edge of the dark harbour. They had a mobile crane and chains straining and hooks gripping somewhere under the car. Our guide said: 'The roof was just barely covered when she settled.' Rain rattled like hail on glistening black capes. Back first, the car came up, water gushing from it, a door crazily swinging open on one hinge, much glass shattered. A searchlight picked out the white digits that had shocked me back to consciousness in the Diamond of the delightful town. Sullivan said nothing to me, but to the police officer in charge, he said: 'I know that number. It's a car from my end of the world.' Out beyond the harbour light-houses the ship was swinging around to point her bows towards the other island. I walked back to Sullivan's wife's car and sat there until Sullivan, covered shoulders to knees in a borrowed cape, came stooping to tell me the body had been found. I didn't ask if they had found one or two bodies or whether it was a man or a woman they had found. For Sullivan would then have asked me whom had I expected to be in the car with Butler. He went away again. My mind a blank, my limbs as if paralysed, I sat until he returned much later, capeless. 'If the pubs are still open,' he said, 'I need that drink.'

The crowd had melted away and I hadn't even noticed it going. We drove uphill and had a drink in a saloon bar across the street from the town hall. The clock said ten-twenty-five. Under fluorescent lighting the walls were a bright ugly, startling yellow. Barmen were shouting time above the din, and rattling tumblers. Sullivan said: 'That little mishap solves your problem.'

'I suppose it does.'

'They're all dead now. Leave it rest.' How many were dead? Three or four? Was the fourth body still down in the dark harbour? I asked: 'Had he a sticky end?'

'What do you think? He must have smashed the wind-screen and crawled out that way. But the car took a twist and pinned him to the wall. He weren't alive much longer than that.' Sullivan took his black Bushmill's whisky with soda in swift electric sips. 'Ribs crushed to powder. Right arm all gashed with glass. A bad cut around one eye. And more like that.'

'We'll never know the truth now.'

'Ah, well. 'Tisn't as if Walsh had any relatives who might want his name cleared.'

'No. He had nobody and nothing. Not even a dog.' 'Years ago he was the great lad for dogs and horses.' 'So I heard.' Had the damage I wreaked on Butler's eyes made him in the rainy darkness confuse the real road with the short road leading to death at the edge of the harbour? To the eternal disfigurement of the grave he would carry the mark I had made on his handsome face. 'There's nothing you can do, Mr. Hartigan. My advice is forget all about it.'

'There's nothing I want to do.'

'Bully man. That's sensible.' But there was something I wanted to do. The light, the noise, the sight of living people, the taste of whisky, were giving me the necessary courage. The telephone was in the wide yellow corridor leading to the gents' and the side door. When I rang Emily a man's voice answered the phone; her father, possibly, the man who on some woman or other had begotten a Deschamps poem. 'May I speak to Miss Emily Rayel?' Was she alive in her bed or dead in the harbour?

'She's not here at the moment. She went out a few hours ago.'

'You don't know when she'll be back?'

'No. Can I take a message?'

'No.' My hand was shaking as I took the telephone away from my ear. Could I run back now to Sullivan and say: Are they certain Butler was alone in the car? At a distance of eighteen inches from my ear the man's voice squeaked: 'Hold on. Hold on. There's somebody coming.' I held on to the telephone and, to steady myself, to the yellow wall. It was slimy with damp. My guts were cold water. The voice said: 'Yes, here she is. Hold on.' Then Emily, breathlessly, but her words still as smooth as silk, said: 'Hello, hello, who's there? Oh, hello, Don. Is that you?'

'It is.'

'Are you well?'

'Very well.'

'I walked around your way, but your place was all dark.'

'I had to go into town on business.'

'I was worried about you.'

'And I was worried about you.'

'And we're both well. Anything strange?'

'Not a thing. Not a thing. I just rang up to see were you well.'

'Never better.' Was her father standing near her elbow so that she couldn't tell me what words or ways Butler had used in his effort to take her with him, and why and how he had failed? I tried to say that Butler was drowned, Butler was dead, but the words wouldn't come. 'Good night, Emily. I'll ring in the morning.'

'Do, please, Don. I've a lot to tell you.'

'So have I a lot to tell you.' She'd read it in the morning papers.

I went back to Sullivan to find that he had persuaded a time-shouting barman to bring us another round. 'Drink up,' he said, 'the way things are nowadays a man's lucky to be alive.'

XIII

Should I have known all the time who was the murderer of Lily Morgan? Should something in the air around pass such information along? But nothing ever does; and you speak to a man day after day, pass him on streets or in corridors, eat with him at the same tables in restaurants, and when he's haled away by the police for murder or embezzlement or unnatural conduct in public urinals, you say: It never occurred to me for one moment; I could have died of shock when I heard the news.

From the hotel in the village I telephoned Emily. There was an awed, hushed air about the place. The king was dead. The kingdom mourned. There could be no successor. I sat alone by the huge coal fire in the back bar, entitled to solitude and sympathy because I had been the friend, the courtier, the black wide-sleeved obsequious secretary of the dead king.

A girl's voice, possibly the voice of the maid who had looked at me with suspicion on the morning of the Morgan murder, said: 'Miss Emily's out. She left a message she'd be back for lunch.'

The king had been my friend, had in a unique way lifted me up and led me into new lands.

I drowned a small gin in blue bubbly tonic-water, sipped it slowly and at twelve-thirty rang again. The maid said: 'She's not here yet, but she's expected at any moment.'

'I'll ring again.' At that moment I wasn't certain if I would ring again or ever see her again. The world was unsteady. What could I tell her about the death of George Buder or about the revelations he had made to me that morning by the river? But I did ring again and this time Emily answered my hello. 'Is that you, Don? Isn't it horrible, horrible? I was weak when I saw the papers.'

'I was there when they took him out.'

'Why didn't you tell me last night?'

'I knew you'd hear soon enough.'

'Oh, Don. Poor George. Why did we do it?'

'We?' How splendid to be dead and pitied and to die by drowning rather than by the merited rope.

'He wanted me to go to England with him.'

'I know that.'

'And I wouldn't, Don. And then he said he'd do what he did.' Her half-choked sobs for the dead monster came to me, carried by wire from the Georgian house, in the air over the artificial lake with the grasses now cold and withered around its edges, then crossing fields not far from Morgan's cottage and so directly to the village.

'What did he say he'd do?'

'Suicide.'

'But, Emily, it wasn't suicide. The corner was dark. He couldn't see where he was going.'

'I wish I could think that. I wish I could think that it wasn't my fault.'

'It was an accident. It wasn't your fault. That's the truth.' 'But how awful, how awful. There's something unlucky about me.' For the first time in my nervous life I felt the conventional noble impatience of the male with the illogical silliness of woman. 'Don't be foolish, Emily. You couldn't help it. It was truly an accident. The place was dark. He had injured his eyes.,

'I saw that. 'You had a fight.' 'Did he tell you that?'

'No. I guessed. And you two were such friends if it hadn't been for me. I am unlucky for people.'

'Oh, no, love, you're not. How could you think so? Come and meet me and talk properly.'

'Not now, Don. Not now. Give me a little while to recover.' I thought: God damn and blast George Butler, dead or alive, he'll keep coming between us. In that mood I gave the dead man no credit or gratitude for having brought us together. I said: 'I'm leaving the hut today. I've packed.'

'Oh.'

'I'm going back to town.'

'But you'll ring me, Don. After a while. Give me a while. How horrible it was.'

What had been horrible; the day on the Forth, the night in the hotel bedroom, or just Butler's violent end in salt water? No charity towards the dead restrained me from telling her the truth about George Butler. But then, like Sullivan's sergeant, she mightn't credit me, might think me crazy. Even if she did believe me she would whine: I brought him bad luck; he did what he did because of me. In some lightless grave-like corner of her mind she might think: He loved me so much that he did murder for my sake.

There was nothing reliable in the world, nothing steady, nothing competently known.

'You'll ring, please, Don. After a while.'

'I will Emily.' I would, too. But the dream was over. It could have been saved if she had come running to me, bringing me her tears and fears. I put down the telephone. A drop of venom from a dead man's finger had fallen into the honey drink we had tasted in the heavenly town. Time might mend matters, but I didn't want to be dependent on time. Time could never root out from my mind the suspicion that in that town she had, known or unknown to herself, been doing something for George Butler; that I had been a quiet, civil, unobtrusive proxy for a violent, terrifying, masterful man.

Back in the hut I took in one hand the mad landlady's springbok-handled toasting-fork. I love you, do you love me, yes, yes, yes, no, no, no, come, come away, then come, follow, follow me to the greenwood, greenwood tree where we shall be alone hypnotizing each other all on a couch in the drunken dark in a basement flat and the noise of a party coming booming up the barrel of the corridor. In the other hand I took Jim Walsh's empty bottle, not a drop left in it, not a sniff, and on a flat stone at the back of the hut I smashed it to pieces. It was as if I, the hangman, had released the trap under his feet, and, all in one blow, smashed Emily's pretty face and Butler's eyes and sent him to his death. If I looked under the eaves would I find protruding the hilt of a skian? My goods and bedding would be collected by a city haulier. I locked the door. Halfway down the lane, avoiding the short cut and the other inhabited hut, I tossed the toasting-fork into the scraggly wood. Like a stone into deep water it ripped out of sight among brambles. The Kavanagh woman might find it on one of her solitary walks if she had now the will or the energy to walk since the yellow saint had found his manhood. For her at least the earth was steady, had rocked itself to a standstill. In the dream long ago my arm around her waist had steadied her.

Bitterly satisfied with my symbols, I walked down the road to the village, around the corner where I had first met Butler running with a fine long healthy enviable stride, carrying his brown leather brief-case, his rainproof draped cloakwise around his shoulders and caught at the throat by one button so that the sleeves as he ran flapped like wings. Eyes looking fixedly ahead, I walked nervously along the wintry road, for I half feared that if I turned around he might be there by my side, throwing back his head to laugh loudly. I wouldn't, couldn't walk at his funeral. I had never known him when he was free from fear. What had he been like then? Had his sympathy for me been only the shadow of his pity for his own predicament?

The wind hissed through brown bare hedges that on an August morning had swayed and closed like green curtains behind the bus Butler and I had missed. Yellow wintry sunlight slanted across the road but brought no warmth. The colour of honey, it spilled through the sightless windows of the gaunt old mill. On a fairy hill Emily and I had sipped our pot of honey. To them that are sick of the jaundice, said old Marcus, that meditative cuckold of a horse-jockey, honey seems bitter. Jaundice yellowed all things, set them shaking, so that at the bridge I could fool myself that I needed a rest. Leaning on cold stone looking towards the narrow lake, I cleared my throat and spat, watched the white blob of phlegm drift out of sight under the arches. There was no sign of life, no cars, outside her father's house. The withered lakeside reeds and crumpled grasses were yellow with old sunlight, dead, tasteless honey. The world was dying of jaundice.

Then I left the bridge and, because I had time and plenty to spare before the train went south to the city, I walked through the beechwood to Morgan's cottage. The walls needed whitewash, but would, apparently, get it in the spring, for as I leaned on the creaking wooden gate I noticed smokepuffs from the chimney, felt the air pungent with the smell of burning turf. Then the door opened and Lily Morgan's mother looked out at me, came towards me down the path between the stained shore stones. She said: 'Good day, Mr. Hartigan.' She was slow-moving, subdued, her hair quite white, her dark stockings and skirt and apron making her look thin, emphasizing the pallor of her face. The resemblance to the dead girl, before only vaguely hinted at, now leaped out at me. 'Good day, Mrs. Morgan. I didn't know you were back. I was just passing on my way to the station.'

'I came back, and why not? Nobody else would live here happily. But the way I looked at it is, my poor Lily's spirit would be no terror to me. My poor Lily.'

'It was tragic,' I said. 'It was sad.' Butler had walked up that path one night when Jim Walsh had gone away with his ring. The door had been open, the woman waiting. Then Butler and myself had walked the path again the next morning. What had he thought or done when I'd left him alone for a while with the swooning widow and her daughter's dead body? 'She was a good daughter to me and I tried to be a good mother to her.' In the city my own mother waited for me. She'd be surprised and happy to see her wandering boy come home. I could never be a good son to her, but I'd live there for a while, endure my sisters for a while until their healthy offensiveness had helped me to forget my friend, George Butler. 'But it's a sinful world, Mr. Hartigan. It's little any of us knows of the wickedness the devil puts into the heart of man.'

'That's true. That's true.'

'Often and often she spoke about you, Mr. Hartigan, after you coming to live in the huts beyond.'

'About me?'

'Indeed, yes. She talked about seeing you in the convalescent home when she was there and about how nice and polite you were.'

'That's true. We met in the home.'

Then, in memory of many silent meetings between wet sleeky rhododendrons and one meeting with words at a bus stop near a cinema, Mrs. Morgan asked me in for a cup of tea. In the warm spotless kitchen I drank strong tea, perhaps from a cup that had once been touched by Lily's lips. Everything had followed from the horror that had happened behind that closed door: a death by the rope, a cry of pain on a fairy hill, a pine bludgeon swinging into a man's eyes, a death by drowning. I promised to visit the village again to call to see her.

The rest of the road to the station two women were alive in my head. Lily lay on the ancient forth in the sunny whin-sheltered corner. Emily on a bed screamed before strangling hands. I played that pleasantly imaginative swapping game until I came to the high bridge above the railway, looked down on the snail-wet wooden platform, heard far away the whistle of the approaching train.